A Note
IN THE
MARGIN

ISABELLE ROWAN

Dreamspinner Press

Published by
Dreamspinner Press
4760 Preston Road
Suite 244-149
Frisco, TX 75034
http://www.dreamspinnerpress.com/

A Note in the Margin
Copyright © 2009 by Isabelle Rowan

Cover Design by Mara McKennen

ISBN: 978-1-935192-66-4

Printed in the United States of America
First Edition
March, 2009

eBook edition available
eBook ISBN: 978-1-935192-67-1

To people who take the time to listen
and find out someone else's story.

CHAPTER 1

THE window of the tiny café had fogged up, making it difficult for John to see the bookstore across the street, but he kept staring anyway. His gaze was unfocused, not really taking in the old-fashioned wooden frames around the windows or the colorful display of recommended Australian authors. The waitress quietly refreshed his tea and smiled briefly when he looked up with the almost apologetic expression of those caught in a daydream.

He took a sip of the tea, sighed, and looked back toward the store. This time his eyes lighted on the small sign next to the door. He couldn't read it from this distance, but he knew the neat handwritten script read "Under New Management".

"Under new management," John mumbled with a disbelieving shake of his head. "My own fucking 'sea change'."

Rubbing a weary hand across his eyes, John remembered the words of his doctor: *"The migraines are going to continue to get worse unless you make some major changes in your lifestyle. What you need is a 'sea change'... in other words, give up the ongoing stress of your current job and get out of Melbourne. Perhaps buy a nice little business in the country or along the coast, settle down, something easier to occupy your time...."*

"Patronizing prick," John cursed quietly, but despite his opinions of the "smug" physician John had known he was right. He also knew he couldn't resign from his hard-fought-for job, but was willing to take a year's leave of absence, have his "sea change" without leaving the city, and then get straight back to business.

So here he was looking at the "nice little business" he'd just acquired. It wasn't in the country, but it might as well be, situated as it was in a quiet back street full of specialty stores and quaint cafés, the sort that could be classed as bohemian without quite making it to trendy.

John drained his cup, paid the bill, and made his way across the small street. A bell jingled when he pushed the door open announcing his arrival to the woman sorting through some bookmarks at the front counter. She looked up. Her first impression was of a designer suit, handcrafted leather shoes, and equally immaculate short blond hair. The overall presentation was of someone expecting to impress. As he got closer Maggie couldn't help but wonder what this man needed from her little store. When he approached the counter she smiled at him and asked, "Mister McCann?"

John returned the smile. "John, please."

"Ah. Welcome, John. I'm Maggie. We spoke on the phone," she said as she made her way around the counter and ushered him to the small kitchen where she gestured for him to take a seat at the table. "Would you like a cup of tea or coffee?" she offered while waving a tin of homemade cookies in his direction. John politely declined both, pulled a folder of papers out of his briefcase, and spread them in an orderly line on the table. Maggie looked at them and her expression saddened. With a small sigh she sat in front of the papers and looked at John. "You know, giving this place up is a lot harder than I thought it would be."

John tried to give her his best "I understand" smile. He was aware that Margins had been a family business and it was only with the death of her husband that Maggie had decided to sell up and return to England to live with her sister.

"Still, at least Jamie will be here to keep an eye on the place for me." She gave a small laugh knowing full well that her son would rather be keeping an eye on the handsome new owner. John had met Jamie during an earlier meeting as Maggie preferred to stay out of the business side of things and knew he had an excellent understanding of the store. "I'm sure he'll be a great help in showing me the ropes and making sure I don't mess things up too badly."

Maggie smiled and patted John's hand. "I'm not so sure about that, but he likes it here and I couldn't convince him to go back to England with his old mum. Jamie was born here; my husband and I were some of the original 'ten quid tourists' in the early sixties. Have you been here long?" she asked, recognizing John's northern English accent.

"Quite a few years now," John replied noncommittally, making it very clear that his private life was not a topic of conversation. This was business.

Maggie looked at the pen John pushed across the table and sighed; she knew this had to be done and the small talk was simply putting off the inevitable. Picking up the pen, Maggie told herself for the umpteenth time that this was the right thing to do and signed the final paperwork.

"I'll finish moving my belongings out of the apartment over the next few days so it should be ready for you in about a week." Maggie smiled gently at the sudden change of expression in John's green eyes, "Don't look so worried, John. It really is all for the best. You'll see." She gathered the documents together in two stacks; one for her and one for John. "Right, then," she announced as she pushed back her chair and stood up. "I'm off now; please let Jamie know I'll be back by tea time."

She picked up her copies of the signed lease, patted John on the shoulder and, with one last look, made her way out the door. John heard the little bell tinkle and began feeling very sick.

He slumped in the chair and stared at his signature on the neatly stacked documents.

"Hey, man, don't look so worried," Jamie teased when he walked into the kitchen. John smiled at the good-looking young man and, though he decided he shouldn't go there, John wasn't totally impervious to the cheeky brown eyes and mess of dark curly hair.

"Your mother said that too," he groaned, then looked up at the figure in the doorway. "Come on. Show me how things work."

"Time to impress the new boss, is it?" Jamie grinned.

"Or at least put my mind at rest that this *isn't* the daftest thing I've ever done in my life." John shook his head and followed Jamie back into the store.

Although the initial impression was of a small cluttered store, it was actually quite large—allowing for even more clutter. Margins tended to be something of a rabbit warren with little alcoves devoted to different formats or genres giving the impression of stepping into separate rooms. Righting a fallen picture book, John knew his attraction to the store was due to its similarity to one he used to visit as a kid, though he could never afford to buy anything there.

"A fucking shoplifter's paradise," John grumbled to himself, shaking off the distraction of nostalgia. Jamie pretended not to hear the comment and guided him to the next section.

John ran his hand down the dark polished wood at the end of one of the tall shelves; they felt old and sturdy under his fingers. They made him feel calm and safe. *But they're not practical.* "These old shelves are a problem; we won't be able to move them easily."

Jamie frowned at John. "Come on, man. Give it a chance. We've managed this long without moving anything."

John understood he'd touched a nerve and softened his voice. "I can see you offer a good range of books...."

"People appreciate that we specialize in hard-to-find books and small local publishers," Jamie interrupted.

"Yes, but is *that* profitable?" John said in an annoyingly officious voice.

"You saw the accounts; we do better than break even most weeks. People come back to us."

John knew to let the subject drop for a while and lay his hand on Jamie's shoulder. "Come on, lad. What's next?"

Jamie led him to a section at the back of the store that was full of secondhand books, mainly fiction, but with a couple of nonfiction shelves. John frowned at the two old leather armchairs and made a mental note to get rid of them. He wanted customers to buy books and leave, not linger like it was a library.

"This area takes up a lot of space with little turnover," John muttered half to himself. "Could be a good spot for discount remainder stock."

John noticed Jamie's look of disgust, but let it go; he actually felt a wave of relief that his business acumen had kicked in and provided a more familiar focus.

"A thought for another day." John turned and headed back to the front of the store. "But for now I have a lunch meeting with a business associate. I'll be back in about an hour and you can fill me in on the ordering system."

Jamie slumped against the wall as he watched John walk out the door. He turned his face to the battered armchairs and sighed. "This is not going to be easy."

LUNCH was spent in an expensive Docklands restaurant discussing the "temporary" handover of John's portfolio. It was familiar territory and reaffirmed John's desire to drag Margins into a higher profit bracket. He refused to let the lure of a childhood memory get in his way. He'd gotten this far from the back streets of Bradford and there was no way he was going back.

It was late afternoon when John pushed open the door and made his way to the bookstore's counter where Jamie was checking through the latest invoices. Jamie looked up at the clock and flashed a cheeky smile. "Must've had a lot of business to discuss."

John scowled, but for some reason found Jamie difficult to reprimand. Instead he took off his jacket and leaned over Jamie's shoulder, eyeing the invoice in hand. "Guess I need to start learning the ropes, huh?"

Jamie turned his face toward him and said with a sly grin, "I'm sure you'll find I'm a good teacher."

"Oh, I just bet you are." John laughed, not sure if Jamie was flirting or just playing up to the boss. "But how about we go through the ordering system first?"

Jamie attempted to look shocked, but failed miserably and giggled. "The order book is out back; I'll go get it."

"No, I'll go. I have to start finding my way around."

Jamie's expression quickly changed and he tried to say no, but John was already around the counter. As he neared the back of the store, John's eyes fell on a very disheveled-looking man sitting in one of the big leather armchairs engrossed in a secondhand novel. John's initial reaction was to look away, but he couldn't help staring at this man. His clothes were a filthy array of layers; his dirty feet were partially tucked under him and a pair of ratty elastic-sided boots sat on top of an overstuffed pack beside the chair. The shoulder-length hair could have been dark blond if it was clean, but hung in mangy brown matted lengths. The man looked up and then quickly dropped his eyes as soon as they made contact with John's.

Jamie had been watching John with a half-held breath and when he saw him take a step toward the chair called out quickly, "Um, John, I need you over here.... Um, there might be a problem with one of the orders."

John hesitated briefly, frowning at the man desperately trying to sink into the leather chair before turning to walk back to Jamie. "What sort of problem?" he muttered.

"Oh... um... no problem really," Jamie wasn't sure how to continue so he took a deep breath and said, "That's David."

John just folded his arms and waited.

"Okay.... Mum saw him looking at the books in the window a few times. She said he looked cold... and sad." Jamie paused to gauge John's reaction, and when there was none he continued. "So she asked him if he wanted to come in. He smiled a bit, but walked away. The next day Mum saw him again. She's not one to give up, my mum; so she went outside and convinced him to come in. Actually she almost dragged him in. She told him it was okay to read the secondhand books and bought the battered old chairs the next day. So David comes in every day to read...."

John frowned at Jamie's babbling and mumbled, "Sounds to me like your mum is a 'soft touch,' Jamie."

Jamie knew that was true but couldn't stand the thought of telling David he wasn't welcome anymore.

"Look, John, I know this is your place now, but David is harmless. Smells a bit, but is quite nice when you can get him to talk."

John didn't look convinced and was more concerned that *David* might discourage paying customers. Jamie shifted anxiously from one foot to the other trying to figure out how to make John understand; finally he came to a decision, took another deep breath, and suggested he introduce him to David. John rolled his eyes and shook his head, but followed the young assistant to the rear of the store because it was obviously important to Jamie.

John felt strangely nervous as they approached the chairs. Despite the hair falling around his face and ratty beard, John could see that the man was around his age, but that was where the similarities seemed to end. John was at a loss to see what he could possibly talk to this man about.

Jamie sat in the chair next to David, who looked up from his book and smiled. "Hey, Davey. Whatcha reading?" Instead of answering David showed him the cover of the book while casting a wary glance at John. Jamie followed his look and said, "This is John. You remember I told you how Mum was selling this place? Well, John is the new owner." David didn't look reassured by this information, but quietly mumbled "Hi" without meeting John's eyes.

For some reason those eyes disconcerted John and he didn't hold the man's look. Perhaps he was a reminder of another path, a "there but for the grace of God" type of thing or…. John couldn't put his finger on why, but David was not someone he wanted near him. With a grunted a hello, John reminded Jamie that he still had to finish showing him last month's orders and walked back to the counter. As he turned his back to them he heard Jamie say in a very conspiratorial whisper, "He'll be okay, Dave. Just seems a bit grumpy 'cause he's not used to us yet."

John raised his eyebrows *and* his voice at the comment. "Jamie! Come on!"

Looking back to see if Jamie was following, John caught him leaning in to whisper something to David before giggling and jogging toward the counter.

"He is a good person, John. Please don't chase him out," Jamie pleaded when he caught up.

"Your mum's not the only one who's a soft touch," John responded, but at least he was smiling. He'd already decided to deal with the David issue another day.

THE rest of the day was spent with John, sitting at the small table beside the counter going through the ordering system, ringing distributors, and introducing himself. He was comfortable with that and gradually began to believe that the next twelve months were at least doable. There'd been a steady trickle of customers throughout the day but he left them to Jamie. John smiled at Jamie's mix of ease and enthusiasm when dealing with people; it was obvious that they adored him, especially the older women. He was a definite asset to the business.

Just before closing, a quiet figure made his way past the counter. John looked up to see David, boots back on his feet and battered pack slung over his shoulder, head down, carefully avoiding John's eyes as he left the store. John frowned. *I must do something about him.*

As he looked away from the door he caught Jamie's worried eyes on him. John refused to acknowledge the look and simply said, "Well, Jamie, we survived our first day together. Time to lock up and head home, I think."

Jamie allowed the knot in his stomach to dissipate, let his breath out, and walked to the door to flip the OPEN sign over to CLOSED. He made a show of turning the lock on the door, looked at John, wiggled his eyebrows, and said, "Tomorrow we let you loose on the customers."

John shook his head and groaned. "Oh fuck."

CHAPTER 2

FINDING the off-street parking was easy enough, but getting out of the car took more courage than John could muster. He'd turned off the engine and removed his seat belt, but rather than exiting he sat silently in the driver's seat. John knew this was the first real day of his life as a storekeeper. He closed his eyes and let his head fall back against the headrest. *A fucking storekeeper,* he thought. *All that fucking work to end up behind a counter. Only a year, Mac, only a year.*

The key slid easily into the lock and with a simple turn the door opened. John stepped inside the still-dark store, flicked on the lights, and entered the alarm code. He took a breath and walked over to the counter. It all seemed so familiar, but *not* at the same time. The business side of things would be easy, he knew that. But the rest….

John ran his fingers over the antiquated cash register and soon they were lightly dancing over the keys; not enough to move them, just enough to feel them against his fingertips. He stopped and looked up through the store. It was quiet. There was a flutter of anxiety in the pit of his stomach and the usual dull pain behind his eyes. Without any real purpose, John strolled through the solid bookshelves, briefly touching the occasional volume before moving on.

It wasn't long before he found himself sitting in one of the leather chairs. He slouched down into worn leather and closed his eyes. The smell of dust and old books was strong. He smiled, feeling like a little boy sitting in the "big" chair at his granny's. She always surrounded herself with books and let John sit in his granddad's chair to read them. John felt his muscles relax. He felt safe.

"You look happier this morning."

John leaped out of the chair as if he'd been caught doing something wrong and glared at Jamie who was leaning, hands in pockets, against one of the shelves. It took a moment for the blood to stop rushing in his ears but he managed to growl, "If you plan on keeping your job, don't sneak up on your boss!"

John stalked past Jamie toward the counter, ignoring the barely concealed giggle of the young man bouncing along behind him.

THE morning passed easily and generally without incident. The early customers tended to be relatively introspective and seemed to know what they were looking for without his help. Jamie informed him that "Customers usually fall into categories according to the time of day or day of the week. The morning is for those on a mission, by eleven a.m. the university students surface, and afternoon is for the browsers and mums with kids." As if on cue a young couple talking loudly breezed past them and headed for the secondhand book section.

Jamie gave John a triumphant look and stated, "Student types. It must be nearly eleven."

John chuckled at the smug look and couldn't resist needling Jamie by asking, "So what time is set aside for our resident transient?"

Jamie's grin faltered and with a quiet "I'll put the kettle on," he left the counter and walked into the kitchen.

A laugh alerted John to the fact that the "student types" were emerging from the secondhand alcove and heading toward him. John braced himself with a mental *be polite* and asked, "Find anything interesting?"

The boy threw a paperback in front of John and grunted, "Does the bookmark come with the book?"

John frowned and picked up the book, opening the page where a slightly tattered red leather bookmark rested. "Um, I guess so...."

Suddenly Jamie appeared from the back room and snatched the book out of his hands. He glanced first at John and then the students, saying in a very hesitant voice, "I'm sorry. This one isn't for sale."

"It was on the shelf!" The boy argued.

Jamie shot another look at John before stammering, "I... I made a mistake. It was requested by someone who phoned earlier and I forgot to pull it off the shelf."

The boy didn't look convinced, but his girlfriend smiled and said, "Hey, that's okay. We all make mistakes."

Jamie smiled and silently thanked her for getting him off the hook with her boyfriend.

"Look, if I get another copy I'll make sure I put it under the counter for you, yeah?" Jamie said, holding on tightly to the paperback.

The girl realized there was obviously more to this so thanked him quietly before dragging her boyfriend out the door. Once they were gone Jamie just stood looking down at the book, his fingers worrying the corner of the bookmark, trying to avoid John's gaze. But he knew the question was inevitable.

"What was that all about?"

Jamie sighed. "The book *is* reserved, John. Sort of."

"Shouldn't it be behind the counter if it's reserved?" John asked with narrowed eyes, well aware that Jamie was trying to get out of answering him.

"Um... yeah, my mistake. I'll put it away." Jamie avoided looking directly at John and reached down to put it under the counter, but John stopped him with a quiet "Now tell me what's *really* going on here, Jamie."

Jamie twitched a bit, realizing John wouldn't be diverted. "Mum gave that bookmark to David to let us know which book he's reading, you know, so we wouldn't sell it until he was finished."

David again! John inwardly growled, but looked at Jamie and said, "Okay. I can live with that, and of course you'll let me know if there's anything else I should be warned about."

Jamie's relief was palpable as he watched John walk back through the store to return the bookmarked novel to the shelf next to the chair. *This isn't going to be easy, but we'll get there.... We have to.* He released a breath and called, "I'm off to buy some lunch. Want me to get you something?"

"Anything's fine." John smiled as he walked back to the counter. "So long as it's none of your vegetarian muck!"

"Okay, sliced corpse on bread for you then?"

"Sounds perfect." John grinned and pulled out his wallet. "Here; take some money."

Jamie waved it away and chuckled as he dashed to the door. "That's cool, mate. I always grab it out of the cash register." Luckily Jamie was through the door before John let loose with a string of very colorful expletives.

John was still shuffling through the accounts when he heard the bell above the door. He was all set to tell Jamie to hurry with his delicious sliced corpse when he saw David come in. Both men avoided looking at each other; David kept his head down and John suddenly found an invoice fascinating. He didn't see Jamie enter the store until a brown paper bag was thrown on the counter in front of him. "Food for the carnivore."

Relieved with the distraction, John grabbed the bag and went into the kitchen. "You want a tea or coffee?"

Jamie continued walking to the back of the store and called over his shoulder, "Can I have two teas, please?"

John frowned as the water rushed into the kettle. "Two teas?" Then he realized with a groan: "David."

With two mugs in hand John walked through the store wondering who the hell was the boss in this place. He could already hear the two men talking when he rounded the shelf and saw Jamie crack up laughing and run his hand over David's hair. It was an innocent enough gesture, but John cringed at the sight. *How can Jamie touch him in that state?*

David stopped talking as soon as he saw John and took the mug with a quiet "Thank you." Jamie flashed John his best smile and said, "Ta, John. Here, sit down and have lunch with us. I'll grab the floor." Jamie started to stand, but John waved him back down and left them to share Jamie's lunch.

JOHN was relieved that his first "real" day was over, although he had to admit it hadn't been as bad as expected. The register tallied, taking into account the lunch money snaffled by Jamie, and the day's takings seemed quite healthy.

Jamie was in the kitchen rinsing out their well-used mugs, leaving John to do the final walk-through of the store before locking up. John methodically straightened up any stray books and checked for discarded sweetie wrappers near the children's books. The last section he reached was the secondhand books and John realized he'd already started to think of this as *David's spot.* "All bloody Jamie's fault," John grumbled as he moved to pick up a piece of paper left on one of the chairs. "I would have flung him out day *one* without Jamie whining in my ear."

John looked down at the paper. It had obviously been torn out of one of the cheap water-damaged sketch books they kept near the counter, like the one he'd seen stuffed in the side of David's backpack. But it was the subject of the sketch that made him frown. He was looking at himself. It was a picture of John at the counter doing the accounts; his chin was resting on his hand and his eyes were unfocused, staring into space.

John was taken aback by the image. *Is that what I look like to him?* It certainly wasn't the face he saw in the mirror every morning. He was still scowling at the sketch when Jamie said, "That's beautiful."

John was startled by the sudden voice and growled, "Fucking hell, Jamie. I wish you would *stop* sneaking up on me!"

"What would be the fun in that?" Jamie grinned, his dark eyes dancing with mischief. "I like catching the boss perving at pictures of himself."

"Come on, you daft git. I'll drive you home." John chuckled and shoved Jamie past the counter toward the door, but not before slipping the picture carefully into his briefcase.

Jamie had fiddled with just about every accessory in the car, both standard and optional, before John had backed out of the car park. Finally he settled on shuffling through John's CDs. "Man, you have crap taste in music."

John just ignored him and indicated to turn into the main street. By the time they reached the third intersection Jamie's attention had definitely shifted to outside the car. John was just about to give in and ask him what he was looking for when Jamie whipped around in his seat. "Hey, pull over!" John instantly did as he was told and turned to Jamie. "What? What's wrong?" But Jamie was already halfway out the window and shouting, "Fuck off, you wankers!" The words were no sooner spoken when John saw a couple of teenagers bolt down the street.

He then saw David walking toward the car and Jamie eased back in the window. "Hey, Dave. You okay?"

"Yeah. They were just drunk kids, that's all," David said quietly as he bent down to the window. His expression rapidly became guarded when he saw the driver of the car. John felt a pang of guilt at the look without being able to pin down why he should feel that way.

David's eyes returned to Jamie as he asked, "It's cold tonight; do you have somewhere to go?"

"Heading to the shelter. It's early; there should still be beds."

Jamie looked at him, hoping that was true, and whispered, "Stay safe, man." David gave him a small smile, shrugged, and walked toward the door of the shelter.

Jamie slumped into the car seat. "I fucking worry about him…."

John didn't know how to respond so remained silent, only asking for the occasional direction. When he pulled on the handbrake outside the small apartment building, Jamie hesitated before opening the door. He turned and said with an almost sheepish expression, "Hey, thanks for driving me man. Um… you wanna come up for a coffee?"

John considered what he assumed was an offer and was tempted, but wasn't really sure if he'd misinterpreted the invitation. Rather than making a fool of himself or embarrass Jamie, he said with a gentle smile, "Rain check, okay?"

Jamie returned the smile and added a wink as he got out of the car. John gave him a good-natured shake of the head and wave as he pulled away from the curb. *Well, McCann, a gorgeous young man invited you up for coffee and you knocked him back. That may just have been the dumbest thing you have done for a while.* By the time he reached the intersection near the shelter, John had decided to take Jamie up on the rain check. Perhaps dinner the next night?

While waiting for the traffic lights to change from red to green he couldn't help looking at the entrance of the shelter. The doors were now closed and it was only by chance that a movement caught his eye and he saw a couple of people huddled in a nearby doorway. His breath caught in his throat when he realized one of the men settling down on the folded cardboard was David.

John didn't notice the lights had changed until he was startled by the impatient drivers honking from behind. He took his foot off the brake and drove away.

By the time he'd reached his apartment John had a sick, heavy feeling deep in his chest. He nodded at the doorman and traveled up the elevator to his floor.

Rather than relaxing when he entered the familiarity of his apartment, John felt agitated and angry. He threw his keys on the table, poured himself a scotch, and flopped down on the couch. The thought of food turned his stomach so he just sat in the quiet room smoking a cigarette. The sense of satisfaction he'd felt earlier had completely evaporated and he rubbed his hand over his eyes, feeling vaguely sick. *Shit! This was all supposed to help.* John groaned at the familiar pressure behind his eyes. *I'm just tired; bed and sleep's what I need.*

John didn't switch on the heating in the room and undressed, ignoring the goose bumps on his flesh. He tried hard to convince himself that it wasn't really a cold night, but by the time he crawled under the warmth of the duck down quilt, he was miserable. His stomach was twisted in knots and his tense muscles were threatening to cramp. His mind kept replaying the scene in the doorway and Jamie's quiet plea: "Stay safe, man."

"Oh, fucking hell," John cursed and threw back the covers. He dressed quickly, grabbed his keys, and made his way back to the garage.

"What the fuck am I doing?" he muttered as he backed his car out of his spot. "David is not some fucking stray puppy."

John found a parking bay near the shelter and walked toward the store doorway, trying to figure out what he was going to say. How was he going to explain why he was there and what was he actually going to offer David?

When he finally turned into the doorway his heart missed a beat. It was empty. John stood in the bare alcove, unsure what to do, and looked around the small space as if he'd somehow missed evidence of where David had gone. He spotted a cop standing across the road watching him. John waved and jogged over to ask, "Excuse me, officer. Did you see a man sitting in that doorway a little while ago?"

The cop gave him a long curious look before answering, "Why? Did he take something?"

"No!" John responded quickly. "No, I'm, um... I'm just looking for him, that's all."

"Moved 'em on. A filthy nuisance they are hanging around here and there's too much paperwork if I haul them in."

John's stomach churned at the cop's attitude, but he forced himself to stay civil. "Any idea where he might have gone?"

The cop looked directly at John and said, "Could be anywhere. Needle in a haystack. Best to leave it and head home."

John knew it was pointless to ask any more and made his way back to his car. He drove fruitlessly around the streets for another hour before the pounding in his head and his rapidly blurring vision forced him to give up and go home.

CHAPTER 3

JOHN had reorganized the books on the recommended fiction display twice within the space of as many hours when he found himself beginning to move the nearest title yet again. He quickly pulled his hand back and shoved it in his trouser pocket as if the rapid action could deny its original intent. He stood and stared at the neat display, then grimaced at his sudden and unfamiliar need to find pointless "busy work". This was *not* his way; yes, he could be methodical, but he always had goals, some sort of end product.

He couldn't settle, and what was worse, had no idea why he felt so restless.

As the day progressed John could feel the little ball of anxiety building in his stomach and Jamie had decided very quickly to give him a wide berth. It was nearly lunchtime when John looked up at the familiar tinkle of the doorbell.

John watched David carefully close the door and was surprised when the knot in his gut began unraveling, shocked that he was relieved to see David. It was then he realized that he was smiling and his hand was motioning a half-wave. Suddenly embarrassed, John dropped his hand, but David gave him a half-smile back before lowering his face and moving to his safe spot at the rear of the store.

Jamie poked his head out of the back room and asked, "Was that, Dave?"

John was flustered, caught off guard, but managed to grumble, "Yeah."

"Cool. Here's your tea, and can you take this one for David? I made him a coffee 'cause it was cold last night."

John hesitated. *Damn it.* He knew Jamie was doing this on purpose, trying to make it harder for John to throw David out. He wanted to say no, that he was busy, but Jamie's look almost dared him to do just that.

John took hold of both mugs and shot Jamie a withering look back. He stormed up to the back of the store, spilling more than the odd drop. He *really* didn't want to do this, but couldn't pinpoint what it was about the man that made him feel so uncomfortable.

David had already removed his boots and was settling cross-legged with a book in his hand. John's attention had drifted to the red bookmark when David lifted his head and gave him a questioning look. Indicating the mug with a nod of his head, John announced, "Jamie made you coffee."

David took the drink quietly and wrapped his fingers around the warm mug. With that job done John started to move away but, for some reason that he couldn't quite fathom, he changed his mind and sat in the spare leather chair.

"Can I ask what was going on last night when we pulled up?" John queried.

David just looked at him for a long while. So long that John started to think there wasn't going to be an answer and was prepared to leave when David replied so quietly that John had to strain to make out all the words. "They were just a couple of kids who'd drunk too much, that's all."

John noticed David's reluctance but continued anyway. "Were they giving you a hard time?"

"It happens." David shrugged.

John narrowed his eyes at what he considered a glib answer and almost pushed for more, but changed tact and said instead, "Jamie's a good kid; he was just about hanging out the car window looking for you last night."

David smiled a little sadly. "Maggie and Jamie have been good to me; I'll miss her."

That was the first time during their conversation that David had made direct eye contact. John was so taken aback by the intensity of the pale gray eyes that he couldn't hold it and looked down at his fingers clenched tightly around his own mug of tea. "Yeah," he mumbled. "You told Jamie you were going to the shelter last night, but I saw you later on."

David's gaze hardened, wondering what exactly it was that John was trying to say. "I did go, but there are very few beds free in winter and there was no room."

John shifted uncomfortably in his seat. This was going into an area he didn't like. It was easier to deal with David when he was simply a smelly derelict who took up store space. He knew those eyes were still on him. Despite his reluctance to hear the answer, John asked in a gentle voice, "So what happens when it's full?"

"Depends on the weather, I guess. Sometimes the park is okay but store doorways are a good option in winter. Cuts the wind and keeps you dry."

"But they don't let you stay there...."

David cocked his head slightly and tucked a strand of hair behind his ear. *Why is this man listening to me?*

"Is that what happened last night?" John looked away from his hands and glanced down the store to where Jamie was pretending not to hover.

David just shrugged as if dismissing it and stated, "Obstruction of a public footpath."

Feeling totally out of his depth, John just shook his head slowly and sipped his tea. He was aware that David was looking at him with some curiosity, but knew his gaze would drop as soon as John met it.

John heard the phone ring and a moment later Jamie called for him. As he stood up, he smiled at David and felt unexpectedly warmed when the smile was returned.

THE rest of the afternoon passed with surprising ease although John couldn't fail to notice that Jamie seemed to take great delight in introducing John to the "regular" customers. Some were civil and polite while others wanted to know every detail about his life, both past and present. He lost track of how many people assumed that John must be related to Maggie because they were both English. "It *is* a very small country, after all." John even survived a quizzing from the local aged pensioners book group.

He was surprised that people didn't seem too worried by David's presence in the secondhand book section; although it was obvious that many customers ignored or avoided him. David just took it all and kept his head buried in his book or his well-used sketch pad. With a wave of guilt, John had to face the fact that *he* was one of the people who would look away and pretend that the dirty man in tatty clothes wasn't really there.

It was wrong that David was invisible to these people, *had* been to him.

When the last customer walked out the door John clasped his hands behind his neck at the wispy edges of his fair hair and stretched his tired muscles. He was weary, but had to admit that he felt good. He grinned broadly at Jamie and said, "I think I'm getting the hang of this."

Jamie gave him an amused look. "Definitely improving, McCann, but a long way to go 'til you reach *my* standard."

"Cheeky bugger!" John laughed as he swiped at Jamie who easily jumped out of his reach. "Hey, want to join me for dinner?"

"This the 'rain check,' huh?" Jamie teased.

"Could be. Any idea where to eat around here?"

"Oh yeah, I know just the place," Jamie enthused, almost bouncing on the spot.

John was laughing at Jamie's seemingly boundless energy at the end of a long day when he saw David walk past and nod good night. Jamie instantly turned his attention to David and said, "Night, Dave. The weather report says it's gonna be mild tonight, so that's good, yeah?"

David paused and smiled at Jamie. "Yeah, that's good."

"Um, listen," John said, looking from Jamie to David. "I'm shouting Jamie dinner. Want to join us?"

Jamie was visibly stunned by John's offer, but not when David quietly thanked him, refused the offer, and walked out the door.

"What's his problem?" John grumbled, angered by the refusal. "I thought he was okay with me now. I mean, he…. Shite. I don't know."

Jamie stood and looked at John for a long moment, trying to get his wording clear in his head. Finally he said in a subdued voice, "I guess he's embarrassed, John."

"Embarrassed? How do you mean?"

"David's not dumb. He knows most places won't let him in. Fuck, even the fast-food joints move them on."

John felt a tinge of shame over his insensitivity. "I didn't think, Jamie. I'm sorry."

Jamie nodded slightly but said, "Hey, at least you're trying. Now, come on, boss. You owe me dinner!"

JOHN laughed when he saw Jamie's *perfect spot*. "I can't believe you found an English pub!"

"You better believe it. My dad used to drag us here for the match of the week." Jamie grinned over his shoulder. "They even serve that fuck awful black pudding from your end of the world."

"Don't knock the puddin', mate." John chuckled as they pushed the door open and walked into the noisy bar. "Fuck! Ale on tap and football on the telly…. I've died and gone to heaven."

"Or died and gone to Bradford. I knew that posh accent was put on."

"You have no idea how much work it took to leave the 'lad' in Bradford."

Jamie was about to reply but spotted a table being vacated near the fireplace. "Yes! Come on," he shouted excitedly and dragged John through the crush of bodies until they reached the table. "Great spot this; warm fire and good view of the match."

The dinner was a near perfect attempt at English fish and chips and they settled comfortably to watch the football match. However, it wasn't even halftime when Jamie turned to John and asked, "So, do you have a girlfriend… or boyfriend?"

John nearly choked on his beer as he managed to gasp, "Shit! You don't bandy your words, do you?"

Jamie just laughed and drained his glass. "Well, you never find stuff out if you don't ask. So, do you?"

John shook his head and let the smile slip from his face. "I have a girlfriend, of sorts."

"What does that mean... of sorts?" Jamie queried.

John sighed. "Marian and I have been 'going out' for a few years, but I suppose it's just convenient for both of us. We're useful to each other."

"Useful? That sounds fucked, John," Jamie said with obvious distaste.

"Well, I never said it was true love," John said with a grimace before emptying his glass. "I also never said we were exclusive."

Jamie stared at him for a moment before breaking into laughter. "Come on then; the match is boring anyway." Jamie jumped to his feet, grabbed his coat, and headed for the door.

John happily acknowledged the pleasant buzz of the alcohol as they left the warmth of the pub and they huddled together against the biting cold of the night outside that was nowhere near as mild as originally forecast.

"Fuck, it's bloody freezing tonight," Jamie cursed as he broke away from John and ran to the car. "Come on, man. Let me in the car before me bits drop off!"

John pressed the button on his key ring and laughed at Jamie's inelegant dive into the passenger seat. As usual, he rifled through the CDs until he found one vaguely acceptable and slid it into the player. By the time John was out of the parking spot Jamie had settled against the headrest with his eyes closed and was singing at the top of his lungs.

He was still singing along to the CD when John pulled on the handbrake outside Jamie's apartment. John gave a quiet laugh as Jamie finished the song and turned his head to give him a cheeky grin.

John matched his pose and asked, "Am I invited in tonight?"

Jamie's grin widened and he waggled his eyebrows before cracking up and laughing, "Oh shit. I can't pull off sexy looks when I'm drunk."

John was about to argue but found himself running his fingers down Jamie's neck instead. He leaned in until his tongue followed the path of his fingertips. Unfortunately John had only just begun in his "grand" seduction when Jamie erupted into a round of drunken giggles.

"Sorry... sorry," Jamie said, trying desperately to suppress his mirth as he buried his face in the crook of John's neck. John was slightly bewildered by Jamie's reaction, but grinned into his hair and said, "Time to get you upstairs, I think."

The journey up the stairs took slightly longer than anticipated. Jamie managed to locate his key and open the door, but as soon as they were inside the foyer he rounded on John, pushed him up against the small bank of mailboxes, and leaned full-length against him. John twined his fingers through Jamie's dark hair and asked with an amused smirk, "Got something in mind? Or am I just a convenient resting place before you tackle the stairs?"

Jamie pushed his hips invitingly against John, wishing they weren't cocooned in such thick overcoats, and giggled more than a little breathlessly. "I have *a lot* on my mind; if I can just figure out how to get up the bloody stairs."

John cupped his hands on either side of Jamie's face and shook his head before laughing and turning him around to face the way up to his apartment. "Lead on, James."

With a lot of laughter and drunken false starts they managed to navigate both the stairs and the front door. Once inside the apartment Jamie fumbled with the buttons on John's overcoat. "Fuck, my fingers won't work," he laughed when he couldn't get a grip on one of the buttons.

John quickly rid himself of his coat and dragged Jamie's off his shoulders, throwing it on a nearby chair. He slid his arm firmly around Jamie's waist and growled, "Coats are gone now."

Jamie grinned and resumed his full-length press against John. "Much better." Reveling in the shared warmth, he moaned lightly and pushed his hand inside John's shirt.

Even though Jamie had earlier argued with himself over the merits and pitfalls of sleeping with the new boss, there was a sadness to John that no amount of bravado could hide. There was something about him that said he needed this tonight.

Besides, Jamie reasoned, *a few drinks and those sexy green eyes....*

A low hum escaped John's lips when Jamie's fingers worked their way up his chest to drag his nails lightly across John's nipple. "Fuck, lad. I think you better show me your bedroom."

Jamie backed off just enough to pull John through the front room and into his bedroom; however, the dynamics quickly changed as soon as they were across the threshold. John's hands encircled Jamie's arms and spun him around until he was pinned against the now-closed door. Jamie barely had time to catch his breath before John had hauled his shirt over his head and removed his own with the same urgency.

Jamie's head fell back against the wooden door as John bit lightly at the side of his neck. He could feel hands working on his fly, his own fingers blindly grasping at John's hair. Despite being trapped between John and the door, Jamie was able to move his hips and legs enough to allow his pants to fall to the floor, all the while trying to pull John in for a kiss. But John was having none of that and quickly pushed him back against the hardwood of the door using his free hand to extricate himself from the last of his own clothes.

"Shit," Jamie moaned, pulling John's hair to make him back off a little. "I'm getting fucking splinters in my arse here."

John chuckled, stepped out of his fallen clothes, and ran his hands all the way down the silken skin of Jamie's sides, stopping only when they reached the gentle crease at the top of his thighs. John hauled one leg up and wrapped it over his hip, steadying himself before he was able to lift the other leg. Jamie moaned and crossed his legs behind John, squirming until he was safely cradled in John's strong hands so he could turn them toward the bed.

With a grunted effort, John managed to get his knees onto the bed where he safely lowered Jamie to the mattress. He lay still for a moment, both to catch his breath and to give him a chance to think and gain some semblance of control. The latter was difficult with Jamie's mouth on his throat and hips rolling rhythmically against his cock. "Oh God. Jamie, if you keep doing that this is going to be over before it begins."

Jamie knew full well the effect he was having on John, enjoying the small amount of momentary power it gave him, but after one more cheeky thrust he unlaced his legs and reached over to the bedside drawer to pull out a condom and lubricant. He tore open the packet and reached down to stroke John's already aching cock.

"No, you don't," John muttered, clamping his hand over Jamie's to still its action. "Turn over."

Without argument, Jamie slid over onto his belly, silently enjoying the delicious friction of the heavy quilt stitching against his already dripping cock. He attempted another languid rub over the fabric but John's arm encircled his waist and roughly hauled his hips off the bed. Jamie arched back into John's touch and the cool fingers that slid between his cheeks.

John paused, taking in the beautiful man pushing back against his hand. *This is not a good idea.* But the desperate ache in his body quickly negated any doubts. He teased two fingers slowly around Jamie's opening before exerting enough pressure to thrust them in.

"Fuck," Jamie grunted, trying to rise farther off the bed, meeting the probing fingers. John's tongue flicked slowly over his bottom lip as he watched Jamie's hips undulate in time with his fingers. He knew he couldn't wait. He quickly removed his fingers and rolled on the condom, cursing as both lube and haste made it slippery.

Jamie braced his head on his forearms when John gripped his hips. The breach was hard and without hesitation, but Jamie remained still. He wasn't usually this passive, but he knew it was what John wanted, *needed.*

It was so difficult to breathe buried deep in Jamie. The heat gripped him and John fought his way back from the edge, exhaling a long shaky breath.

His fingers tightened their grip around Jamie's hip bones and with a near desperate growl John pulled back just enough to allow him to snap his hips hard into his compliant partner. "Oh, fuck." Jamie gasped against the sweaty skin of his forearms but pushed back, urging John on as he matched the initial thrust with a second and a third.

The room faded from John's vision as all his concentration focused on the smooth skin in front of him… *male* skin… something he'd denied himself for too long.

Above his own labored breathing Jamie could hear John's almost pained grunts and he knew neither of them was going to last at that rate. With a little effort Jamie managed to squeeze one of his hands beneath them and took hold of his own need. Each movement brought on a gasped moan as Jamie pumped his cock in time with John's increasingly erratic rhythm.

"Oh God. Almost there… almost." John panted breathlessly.

Jamie wanted to answer, but was too near his own completion to formulate words; he barely managed a mantra of incoherent noises as the tension built in his body. He rocked back, vaguely conscious of John's sweat wet between his thighs and the steady echoed slap of their damp skin. His hand gave one last twist as his orgasm hit, leaving him only barely aware of John's strangled cry and shudder before he slumped forward onto Jamie's back.

"Fucking hell, Jamie, I think you killed me," John gasped into Jamie's ear.

"Well, you're squishing me, John." Jamie chuckled breathlessly.

John carefully eased out and sat back on his heels to peel off the condom. "Sorry. Um, where can I put this?"

"Bin next to the bed." Jamie pointed as he rolled over to watch John.

"So tell me, Jamie, do you always fuck your boss?" John grinned as he leaned back against the headboard and lit a cigarette.

Jamie sat up and twisted around until he was cross-legged facing John. "Eew…. Think about what you just said, John!" he exclaimed and pulled a face of disgust.

John looked blankly at Jamie for a moment before it dawned on him who Jamie had previously worked for. "Oh fuck. I'm sorry," he blurted out, embarrassed by his mistake, but Jamie simply grinned and shrugged.

"It's okay. So when does your girlfriend get back?" he asked and reached over to take the cigarette.

"Not sure. Soon, I think," John said quietly, not particularly keen on the idea of discussing Marian while he was still in Jamie's bed. "She is not going to like my new apartment though. Speaking of which, it's time I headed home."

With that, John got off the bed and started to dress. Jamie raised his eyebrows at John's haste, but made no move to follow and lay back propped against the pillows to watch him. He took a long draw of the cigarette before stubbing it out in the ashtray. "You know, you shouldn't stay with someone you don't love, John."

John stopped buttoning his shirt and looked at Jamie. "Meaning?"

"Just that, John," Jamie said quietly.

"What makes you think I don't love her?"

"Well, the fact you just fucked me through the mattress is a bit of a giveaway."

John gave a short laugh and finished dressing without answering.

Driving home, he *did* give some thought to Jamie's words; he *knew* he wasn't in love with Marian and she didn't love him. They were both okay with that because neither had time for the distraction of a "real" relationship.

Even though thoughts of Marian and work had occupied him most of the drive, by the time he was nearly home John realized he'd been subconsciously scanning the street looking for David, and had been since leaving Jamie's.

CHAPTER 4

JOHN watched Jamie come through the front door of the store and had all his excuses ready, ranging from *Man, we were so drunk last night* to.... Actually, *that* was his only excuse other than admitting that he'd been lonely. As Jamie approached, John cleared his throat and said gruffly, "Morning, Jamie."

Jamie just looked at him with a grin and replied, "Good morning, John." When he thought John had squirmed enough he laughed. "It's okay. I know it was just a fun night and nothing more. My arse is sore but I'm not going to pine away until you swear your undying love for me."

John definitely looked relieved but had to ask, "It was just your comment before I left.... I wasn't sure?"

"Oh fuck, John. I didn't mean me. I may look it, but I'm not that naive," Jamie exclaimed, slapping John across the shoulder. "Although I do think you're missing a lot of... of... I don't know, *stuff*, the way you live."

"Oh yeah, much clearer now, Jamie." John smiled and raised an eyebrow.

"Oh shit. Um... okay, I'll tell you why the name of the store is Margins; that might help, yeah?"

John folded his arms and leaned back against the counter waiting for Jamie to tell his little story.

"I remember when I was little I got really upset about something—can't remember what now—but my dad asked me if Mum had ever told me why they called the store Margins. I said she hadn't and...."

"Get to the point, Jamie," John sighed.

"Anyway, he explained that the most important things aren't always in the main story; sometimes the real meaning is scribbled in the margins. You know, when you pick up a secondhand book and people have written stuff in it. Um, read what other people think is important. Maybe they underline a sentence or just a word. Sometimes it has nothing to do with the story but how they feel at the time." Jamie frowned because he could see John was not getting his point. "All I'm saying is that there is more to life than the main story. Check out the notes in the margins because maybe they're even more important."

"So tell me, what scribbles are important here, Jamie?" John asked sarcastically.

"Oh, I don't know." Jamie shrugged, frustrated but not defeated. "Um, okay. Look how you are so caught up with profits and meeting deadlines, yeah... and then you meet someone like David. He's not part of your story, but he means something. He might be important."

"Oh, that is total shite, Jamie," John grumbled, his good mood starting to slip. "Go and put the kettle on. You're making my head thump."

John fished in his pocket for his headache pills while Jamie's words replayed themselves. *And then you meet someone like David. He's not part of your story, but he means something.* He lay the pills on the counter ready for his tea and mumbled, "How the fuck could someone like David mean anything?"

Jamie had touched a nerve and John knew it.

BETWEEN accounts and customers John managed to shrug off the mood Jamie had put him in with his story and was chatting happily to a young female customer when David entered the store. He faltered slightly in his sentence at their brief eye contact. David gave a small smile and nodded hello. John nodded back, but David had already looked away. John felt a twinge of guilt and wasn't sure if it was sparked by his previous dismissal of David's importance or the fact he'd fucked Jamie.

He returned his attention to the woman and handed her the brown paper bag containing her child's picture book.

"Was that David?" Jamie asked as he all but danced past John and headed to the back of the store. John glowered at the young man's retreating back and muttered, "You fucking know it was, so why ask?" Suddenly he felt sick to his stomach, sure that Jamie had rushed to tell David the events of the night before. *So what.* He scowled and turned to the inventory book. *I seriously have to get some fucking computers in this place....*

The numbers had only just started to swim into focus when John heard Jamie's laugh and he slammed the accounts book shut. Stalking through the store toward the second-hand section, John growled at Jamie, "Are you doing any work today?"

But as usual Jamie took John's mood in stride and grinned. "Oh come on, John. It's a half-day today and we're closing soon. I was just telling Dave that we're moving you into Mum's place this afternoon and that you couldn't put up with the 'little old lady' furniture."

John relaxed a little; his evening with Jamie had *not* been the topic of conversation. "Give me a break, Jamie. *You* moved out," he said, making sure to keep his gaze away from David.

Jamie laughed, slid his arm in David's, and asked, "Come on, Dave. Wanna give us a hand moving John's stuff upstairs? I'll make him buy us dinner."

David looked briefly at John, not sure how the suggestion would go down with the dour man now watching them, but when Jamie gave his arm a tug he shrugged and said, "Yeah... okay."

MOVING a selection of John's possessions took most of the afternoon. Although Maggie had left the apartment fully furnished, John decided to put her furniture into storage and move in some of his own. The bulk of his belongings remained uptown in his *real* apartment; that way when the year was over he could simply settle back into his old life.

By early evening only a few boxes of clothes and peripheral items remained in their neatly printed cardboard boxes stacked near their final destinations. Looking at their progress John had to admit that although he'd initially been reluctant to let David help he'd worked hard and done the majority of the manual work. Jamie seemed to start a lot of jobs, but always found something else more interesting to do and spent most of his time looking through the boxes providing a running commentary rather than actually unpacking them. Finally John called a halt and sent Jamie for beer and takeout.

With nothing left to do, David stood uncomfortably near a stack of collapsed and folded packing boxes waiting to see what John wanted him to do.

When John turned away from the door he instantly saw David's discomfort and gave him an equally nervous smile. "Jamie won't be long. How about you give me a hand and we clear away some of these boxes to give us room to eat?"

David didn't answer as he began moving the cardboard.

LITTLE more than an hour later, the three men had managed to empty all the takeout cartons and the debris was now strewn on John's coffee table.

"Man, I'm stuffed," Jamie groaned, rubbing his hands over his very full belly.

"I'm not bloody surprised," John laughed. "For a skinny guy you can sure put it away."

I saw you knocking back an entire carton of satay," Jamie pouted. "And I am *not* skinny, you wanker!"

"Oh come on; you're a twig," John said as he leaned over to reach Jamie and pulled up the T-shirt to expose his belly. "Look at this! Nothing wobbles!"

Jamie shrieked as John proved his point by giving him a round of playful slaps. "Fuck off, you bastard. Help, Dave, make him stop."

David sat on his side of the table and laughed at the antics of his friend. The sound made John abandon torturing Jamie and look up. He was stunned by the change in David's features when he laughed and found himself smiling as David met his eyes.

David's own smile quickly faded under John's scrutiny. He decided then that it was time to go and got to his feet, looking around for his jacket, boots, and pack. Jamie saw the sudden change; he'd half-expected it because David always did this when he started to drop his guard. It had taken David months to even tolerate Jamie sitting next to him and longer still for him to accept Jamie's touch. That was the hardest thing for Jamie to deal with; remembering to give David space and resist his inability to *not* touch and hug people.

"It's gonna be cold tonight. Find somewhere warm, okay?" Jamie said as he got to his feet to see David to the door. He knew David had little choice over his sleeping arrangements, but hoped the hot dinner would help.

"Yeah, thanks for the help today," John called as David closed the door behind him.

When Jamie turned away from the door it was obvious that his previous light mood was gone. Seeing his expression, John frowned and said, "Come on, Jamie. He's had his nightly weather report. He'll be okay."

"It's a cold night, John, and it's late." When it was obvious John didn't get the intent of his words Jamie continued. "It's late, John. The shelter will be closed. David knows that and he has nowhere to go."

"*Then why* didn't he fucking say so?" John rolled his eyes and growled. "Why didn't he *ask…*?"

Jamie shot John a withering look and said, "Would you?"

John felt the air leave his lungs. Of course he wouldn't. His fucking pride wouldn't let him, but he still tried to reason. "Look, he'll find somewhere."

"Yeah, John… and he can always call the hypothermia emergency line if he can find a phone that hasn't been vandalized!" Jamie spat out.

"Come on, Jamie. I'll drive you home," John said quietly, wondering if there *was* such a thing as a hypothermia emergency line.

It was bitterly cold and had started to rain by the time they reached the car, but neither man acknowledged it. They sat in silence while John peered through the fogged window waiting for the demister to clear the glass. They were several blocks down the main road when John pulled sharply into the curb. He hit the button that lowered the electric windows, leaned across Jamie's lap, and shouted, "Get in!"

The icy wind rushed in through the open window, making Jamie's eyes water, but he was still able to make out the somewhat surprised and confused expression on David's face. He just stood there staring at John unsure what to do. Jamie had no clue what John had in mind, but he mentally willed David to walk to the car. He could feel John growing impatient when David didn't move so he called, "Come on, Davey. Please get in."

Jamie held his breath for what seemed an age until he saw David start to walk toward them; he quickly twisted around in his seat to open the back door. David lowered himself into the car and didn't say a word. He just sat and waited for John to explain the invitation.

John hadn't really thought that far ahead, but managed to come up with, "Look, it's fucking freezing and um... you may as well crash on the couch tonight. After all, you did help move it." Jamie knew it sounded pretty lame, but he gave John an appreciative smile when David closed the door and mumbled his thanks.

Jamie chattered happily the rest of the way to his apartment making sure to cover up the silence in the rest of the car. When John pulled up out front Jamie mouthed *thank you* to John before making a dash through the rain to his front door.

John could *feel* David sitting quietly behind him and wondered what the hell he was doing taking this man home. After a moment or two he turned around and asked, "Want to sit in the front? That way I'll feel less like your chauffer."

David looked at him before giving a small nod and stepping out of the car to swap seats. He wasn't totally sure what was going on here but John seemed okay, and Jamie liked him. Once the car was in motion John commented on how quiet it was now that Jamie was gone and went on to tell David about Jamie's ability to talk nonstop without taking a breath. David visibly relaxed and smiled at John's observations.

They were nearly back at John's when he stopped outside a pharmacy and said, "Need some supplies if you're staying over. Not be a minute."

David felt his stomach plunge as he watched John jog into the store. *There's always a cost.... Even for a night on the couch.* He squeezed his eyes shut and contemplated just getting out of the car, but was too tired and simply didn't have enough energy to move. David didn't look at John when he got back into the car but eyed the small paper bag warily before it was tossed onto the backseat. He spent the rest of the trip in sullen silence despite John's attempts to make conversation.

When they got to the apartment he walked quietly behind John and stood still as the door was closed behind him. David felt the familiar wave of helplessness as he waited for the inevitable rough touch.

John was confused by the change in David. He'd not moved since John closed the door and his entire body language radiated fear. John knew he was out of his depth with this man; he hadn't meant to make him feel so uncomfortable. He passed the bag over and said in a hesitant voice, "I didn't know what you had so I just got some of the basics. Look, I'm sorry if I've offended you, but... oh fuck, I don't know...." John's sentence trailed off as he closed his eyes and wearily rubbed his hand across his forehead.

Slightly stunned by John's words, David looked down at the paper bag in his hands. He cautiously unfolded the neat crease to find a toothbrush, bar of soap, and a razor. He felt a rush of both relief and shame; relief that he was wrong and shame for not trusting John's intentions.

"Thank you, John. I appreciate it," David murmured, still looking at the contents of the bag. "Can I use your bathroom?"

John gave him a small smile even though David hadn't raised his eyes above the bag and fished a couple of fresh towels out of a nearby cardboard box efficiently labeled "linen closet".

David took the offered towels and ran his fingers lightly along the soft loops of the fabric. Eventually he looked up at John and quietly asked, "Would it be okay if I have a bath?"

"Of course it's okay." John's smile broadened and he motioned toward the bathroom.

John let out a relieved breath when he heard the bath taps running and went to retrieve bedclothes from the relevant box in his room to make up a bed for David on the couch.

Once the bath began to fill, David carefully took the items out of the bag and placed them neatly on the small counter next to the sink. He then started removing the layers of dirty clothing, pausing only to check that the door was still locked. David finally stood naked in front of the mirror and stared at his reflection. Both disgust and despair filled him at what he saw. *How could you think John would want anything from you?* He'd avoided looking at himself for so long he hardly recognized the person looking back.

David raised a hand to his face as if to convince himself of its reality. He closed his eyes against the image, fighting the urge to haul his clothes back on and walk out of the apartment.

It took David several minutes before he'd convinced himself to open his eyes. This time he resolutely met his own gaze before rummaging through the hastily filled bathroom drawers until he found a pair of nail scissors and began to methodically cut some of the matted knots from his hair. By the time the bath was full he'd finished on his hair and rubbed a hand over his beard.

After making up the bed on the couch, John carefully sat on it to test its comfort, despite the fact they'd been sprawled on it most of the evening. Being alone with David made him nervous. He wasn't afraid he'd wake up with his things stolen or anything; it was more the small but insistent flutter that had started low in his belly. He stood up and smoothed his hand over the blanket, straightening out the creases he'd just made. Satisfied with the result, he looked through his neatly folded clothes until he found track pants and a long sleeved T-shirt that might fit David.

When he heard the water gurgling down the drain, John waited a few minutes, then knocked on the door and called through the wood, "I have some clothes for you to sleep in. I'll just leave them by the door." John turned away and wandered into the kitchen, not that he had anything to do in there, but to give David a chance to retrieve the clothes. For want of something to do he started to organize the cutlery in the kitchen drawers until he heard the bathroom door open and close for a second time.

John felt strangely apprehensive about returning to the living room but with a deep breath he braced himself and pushed the kitchen door open. David was still standing next to the bathroom.

John had had every intention to ask David if he wanted a drink, but the words seemed to dry up in his mouth when he saw the other man. The old clothes hung a little too big on him, his hair was still damp, and he was clean shaven.

Beautiful.

John kept his eyes on David but waved his arm toward the makeshift bed. "I... I hope the couch is okay. You should be warm enough, but if you need another blanket I've put them in the closet in my room. Do you want me to get one? I can leave it here for you."

David walked to the couch and sat down. "This is good," he answered quietly, looking directly at John. "Thank you."

John was flustered. "Good, good.... Look, I have a pair of jeans and a flannel shirt I used to use for gardening; don't get much chance to use them anymore. Give me your things and I'll get them cleaned."

"It's okay, John; you don't have to do that." David frowned slightly at John's reaction to him.

John finally smiled. "Don't be daft," he said in a more relaxed voice now he had a purpose, and went into the bathroom. David's clothes were folded on the bathroom floor. He picked up a pair of old jeans and two tattered T-shirts. He left the jacket hanging on the back of the door. Not much he could do with that because he had nothing suitable to replace it. John frowned when he realized that there were no socks or underwear. He put the clothes in a plastic bag and then in his laundry hamper. As he walked through to the bedroom to find his "gardening" clothes, he could see David hadn't moved but was sitting watching his hand as it slid thoughtfully over the white pillowcase.

He put the change of clothes on the coffee table in front of David. "Here. These will do for tomorrow."

John could see the muscle in David's jaw tighten as he obviously fought for a reply; finally he just looked from the clothes to John and said, "Thank you."

"I... I couldn't find your underwear?" John asked and then gave himself a mental kick at the look of shame that crossed David's face. "Sorry. I didn't mean to pry," he quietly apologized and started to walk away.

"I *had* underwear," David murmured. John stopped and turned back to sit on the coffee table in front of David. "It's hard to keep stuff clean after a while. The water is so cold in winter. Nowhere really to wash. I had to throw them out."

John looked down at his hands; it must have taken David a lot of courage to admit that to him. When he looked up he had to know. "What happened, David? Why do you live like this?"

David sat for a while, also watching John's hands. His gaze turned to his own. He'd washed them, scrubbed them in the bath, but he couldn't rid himself of the ingrained dirt. They still weren't as clean as John's. He swallowed hard and looked away. "I was clean at the start, John, and I tried so hard to stay clean, but weeks became months and... and I just got dirty. I wanted a shower, but the line was always so long or by the time I'd get in the hot water was gone. You never seem to get properly clean in a cold shower, do you?"

The words had come out in a rush and then just trailed off. John's chest ached as he listened. They didn't answer his question, but that didn't matter. He hoped David would talk to him when he was ready. As out of character as it was, John wanted to put his arm around David and tell him it would be all right, but the touch may not be welcomed and he also knew it would be a lie. Instead, he took a breath and said, "You're always welcome to come here. I mean, if you need a bath or to wash your clothes."

David chewed on his bottom lip and blinked several times before he could answer, and even then he could only manage a small nod. John's discomfort increased with David's response so he quickly stood up and said, "Well, we better get some sleep because I know we're going to face a barrage of questions from Jamie in the morning. Good night, David."

The mention of Jamie brought a small smile to David's lips and he replied, "Good night, John."

David waited until John closed his bedroom door before he settled down under the covers of the makeshift bed. John's clothes were clean and soft against his skin. Even though they'd obviously been laundered, they smelled vaguely of their owner. David turned onto his side and pulled the blanket up over his shoulders. He was clean, warm, and felt safer than he had for a long time.

Although sleep came swiftly for David, John found it difficult to settle. He lay in his bed and thought through the events of the past couple of days. So different from what he'd expected. The store was okay; actually, he had to admit he was almost enjoying being a storekeeper.

Sex with Jamie had been great and something of an unexpected bonus, but more importantly he was turning out to be a good friend. So why was he still lying awake with his mind racing? *David....*

With a frustrated groan, John sat up and moved to the edge of the bed. He rested his forearms on his thighs and looked at the window. With a long sigh he stood up and moved over to the curtains, parting them slightly. The street below looked cold and wet. John leaned against the window frame and allowed his mind to imagine life on the other side of the glass; a life that didn't include the security of a warm bed at the end of each day. He was relieved that David had come home with him tonight, but knew he'd be back out there tomorrow. John turned away from the window and reached for his cigarettes. *Shit!* The packet was empty. Walking over to the closed door, he debated crossing the living room to get the fresh pack from his jacket pocket. His hand hovered over the doorknob before gripping and turning it.

John tried to keep his steps quiet when he passed near the couch and stretched his hand out to retrieve his jacket from the back of the chair. He could hear David's steady breathing and knew from its soft regularity that David was asleep. John looked down and could just make out David's feature in the dim light of the room. His arm was curled around the pillow, his hand resting gently against his face. His lips were parted and each breath ruffled the stray hairs nearby. John felt himself flush when he had to fight the temptation to brush his fingers over the fine hair and push it back off David's face. The same hair that had disgusted him merely days ago. John shook his head, turned his back to the couch, and made his way back to bed.

CHAPTER 5

THE pale light had barely managed to illuminate John's room when he opened his eyes. He blinked until the sleep haze dissipated and he was able to focus on the nearby clock to see he'd woken about half an hour before the alarm was due to sound. It took him a few moments to adjust to the unfamiliar surroundings of his new bedroom, but then his thoughts instantly turned to the man in the other room. John felt a low heat in his stomach at the thought of David in his clothes, on his couch. Rubbing a hand over his eyes, he banished the nagging ache in his body. *Oh, don't even go there, McCann!*

He ignored the fact he was half-hard, told himself it was morning and had nothing to do with David, and swung his legs over the side of the bed. "I'll make him breakfast, then send him on his way," John muttered as he pulled on clean jeans and made his way into the living room, contemplating whether or not to splurge on a big fry-up breakfast and if the nearby market would have decent bacon. His thoughts stopped short when he approached the couch. The blankets were neatly folded next to the stacked pillows; David was gone. John didn't even consider that he might simply be in the bathroom because he could see one of David's drawings sitting on the coffee table.

John hated to admit it but he was disappointed that David had taken off before he had a chance to talk to him, spend some time with him. He thought David had started to trust him a little last night and though he loathed admitting it, David's trust was becoming important to him.

Picking up the drawing, John sat heavily on the couch. It was a near perfect rendering of himself and Jamie; they were both laughing. John let his fingertips lightly touch the broad smile of his portrait, careful not to smudge the fine pencil work, and wondered if that was how he looked to David. He slumped back and sank into the soft cushions. *What would it take to see David laugh like that?* He let out a heavy breath and put the sketch back on the table.

JAMIE entered the store with a huge grin, sidled up to John, and asked, "Well?"

John knew what he meant, but tried to ignore Jamie's implications with an almost aggressive "What?"

Jamie rolled his eyes. "Did David stay over? Where is he?"

"Yes, he stayed over, and he left before I got up," John replied abruptly, not really wanting to discuss this.

Jamie was tempted to make a comment about John's rapid exit from his bedroom the night before last, but decided not to push his luck. Instead he simply asked, "Things go okay?"

"*Things* went fine, Jamie. Now can we get some work done?" John turned away to reinforce the fact that the conversation was over.

Jamie looked at the back of John's head and grinned with the knowledge that David was definitely starting to get to his boss.

John spent the morning on edge, his anxiety building with each person who entered the store that *wasn't* David. He knew the time David usually wandered in, but that didn't stop him from looking from the first customer of the morning.

Finally David pushed the door open. The change in his appearance still took John's breath away.

David hesitated as he passed the counter. He wanted to thank John. There was so much he wanted to say to him, but he still couldn't quite find his voice. Instead he reminded himself that John was just a kind man who had taken pity on him. *That's all it could be… nothing else.*

John watched him hesitate and almost stop as if he wanted to say something, and *he* desperately wanted to hear David. So John just stood and waited with his fingers clenched around a now very crumpled invoice.

The moment was instantly broken with a loud cry of "David!" Jamie ran out of the kitchen and threw his arms around him. "See, I told you you're beautiful," Jamie whispered as he embraced him impossibly tighter. David attempted an indulgent smile and tentatively let one of his arms encircle Jamie's shoulder.

John chuckled at the pained expression on David's face. "Come on, lad; give him some breathing room."

Jamie loosened his grip, beamed at John, and grabbed David's hand. "We just got a whole new bunch of secondhand books. I pulled out a few I thought you might like. They're next to your chair. There's even a *whole* trilogy. Usually we just get the third book in a series, which is a real pisser, but we got them all this time...." Jamie proceeded to drag David to his section of the store where John could still hear him babbling happily about books with the occasional *Man, you look good* thrown in.

When a new customer approached the desk, John realized he was still looking toward the secondhand book section with a broad grin on his face. He knew he felt better today than he had in a long time.

THE day was a fairly busy one, with visits from both the local book club *and* the aged pensioners to contend with, but John was pleased with the distraction. Plus, it meant that Jamie's attention was elsewhere, allowing both him and David some much needed peace and quiet.

When the string of customers waned John stretched and heard his neck give that satisfying crack. He looked at the clock; it was already four and definitely time for a break. Three mugs of tea were soon made and he carried them carefully out to the front counter where he managed to catch Jamie's eye and nodded down to his steaming brew. Without a word, he picked up the other two mugs and walked to the back of the store.

David was sitting in his usual position, legs curled beneath him and head bowed as he read. When John approached he sat up straighter and took the mug with a smile that said "Thank you."

Taking the seat beside him, John sighed. "I don't know what's got into Jamie today, but he's driving me mad."

To John's surprise David actually gave a low chuckle and shrugged. "He's just happy, I guess."

John shook his head and laughed. Neither spoke for a moment, but this time the silence was not strained. Both men sat and sipped at the too-hot tea, comfortable in each other's company until John looked up and said, "Thank you for the picture. It's really beautiful."

David gave a slight smile and replied very quietly, "You looked good together."

You looked good together. John frowned. It bothered him that David thought he and Jamie were a couple. "We're *not*... um, *together.* It's nothing like that."

"I know, John," David murmured, looking at John to see if he should continue. "But I could see last night that you were...." David sighed, not sure how to put into words what he saw in their friendship. "You already care about each other."

"Care about that brat? I hardly even know him," John joked, feeling very relieved. "Actually he doesn't give you much option, does he?"

David smiled and shook his head. "He has a good heart." His expression became more serious as he looked down at the mug. "And so do you. Thank you, John. Thank you for finding me last night and letting me stay."

John swallowed hard. He wanted to reach over and touch David, to let him know it was okay. It always seemed so easy for Jamie, but he held back. "Any time, David. I meant that," John muttered quietly. He felt the need to lighten the mood and relieve his sudden discomfort. "Although you did miss out on the perfectly good breakfast I'd planned to make."

"You were good to me. I didn't want you to feel uncomfortable with me still there this morning."

The temptation to lie was strong and John was about to protest that he hadn't felt awkward about David's presence in his new home when he heard a female voice calling from the front of the store.

"Well, McCann, stop hiding in the back. I can smell that god-awful cologne of yours so I know you're there."

It was obvious that John recognized the voice. He looked at David, unsure of what to say, so he simply excused himself and made his way to the counter.

"So this is what you've come down to." Marian laughed when she saw John approaching. She was of medium height and slight build with short wavy hair that was almost strawberry blonde, but not quite. She could have been pretty, but instead she looked "efficient".

John gave her a hug and laughed. "Bloody hell. You don't see me for a couple of months and the first thing you do is give me a hard time."

"I'm sure I can make up for it tonight after dinner."

"You haven't changed, Marian. Still making assumptions that you'll always get what you want."

"I *do* always get what I want, and tonight that's you! Come on, McCann. Get your assistant to lock up. We have a lot of catching up to do."

John cringed at the term "assistant," but still called to Jamie, who was pretending not to watch them from the kitchen. "Can you lock up for me, Jamie? Thanks."

He left without waiting for a reply.

David sat in the chair listening to the exchange. He heard how easily they flirted with each other before leaving together… and he knew he'd been kidding himself yet again.

He put his mug on the floor next to where John had left his. He closed his eyes and rubbed a hand wearily over them, reminding himself of what a fucking fool he was.

After John had gone David heard Jamie sit in the chair beside him. He didn't open his eyes when Jamie asked him if he was okay and flinched away from Jamie's hand on his hair.

DINNER was an easy mix of catching up on shared friends and bitching about work colleagues. Marian filled John in on the progress, or lack of progress, in his division and who was doing whom on staff. They talked about her recent trip to London and her plans to stay in town for the next few months. However, for some reason, John was reluctant to discuss Margins. Marian acknowledged John's reasons for "opting out" for a year, but seemed totally unwilling to understand that the little store could actually be anything other than a minor short-term distraction.

It was late by the time they'd drained their last cups of coffee and John wrapped his arm protectively around Marian as they walked back to the car through the park. He was relieved that dinner had gone well and they'd quickly fallen into their old routine of arguing over whose apartment they would end up in. John knew it was all power play between them but enjoyed the familiarity of it.

He'd just managed to sway her into "slumming it" at his place when John noticed her looking toward the nearby public toilet block.

"That is disgusting," she hissed.

John followed her line of sight and saw a man in a cheap suit obviously paying for a quick fuck or blow job. He curled his lip at the scene and was about to echo Marian's sentiments when his eyes rested on the sleeve of the man taking the money. Just below the frayed jacket cuff he could make out green flannel. It was his shirt. John stopped midstride and watched, horrified, as a man pushed money into David's hand. As his fingers closed around the note, David glanced over and saw John.

With eyes wide, David suddenly felt like all the air had been squeezed out of his lungs. John could read the shame on the other man's face, but all he felt was anger. He clenched his teeth and glared.

David's stomach cramped as John's disgust rolled over him. He wanted to throw the money back at the man and go to John, but that wasn't real…. It didn't happen that way. He was paralyzed, pinned by John's eyes until the man grew impatient and gave David a brutal shove toward the toilet block.

Marian looked curiously at John and asked, "Do you know him?"

John looked away from the scene and spat out, "Why the fuck would I know someone like that?" He grabbed her by the arm and stormed to the park exit.

JAMIE figured out pretty quickly that things did not go as planned on John's date although he knew better than to ask. John was in a *filthy* mood. Instead, to avoid John's wrath, he sequestered himself away in the back room where he could unpack and check the latest shipment of school booklists.

David hovered around the front of the store, trying to find the courage to open the door. He'd almost decided not to go in, but knew his regular routine was the only thing that kept him on track, kept him together. He knew he *needed* to spend the day in his chair in the little store despite the risk of John's condemnation. David closed his eyes briefly, pushed the door open, and hoped that Jamie would be at the counter. The doorbell was too loud today and set his nerves jangling. His breathing quickened as he looked at the counter and saw John.

John looked up at the same moment.

David desperately wanted to turn around and leave or put his head down and make it past the counter, but his sketchbook was full. He *had* to have a new one before he could hide in his chair.

John watched as he walked slowly toward the counter. David slipped his hand into his jacket pocket and slid a crumpled twenty onto the counter. His hesitant request for a new sketchbook was barely audible.

Pulling one of the water-damaged pads from under the counter, John slammed it down hard in front of David. He was almost trembling with anger. David cautiously picked up the book and pushed the money forward.

Even the sight of the money twisted John's gut. In that instant all he wanted to do was wrap his fingers around David's collar and shake him, but instead he picked up the note, crushed it in his fist, and threw it back at David, watching as it bounced uselessly off his chest.

"I don't want this fucking money," John barked at him. "I saw how you earned it!"

The words had the impact of a physical punch and David stumbled back from the counter.

Hearing the shout, Jamie ran out of the back room to see what was going on. He looked from John to David trying to figure out what had happened between them, but neither returned his look. He took a few steps toward David and asked quietly, "What's wrong?" David didn't react to Jamie's question and continued to look at John.

With a gentle hand on David's arm, Jamie asked again, "Davey, *please* tell me, what's wrong... what's happened?"

This time David turned and looked at Jamie, and the pain in his eyes was evident.

When Jamie saw this he tightened his grip. "*Please,* Dave...."

David shook his head so slightly that Jamie wasn't sure it happened before he wrenched his arm free and fled out the door.

John was standing looking at both the sketchbook and crumpled ball of money lying on the counter when Jamie rounded on him. "What the fuck happened, John? What did you say to him?"

John's grip on his emotions was so tight that his voice came out flat and controlled. "I told him I didn't want his money."

Jamie eyed him warily. Something was really wrong. "Why not, John?"

"I saw him, Jamie, whoring himself out in a fucking public toilet." John's hold slipped as he managed to get the words out.

Jamie stared at him, allowing the words to sink in. He could feel his own anger taking hold. "Fucking up-market morality! Bloody hell, John. David doesn't have a healthy bank account to dip into when he needs something... or even a fucking welfare check to cash. I can't believe you did that to him! Do you think he *wants* to sell himself?" Tears of frustration and anger built behind Jamie's eyes. "Can you even *imagine* what that must do to him every time he has to let someone...?" Jamie clenched and unclenched his hands as he fought for control. "I can't believe you did that."

Jamie turned his back to John and walked out of the store to look for David.

CHAPTER 6

SITTING in the old leather chair sharing his lunch with David had become something of a routine for Jamie. He enjoyed the quiet conversation, the fact that he could confide in David and know that he'd never be judged.

It had taken quite a while to get to that point. Jamie remembered David's first reluctant venture into the store; once Maggie had convinced him to come in he spent his time moving around as if he were looking for something. He wandered from shelf to shelf lifting his hands to the books, but not letting his fingers make contact. Jamie wanted to go and speak to him and ask what book he wanted, but Maggie had held him back with the advice to give David time. He didn't stay long the first day, but appeared at the door the next morning. Maggie smiled from behind the counter and clasped Jamie's hand as a warning not to invade his space.

After he made his slow walk through the shelves, Maggie quietly approached David and calmly pointed out the secondhand book section with the invitation to stay and read. He wouldn't make eye contact but looked in the direction she'd indicated and twitched his lips in what Maggie had decided was an attempt at a smile. She left him alone to explore and returned to the front desk, whispering to Jamie that it was going to be all right.

Jamie absently chewed on his sandwich; he'd spent a lot of years helping in his parents' store before David appeared, but it still seemed wrong now without him. The second triangle of bread sat on the empty chair. Jamie couldn't eat it.

TWO weeks had passed since David had left. Jamie had tried to find him after he ran out of the store but quickly learned that many people, either through conscious choice or apathy, didn't see people like David. Jamie had given each homeless person he met ten dollars and his phone number with the request that they call him if they saw David. He knew some would spend it on drink, but he didn't begrudge them that.

He'd spent most of his wages, even a large chunk of his rent money, but there'd been no phone call.

Initially Jamie had been furious with John, but now he could see that no matter how hard John tried to hide it he looked up hopefully every time the doorbell jingled. It became very obvious to Jamie that John missed David and was worried about him too, even though he would never admit it.

John walked to the back of the store and saw Jamie sitting quietly eating his half of the sandwich. He was shamed by the sight of the uneaten sandwich on the otherwise empty chair, but as had become habit over the past couple of weeks John resorted to anger and snapped, "Get rid of those fucking chairs, Jamie. I am fed up seeing them here taking up space."

He turned and walked back to the counter, his hand fumbling with the strip of headache tablets in his pocket.

WITH Marian back in town, John fell into their familiar routine of dinner at an up-market restaurant followed by drinks and sex at one of their apartments. They never spent the entire night together. Both John and Marian avoided lingering in the bedroom once their liaison was over; they usually dressed quickly and said their good nights. It wasn't that they didn't care about each other, but they couldn't see the point in complicating a *useful* relationship. Tonight it was John's place and, as usual, the dinner was expensive and the sex was passionless but had served its purpose.

"You know, you have to get out of this area, John," Marian complained and shook her head at him as he closed the bathroom door behind him.

John rolled his eyes at her and grinned. "I know…. It's too small, too depressing, and the parking is a bugger."

"Well, all those things are true," Marian continued. "But I'm more concerned with the fact you have vagrants turning up on your doorstep after midnight."

John looked at her blankly but a vague sick feeling started to creep through him. "What do you mean?"

Marian picked up their empty glasses and started to walk to the kitchen. "While you were in the bathroom a filthy man turned up, bleeding on your doorstep."

John quickly crossed the room and grabbed her arm to stop her. "What happened? Where is he?"

Marian gave John a curious look. "It's all right, John. I told him to leave."

"What did he say, Marian?" John asked through clenched teeth, fighting to remain calm.

"Not a thing actually. He just stared at me when I opened the door. I asked him if he needed help. I'm not *totally* heartless. But when he wouldn't answer I told him to leave and I locked the door."

John instantly let go of Marian's arm and rushed out the door. His heart pounded heavily as he vaulted the steps two at a time, nearly tumbling over the figure sitting huddled at the bottom of the stairwell.

Quickly regaining his balance, John attempted to steady his breathing and crouched in front of the still figure. "David?"

When David didn't respond, John could feel his panic build. He put his hand carefully on the downturned head, slid his fingers through the greasy hair, and whispered, "Dave, *please?*"

Slowly John cupped David's chin with his other hand and carefully raised the bloodied face. David's lip was split and blood flowed freely from a cut above his eye. Gently rubbing his thumb along David's jawline, John watched and waited anxiously while David tried to focus on the face near his.

Relief washed through John when he saw recognition flicker into the gray eyes, but it was soon replaced with a mixture of guilt and pain when David mumbled, "I'm sorry, John."

"Oh fuck, David, you have *nothing* to be sorry for. I was a fucking bastard," John said just as quietly before he eased his hands away and stood up. "Come on, mate. Let's get you inside." John looked around for David's pack but the only possession he could see was a single torn sketchbook held white-knuckled to David's chest.

It was clear that David was exhausted after making it to the apartment so John leaned down, tentatively put his arm around David's waist, and, with some effort, was able to get him to his feet. John tried to support him as carefully as he could when they started up the stairs. David grunted slightly at the pressure of John's arm around his body, but still leaned appreciatively against him.

By the time they reached the door, David's face was ashen and his sweat mingled with the blood on his pale skin. John eased him carefully through the door and onto the nearest chair, ignoring the disapproval on Marian's face.

"Where are you hurt, David?" John asked as he pushed David's hair off his face, relieved that the cut seemed superficial despite the blood flow. He needed to check if David was injured anywhere else, but hesitated. The physical contact of helping him up the stairs was different; he wanted David to let him know *this* was okay. "I need to see if you're hurt, David. Can I take your jacket off?"

David didn't answer; his concentration was centered on keeping his breathing steady rather than listening to John.

"David, *please.* I need to know if this is okay."

Perhaps it was the tone of John's voice that broke into David's consciousness, but he started slightly and turned to look at him.

"Come on, Dave. I need to see where you're hurt. I have to take your jacket off."

David looked down at the hands clenched around the sketchbook and slowly loosened his grip, letting John take the pad and place it on the table. John carefully pulled the jacket off David's shoulder and down his arm and then repeated the process on the other side. There was no sign of blood on the torn flannel shirt.

David flinched and glanced up when Marian walked over and said with some impatience, "Look, John, I don't know why he came here, but you don't need to be doing this. Stick him in a cab to the hospital. Let them deal with him."

John turned his head and glared at Marian. His teeth ached from the tight grind of his clenched jaw. *How could she simply dismiss him like that?* He turned his attention back to David, but said to her in a deceptively calm voice, "Go home, Marian. This has nothing to do with you."

She narrowed her eyes and opened her mouth to reply, but quickly closed it again. With as much dignity as she could muster, Marian located her handbag and coat and walked out of the apartment. John listened to her leave, knowing he would have to apologize later, but right now David needed him. Marian didn't.

He sighed and focused his attention on David's shirt. Several of the buttons had been torn off, leaving only a couple for John to undo, exposing the remnants of a threadbare T-shirt. He glanced up at David's face to gauge whether or not to continue; his expression was difficult to read, but the desperate fear had left his eyes. John lifted the hem of the T-shirt and swore at the mass of red and purple bruises covering David's midriff. "Shit, David. I'm phoning a doctor. This needs to be looked at."

David lifted his hand and put it on John's, determined to push the worn fabric back down. "I'm okay," he mumbled. "Just need... need to clean up... please."

John looked at David's hand covering his. "You really need a doctor, David."

"Please, John," David whispered, tightening his grip.

Although unconvinced, John nodded and David quickly withdrew his hand as if embarrassed by the contact. John rose silently and walked into the bathroom. He turned the taps on full and watched the steady rush of water as it began to cover the bottom of the bath. The room was already filling up with steam when John returned to crouch by David's side. "The bath is running if you want to go through."

David nodded and took a pained breath before standing. He gripped the back of the chair and closed his eyes. John slowly stood and placed a gentle palm on David's back. "It's okay. I'll give you a hand."

It surprised John when David gave another small nod, opened his eyes and began to walk to the bathroom.

The bathroom had nearly filled with steam, diffusing the harsh light above the mirror as John leaned over to check the temperature of the water. It was nearly ready. David began to fumble with the buttons on his shirt cuffs, but the constant tremor of his hand made the small black button slip out of his grasp. The more he tried the more distressed he became until John's fingers closed softly over his hand. John didn't say anything as he gently moved David's hand away and slipped the button through the hole. He paused briefly at the tiny red heart tattooed in the creases of David's wrist, wanting to ask about it, but knowing this was not the time or place. He undid the other cuff and slid the shirt off, laying it on a little wooden chair.

David let John remove his T-shirt, but dropped his head as the hot flush of shame crept over his face. He didn't want John to see him like that; too thin, dirty, and blemished with bruises old and new. David swallowed repeatedly when John knelt on the floor and carefully removed first one boot and then the other. Although he was forced to grip John's shoulder to keep his balance, David quickly let go as soon as the task was completed. *It was one thing for John to touch him....*

"Um, you need to take off your trousers," John said quietly before he straightened and turned to shut off the water flow. "Do you want me to leave?"

The thought of John seeing him naked horrified David, but he knew he'd need help getting into the bath. He attempted to slow his breathing and with gritted teeth set his fingers to work on his fly. The button was larger and he was able to unfasten it with relative ease; he slid the zipper down and lowered his pants, wobbling slightly as he stepped out of them.

Glancing over, John experienced a mix of anger and regret at the sight of David's body. *It could have been so beautiful under different circumstances.* But he quickly looked away, seeing David's embarrassment. "It's okay, Dave. Come on." John held out his hands and supported David while he tentatively stepped into the bath.

Once in the warmth of the water, David's resolve left him. He pulled his knees up and turned his face to the wall. *I shouldn't have come here.... I should have stayed in the park. It's wrong for John to have to do this.*

John stood and watched him for a moment at a loss of what to do. He knew he should give David some privacy but didn't want to leave him. He hovered at the edge of the bathroom door before making a decision. "I'll get you something to wear. Take your time."

A barely perceptible nod of the head was the only indication that David had heard him.

John walked to his bedroom, where he gathered the same clothes he gave David to sleep in the last time and some bed linen to make up the couch.

While tucking in the blanket John kept playing one thing over and over in his head. *He came to me. After the way I treated him, he still came to me.* By the time the bed was made John almost itched to be back in the bathroom with David.

When John carried the clothes to the bathroom he saw that David had managed to lift himself out of the bath and was sitting on its edge wrapped in John's favorite bath sheet. He was clean and the cut had finally stopped bleeding. He looked up at John, exhaustion clear in his eyes.

"They're the same ones as last time," John said for want of something better to say and left the track pants and T-shirt on the chair. He gave David an almost shy smile and left him to dress.

Once out the door, John didn't venture far from the bathroom and leaned against the wall watching his hands rub nervously together until David emerged. David was slightly startled by John's close proximity, but settled when he saw the bed made up for him; he needed to sleep.

John straightened up quickly, his hand raised as if to touch David's arm before dropping equally fast to his side. He saw David looking at the makeshift bed and shook his head. "Oh um, that's for me. You can have… ah, my bed tonight." John blushed a little at the mention of his bed and mentally kicked himself for wording it that way. David looked at him curiously, making John feel even more flustered. He attempted a quick cover-up with the action of moving into the bedroom, hoping David would follow. "The bedroom is through here. It's a warm bed, but the heater switch is there if you get cold." John suddenly ran out of words, feeling very self-conscious standing so close to David in his bedroom. Sensing John's discomfort, David misinterpreted its origin; he lowered his face and mumbled "Thank you."

John nodded and left the room, closing the door quietly behind him. He let out a breath he hadn't realized he'd been holding and grabbed a glass, which he promptly filled with scotch. He gulped a couple of mouthfuls before rubbing his fingers wearily over his eyes. *What the hell are you doing, McCann?*

THE green glow of the DVD display was the only thing John could see when he sat up startled out of a troubled sleep. He didn't know what had woken him so suddenly and found it difficult to orientate himself in the gloom of the windowless room. He sat on the edge of the couch waiting for the rush of his heartbeat to cease in his ears so he could listen to the sounds of the apartment…. Nothing. He stood up and moved nearer to his bedroom door. When he heard no obvious sounds John carefully opened the door. The stream of moonlight through the open curtains made the room seem bright in comparison to the living room; John could easily see David asleep in his bed. He stood quietly in the doorway watching the rise and fall of the quilt matching the steady wheeze of breathing. John grimaced at the tightening of his chest and the need to make an admission. *Fucking hell, I'm in trouble here.*

CHAPTER 7

CONSCIOUSNESS slowly invaded David's sleep and along with it came the steady thump of a headache. He lay still, taking the time to wake up fully before even attempting to open his eyes. Rather than preparing for the usual regret of waking, David allowed his body to relax in the warmth of the bed. The sheets smelled vaguely of John. Turning his face slightly into the pillow, David rested his nose against the pillowcase and breathed deeply. It was only then that he noticed the sound of light snoring. He must have heard it before but it hadn't registered. He was used to the sound of snoring bodies nearby; frequently it was only exhaustion that enabled him to sleep among the noise of the men's shelter. He frowned and instantly regretted the action when the dried cut in his hairline threatened to split.

David opened his eyes; the morning light sent a bolt of pain shooting into his already aching head. He groaned and squinted until his eyes acclimatized to the intrusion of daylight.

The other side of the bed was empty. Stretching his hand out under the covers, David slid it across the mattress. Seeing the movement of the quilt charting its progress he wondered vaguely which side of the bed John usually slept on… which was his pillow? David sighed. It was ridiculous that he was thinking such thoughts.

A snort suddenly interrupted the snoring before settling back into a steady and louder rhythm. David realized it was behind him. He carefully pulled his hand back and braced it against the mattress to turn over. Every joint and muscle complained at the movement; the pain of rolling over momentarily took his breath away. But now he was looking at John.

John was asleep in the wingback armchair in the corner of the room, the blanket from the couch draped over one shoulder and down across his knees. One leg was tucked under his body and his head tipped to one side, resting on his palm. David couldn't help but smile at the sight of John open-mouthed and snoring at full bellow. Completely unguarded in his dreams.

David had lost track of how long he'd been watching John sleep when he was startled by the shrill buzz of the alarm clock. John woke with a grunt, almost tipping the chair as he jumped up, eyes darting unfocused around the room. It took him a few seconds to realize what had happened and then he walked over to the nightstand. He gave David a sheepish grin and shrugged. "Ah, sorry. I forgot to switch that off last night."

A wave of self-consciousness flushed through David as he lay in John's bed. He glanced away and mumbled a quick "It's okay."

John silently cursed himself for not waking sooner so he could creep back to the couch unnoticed; he moved away from David to look out the window. The morning was gray and the thin light had a harsh edge. He absently raised his arms above his head, a hand on each elbow, and stretched, twisting his head until he felt that satisfying pop of his joints. He ached from the night spent in the chair but played it down with a shrug. "I'm getting too old for that." He smiled, tilting his head toward the wingback.

David frowned and looked at John, who now felt the need to explain. "Look. Last night I was worried. You didn't seem too... um... *together,* and I kept thinking I should have called a doctor." His explanation trailed off.

David thought about this for a moment, then looked at the chair and said quietly, "I'm okay now. I'll get dressed and go." He made to get out of the bed, but his clenched jaw gave away how the simple movement had sent pain rocketing through his rib cage. John instantly held out his hand in an action reminiscent of someone trying to soothe a frightened animal; his voice came out louder than intended. "No... what I mean is, this time you have to let me make you breakfast."

Although momentarily stilled, David mumbled, "I don't usually eat breakfast."

"Well today you do. You missed out on a good fry-up last time," John countered, not willing to give up.

David's stomach rolled at the thought of eating, his head pounding sickly. He ran his fingers tentatively over his forehead and said, "Please, John… just coffee?"

John smiled, nodded, and headed into the kitchen. *Shit, stop overcompensating and give him some fucking breathing room.* He leaned palms-down against the bench in an attempt to gather his thoughts. *Okay, calm down. Make him a drink.* Maybe he could manage some toast and actually talk to the man!

With the coffee brewing, his tea in the pot, and bread in the toaster, John finally started to feel like he had some control over the situation. He set up a tray with two cups, napkins, a glass of water, and a strip of aspirin… not for himself for a change.

While spreading a generous layer of marmalade on the hot toast, John started to understand that David's first meal of the day was probably the sandwich he shared with Jamie and that he'd never actually considered what David did when the store was closed on Sundays. In fact he knew *nothing* about David.

With the tray set up, John made his way back into the bedroom. When he came through the door David pushed himself upright in the bed, grimacing until he eased back against the headboard. John used the edge of the tray to move the clock and lamp back to make space on the nightstand for their breakfast. When it was safely situated he pulled the wingback chair closer to the bed. It was heavier and took more effort than John had anticipated, but he was determined not to let David see that he struggled with its weight. That done, John smiled briefly before sitting down and swallowing a large gulp of his tea.

Up until then David had been sitting quietly watching John organize their breakfast setting. He looked at the tray, feeling a little overwhelmed that John had gone to so much trouble for him. He reached for the aspirin, hesitated, and glanced up at John as if seeking permission before downing three tablets. He closed his eyes for a moment as a wave of nausea followed the pills. John saw David's response to the medication and said in a very soft voice, "Try to eat something; it'll help."

David picked up a piece of toast and tentatively bit the hard crust, chewing slowly and carefully. "You know, maybe you should stay here today? Take it easy?" John suggested, staring at his fingers holding his cup a little too tightly. "Jamie is going to be an absolute nightmare when he finds out you're back."

Still chewing his first bite, David smiled at the thought of Jamie pestering John for details, and had to admit the offer sounded good. "Thank you, John. Please tell him I'm okay."

John nodded but didn't smile back as he asked, "What happened last night? Who did this to you?"

"Just kids. Drunk and looking for an easy target, I guess," David answered with a dismissive shrug.

"Fucking hell, David," John cursed. "How can you treat it like that?"

Keeping his eyes down, David lay the slice of toast back on the plate and picked up his coffee. "It happens."

"To you? Has it happened to you before?" John asked, leaning forward in his chair. David just nodded and took a sip of coffee.

John couldn't believe it; he felt physically sick that anyone could find entertainment in beating someone up. He replaced his cup on the tray and caught the time on the clock behind it. "Shite. I gotta go or Jamie will be up those stairs looking for me. I'll see you later, okay?" He waited until David agreed then grabbed some clothes and dashed into the living room to change before heading down to the store and the barrage of questions he knew would be waiting for him once he admitted to David's return.

JOHN was just unlocking the front door of the store when Jamie walked up behind him. "You're running late this morning," Jamie said, stamping his feet against the cold.

John braced himself for the onslaught and said without looking around, "David's back."

Jamie's feet instantly stilled. "When? How do you know? Where is he?" He whirled around as if David would magically appear near him.

John rolled his eyes and said, "Inside first; it's bloody cold."

He couldn't help but grin at Jamie, who virtually bounced through the door and past him to the counter. "Okay, we're in. Tell me!"

"David turned up at my place last night," John paused, unsure how to tell Jamie what had happened. "He'd gotten into a bit of trouble; been in a fight."

"No way! David wouldn't hit anyone," Jamie stated adamantly.

John shook his head, sighed and explained, "*They* hit *him* but he's okay. Just bruised and sore."

"Fucking bastards. Where is he?" Jamie asked, pretty sure that John wouldn't have sent him away, but needed to be certain.

"He stayed the night and is upstairs finishing his breakfast," John said in a voice that managed to sound a lot calmer than he felt about it all.

Relieved, Jamie broke into a huge grin. "He came to *you,* John."

A whole swarm of butterflies suddenly took flight in John's stomach. He turned away, blushing furiously, and grumbled, "Get the register set up, Jamie, and keep your mind on the day's business."

Jamie cracked open a roll of coins and hummed happily, not even trying to hide his amusement at John's embarrassment.

JOHN was on the phone with a supplier when he saw David enter the store. He was dressed in his old clothes, the torn shirt just visible under his jacket. Although steady on his feet, John noticed how pale David was, emphasizing the ugly bruise coming out around his left eye and cheek. He smiled and nodded "hello" at David, who returned the gesture.

As David started to make his way through the store, Jamie spotted him and with a shout of "Davey" dashed over. Mid-movement, Jamie stopped himself from launching into a hug and gently stroked his hand down David's damaged face instead. He whispered sadly, "Shit, Dave…," but was unable to finish the sentence, finding himself uncharacteristically lost for words.

David lifted his hand and placed it over Jamie's. "I'm okay."

Jamie knew to leave it at that and said, "I'll make you some tea to have with lunch, yeah?" David nodded and smiled at Jamie before turning to find his bookmarked novel and sitting in his chair.

John had left David alone for most of the day, starting to understand his need for routine; however, when he went to the back of the store to retrieve an order he noticed that David had fallen asleep. John quietly crouched beside the chair, lifted the paperback, and carefully replaced the red bookmark. When David didn't stir, John put his hand gently on David's arm and said, "Come on, Dave. Here are my keys. Head upstairs." He fished his keys out of his pocket and put them on David's open palm. David blinked awake and looked blankly at the keys sitting in his hand, not quite comprehending what was happening. John curled David's fingers over the keys and stood up with the instruction, "Upstairs, Dave. You need to rest. I'll be up after we close."

John was surprised that David didn't even try to argue, but took the keys and slowly headed out the door.

JOHN tested the doorknob before he raised his hand to knock; it was unlocked and he was pleased Jamie wasn't around to witness how nervous he was entering his own apartment. The fluttering in his stomach turned to anxiety when he saw both the living room and kitchen were empty. *Fuck!* He listened carefully to the silent apartment as his eyes traveled to his bedroom door. *Bloody idiot, McCann. You told him to rest.* John pushed the door open just a fraction and peeked around. When he saw that the curtains were drawn and David was asleep in the bed he smiled and quietly closed the door.

The torn sketchbook caught John's eye. It was still sitting on the table where he'd left it the night before. He sat down on the couch and looked at the remnants of the book. The back cover was ripped in half, several of the pages were ragged and creased, and the spiral binding wire was mangled away from almost half the book. *David had fought hard to keep this,* John thought as he ran his fingers down its edge. He knew it was none of his business, an invasion of David's privacy, but John needed to know. He sat in silent conflict for several long minutes before picking it up.

Opening it randomly, he saw a page filled with images of himself; studies of his eyes and hands. The next picture was of John reading. There was a tranquility to the rendering that John barely recognized. There was one of Jamie. He was smiling and the eyes looked directly at him. John briefly wondered if he'd posed for this and pushed down a fleeting pang of jealousy.

His frown deepened when he turned the page. The sketch was of a teenage boy laughing at some unknown joke; John didn't recognize him. There were many more pictures of this boy throughout the book, some hurried outlines, others painstakingly detailed. John closed the book and put it back on the table, unsure what to make of its contents.

The sketchbook had him unsettled and John needed to get up and do something. He walked purposefully into the kitchen and pulled a large pot out of the cupboard all the while trying to remember the ingredients of Gran's favorite vegetable and barley soup. *Soup therapy.* He grinned as he started to dice carrots and drop them into the simmering chicken stock.

Within an hour, John was ladling steaming soup into two bowls, pleased with his effort even if he did have to substitute rice for barley.

David stirred when John switched on the bedside lamp. He yawned and mumbled, "Sorry. I was just so tired."

John lifted his bowl off the tray and settled in the chair; he looked at David and said, "Bloody exhausted more like it. Now get some of that soup into you."

David shuffled up in the bed, lifted the tray down, and took a sip of the soup. Making an appreciative sound, he refilled his spoon. John smiled and ate his soup while filling him in about the day's events in the store. By the time both bowls were empty David's eyelids were heavy and John had managed to convince him to stay the night. Actually he gave him no other option.

John couldn't stop grinning as he scrubbed the soup pot.

IT was late when David woke up to see the dark figure moving carefully toward the chair. He watched John start to cover himself with his blanket and said softly, "I'm okay, John."

John looked over at the bed, pleased that David couldn't see the pink spreading up his neck, and answered as gruffly as he could. "So you say, but indulge me, all right?"

A gentle warmth spread through David's belly knowing that John cared enough to endure another uncomfortable night propped in the armchair, but he couldn't let John do it... *not for him.*

His thoughts were still tangled when he finally got the courage to say, "Poverty isn't catching."

John peered at him through the darkened room and said in a totally incredulous voice, "Did you just make a joke? You bloody did, didn't you?" The chuckle that followed spread the heat rapidly through the rest of David's body and he shrugged. "Well, it's a big bed." His smile was small but he knew the dark of the room hid some of his insecurities.

After a moment of hesitation, John moved to his side of the bed. He tentatively climbed in, holding his breath as he tried not to jostle David too much. Settling back against the pillow, John allowed his back to slowly straighten out. His mattress had never felt so good.

John could sense David's tension as he lay very still beside him and, staring up at the ceiling, he did something he'd not done for too many years: thought about his life before he'd covered it with a corporate suit. "*I've* been poor, Dave."

His peripheral vision caught the movement of David's face as it turned toward him to listen. "I didn't really understand that we were poor when I was little. I just knew that sometimes I was hungry and my mam would cry if I said anything. She died when I was six and we went to live with my grandparents; my mam's parents. I loved it there with them, but my dad wasn't working and they fought a lot. I often heard my granddad arguing with him. He used to stay out late and come home drunk, and then one night he just didn't come home at all. I realize now that he missed my mam and didn't know how to cope without her, but at the time...." John took a breath; he didn't know why he was spilling this all out to David but now he'd started he knew he wanted to get it *all* out. "My life wasn't bad. I'm not saying that. I loved my grandparents but they struggled and as I got older it hurt to see that. I decided then that I wasn't going to live that way so I packed what little I had and blew all my savings on a plane fare here. A new life in 'sunny Australia' was the dream. I left my old life behind, but every fucking day I'm terrified of falling back into it." John's voice cracked slightly and David leaned over to lay his hand on John's shoulder, but let it hover inches away before pulling it back.

John closed his eyes briefly at the missed touch and gave a small bitter laugh. "I'm sorry, David; it all sounds like a bloody Catherine Cookson novel."

"It's okay, John," David murmured. After a brief pause, he added, "I had money... and *something* of a life."

They lay side by side in the dark for several minutes. John wasn't sure how much to push so he just waited for David to continue. When David turned onto his side away from John, he assumed that was all he was going to be told. Then David said so quietly that John wasn't sure he'd heard correctly, "I have a son, John."

John instantly thought of the young man drawn so lovingly in the sketchbook. He knew that David was waiting for a response but found he didn't have one. Instead of risking the wrong words, John rested his hand lightly on David's shoulder.

Blood pounded in David's ears as he'd voiced his admission. He'd spent the past few years burying his past life so deep that it might not be able to hurt him anymore. If he didn't talk about it, it didn't exist. But his son *did* exist and he experienced the shame of missing him each and every day he couldn't go and see him... *so maybe telling John would be okay?* John's hand was warm through his T-shirt and the gentle stroking motion of his thumb felt surprisingly safe.

John leaned his face close but not quite touching David's hair and asked softly, "What's his name?"

David closed his eyes and took a breath. He couldn't make himself answer.

John moved closer and slid his arm slowly across David's chest to gently pull him back. When he felt David's weight against his chest, John whispered, "It's all right. You don't have to say any more tonight. Try to get some sleep."

Even though there was no reply, John could feel the tension gradually leave David's body. It took John quite a while to drift off to sleep but his final thought was, *Time, Dave. Please give us some time....*

CHAPTER 8

JOHN hardly ever slept through until his alarm, yet he always set it. The faint gray light of dawn signaled the first stirrings of awareness, but John knew instantly that something was very different this morning. There was someone in the bed with him, close to him. He could hear breaths that weren't his own and the weighting of the mattress was different. John had always avoided this moment; it was too intimate to wake up next to someone and left him too open.

John hadn't actually thought this far ahead, waking up beside David.

He closed his eyes and listened to the steady breathing behind him. Although there was no physical contact, he knew David was close. Suddenly, knowing wasn't quite enough. He wanted to turn over and see David asleep in his bed only inches away from him. *Shit, why did I have to think of that?* John cursed silently as he felt the heat from David's body create its own heat in his body. He tried to lie still, ignore his growing erection. *Oh God.* He wanted to just quietly and slowly slide his hand from under his pillow and down along his body to touch himself. He started to move, not sure whether he was going to let his fingers travel or simply rearrange himself to release some of the tension that had rapidly built in his body.

David groaned slightly in his sleep, which immediately halted John's movement. He exhaled a slightly shaky sigh. *Fucking hell; the man trusts you. Stop reacting like a fucking teenager.* Sobered by this thought, John began to wonder just what it meant that David trusted him; he had to admit the thought both warmed and terrified him.

He had no idea what this thing with David was or where it was going. The only thing he did know for sure was that he didn't want David to go back to the streets. Problem was, he was running out of reasons for him to stay, and John understood that, despite his circumstances, David was a proud man and would be uncomfortable accepting charity. *Perhaps I could clear out all the store junk from Jamie's old bedroom and offer him that. Maybe he would help out in the store so it wouldn't be seen as charity?* His thoughts were instantly cut short when David moved in closer. The rise and fall of his chest was hot against John's back. He could feel David's breath against his neck. An involuntary moan escaped John's lips. It was quickly stifled when he heard the cadence of David's breathing change. *Shit, I woke him up.*

John cleared his throat and said quietly, "Morning. You okay?"

As soon as he uttered the words, David pulled away from him and whispered, "Sorry, John."

John regretted speaking as soon as David broke contact, but he knew he couldn't lie there like a horny teenager until the alarm went off. He carefully turned over and settled back against his pillow but found looking directly into David's eyes very disconcerting, so focused his gaze on the yellowing bruise instead. "Your bruise is already starting to fade."

David lifted his hand briefly to his face and mumbled, "It doesn't take long."

"It shouldn't happen at all," John said, more to himself than David. He carefully touched the discolored skin before halting his actions and saying in a louder voice, "Time to get up, I guess."

John quickly turned away from David, flicked the alarm off before it had a chance to sound, and swung his legs over the edge of the bed. "Take your time getting up. I have to go to the store early to do some paperwork."

JOHN arrived back at Margins after telling Jamie he was taking a break carrying a large white shopping bag; the kind made of extra-reinforced paper with raffia handles, indicating fashion rather than produce. Jamie didn't say a word, but eyed the bag curiously. Noticing the look, John quickly growled, "Mind your own business."

Jamie just raised his eyebrows in an attempt at total innocence and followed John into the kitchen. "You are such a clothes horse, John; you know you want to show me." Jamie grinned as he headed for the bag.

John quickly pulled the bag away from Jamie, ignoring how his faced colored as he said, "Look, Jamie, they aren't for me. Just leave it, okay?"

Jamie's smile softened. "I figured that, John. I knew they must be for David, but I wanted to see if you'd own up to it."

John shot Jamie a filthy look and said in an exasperated voice, "Fucking hell, Jamie! Give me a break, will you?" He took a deep breath, looked at his young friend, and admitted, "I'm struggling here, Jamie. Okay?"

With a quick glance over his shoulder to check the store, Jamie moved away from the door to join John at the table. He pulled up a chair next to John, where he could ask quietly, "What's up, John? What's wrong?"

John gave a mirthless laugh and shook his head. "That's the problem, mate. Nothing is actually wrong. I'm just in new territory here and it scares me shitless."

Despite trying very hard not to smile, Jamie couldn't help himself. "You've never really been in love, have you, John?"

John's stomach did an inelegant flip and he suddenly felt light-headed, but he pushed all that aside and said, "Leave it out, Jamie. I am not in love. He just... I'm just worried about him, that's all."

Jamie stood up, stroked his hand down John's hair, and said with a gentle smile, "Yeah, I know, John," before walking back into the store.

JOHN was in the process of juggling his shopping and the packages of takeout food before reaching for the doorknob when David opened the door. "Thanks," John managed to say before bundling a carton of steaming noodles into David's hand. "Here, grab this. You know, the woman at the noodle place and I are on a first-name basis now."

David grinned, carried the food over to the table, and then helped John with the other cartons. John looked at the mass of white containers and chuckled. "I think I over-catered a bit."

David shrugged and said, "Maybe you catered with Jamie in mind?"

"Fuck," John laughed. "It always amazes me how much he can eat and stay so skinny. Come on. Sit down, and we'll see if we can make a dent in this."

After three cartons of noodles, they finally had to admit defeat and sat back in their chairs; although John did notice that this was the most he had ever seen David eat. David looked at the remnants of their dinner and started to stack the containers, but John shook his head. "Leave that. I'll do it later."

John signaled for David to go sit on the couch and said, "Grab a seat; I'll put the kettle on."

David sat quietly, waiting for John. His eyes dropped to the sketchbook on the table. He picked it up carefully and held it close. "That must be important," John said quietly as he sat down beside him. David just nodded. John desperately wanted to ask him about the contents, but didn't want to admit he had already looked through it, so he waited.

David looked at the torn cover of the book, took a breath, opened it, and said very quietly, "These people are important to me." He hesitated briefly before he passed the book into John's hands.

John looked down at a sketch of the teenager and asked, "Is this your son?" David didn't raise his eyes from the image as he nodded.

"What's his name?" John asked, glancing sideways at David, hoping that this time he would tell him.

David clenched his jaw for a moment while he decided whether or not to answer. Finally he said the name so long kept to himself. "Adam."

"Adam," John repeated gently, hoping to reassure David that this was okay. "How old is he?"

David sighed and said with a shake of his head and a tone of incredulity, "He'll be sixteen soon."

"Do you still get to see him?"

David's expression closed again so John was surprised when he gave an answer. "Sometimes… sometimes when I have enough for the bus fare I go to his school. I never let him see me, but if I'm there at the right time I see him arrive and meet up with his friends. He has a lot of friends."

Shit. John couldn't imagine what it would be like to have a child and not be able to see him when he wanted. He turned the pages in silence until he came to one with his own image, then, slightly embarrassed, he closed the book and handed it back to David. "These are beautiful, David. I can understand why you wouldn't let them go. Look, um… I know you lost all your stuff so I hope you won't be offended, but I… um… got you a few things."

He reached down the side of the couch for the bag and placed it on the coffee table. John tried to make the unpacking seem as casual as possible, but his heart was hammering so hard he was sure David would hear it.

David took each parcel with very deliberate care and laid them on the coffee table: a pair of jeans, two T-shirts, two pairs of socks, and underwear. David couldn't say anything; he looked at the underwear and didn't trust his voice to say thank you. From where he was sitting John couldn't read David's expression and began to worry that he'd done the wrong thing. "Are they okay, Dave?"

David nodded, but dropped his head into his hand and kept his eyes covered until he was sure he had himself under control enough to answer. His voice was small and strained as he said, "I'm sorry, John. It's just… shit… I'm such a fucking mess." He turned away quickly, not wanting John to see the effect the small act of kindness was having on him.

John hesitated, wanting to comfort him in some way, but stood up awkwardly instead and went to pick up the now empty bag. Before he crushed it to put it in the trash David turned and asked very quietly, "Can I have the bag too?"

John frowned at the question but said, "Um, of course you can."

David took the bag, mumbling, "I don't have my pack… I need it to carry my stuff."

It was as if a sledgehammer had just hit John full force in the chest; David was going to leave. It hurt like hell, but John couldn't stop him. He nodded and said in a carefully controlled voice, "Sure, David. Come on; get a decent night's sleep."

DAVID changed quietly and climbed into the bed, his back to John.

The silence in the room was oppressive; John had things he wanted to say, things he wanted to ask, but the barrier of David's back stopped him. It was obvious that he'd done something wrong to make David want to leave and the thought of him back on the streets made John's stomach cramp. He turned onto his side and looked at the back of David's head; he couldn't just let him go without even trying.

Reaching over, John slowly let his fingertips slide down David's hair. He felt the initial flinch and then David seemed to relax back into John's touch.

"You don't have to go, Dave," John whispered. "I can understand that you don't want to share my bed, but I can clear the spare room. It's just being used as extra storage for the store and Maggie's furniture. Please stay."

David turned over to look at him. His eyes traveled over John's face before saying, "I want to share your bed, John."

Both men lay in silence; it seemed that neither knew how to proceed. Then John's hand gently cupped the side of David's face. He leaned forward until his lips brushed David's, waiting for him to pull away. Instead David's lips moved softly against his, allowing John to slide his tongue between now-parted lips and deepen the kiss. The blood was rushing through John's ears as he shuffled his body closer.

He slid his hand slowly under the hem of David's T-shirt and stroked his fingers through the swirl of belly hair. David gasped lightly into the kiss when John's hand moved up until his fingers teased an already erect nipple. Gently breaking the kiss, John pulled back so he could see David's face as he passed his finger back and forth over the sensitized flesh.

John was overwhelmed by how beautiful David looked under his touch; his eyes were closed and his lips parted. John ached for him. He removed his hand from under the T-shirt and met David's eyes when they opened. John held his gaze while he gripped the hem of his own T-shirt and pulled it over his head. David watched him steadily, his breathing increasing as he sat up enough for John to repeat the action on his own T-shirt.

Bending down, John gently pressed his lips to the center of David's chest, increasing the pressure to carefully ease them back onto the bed. He created a slow path of kisses up to the hollow of David's throat where he hesitated, suddenly aware that none of his touches had been returned. Resting back on his elbow, John traced the trail of his lips with the back of his hand and asked, "Is this okay?"

David gave an almost imperceptible nod, never taking his eyes from John's.

That was all he needed to know. John lay down on the bed facing David and pulled him closer, moaning at the sudden heat of David's skin against his own. Lowering his face to David's neck, John ran the tip of his tongue up to the stubbled jaw-line.

David's hand hovered in midair, fingers flexing, before dropping onto John's head and tightly clutching his hair. The almost painful grip on his hair sent a bolt of lust through John. He groaned and pushed his hips against David, hissing into already sweat-dampened skin as his erection ground against David's. John was so hard that the sudden friction sent shockwaves through his cock; he lifted his mouth to David's ear and gasped, "Need you... need you now." John's hand started to push urgently at the waistband of David's track pants and he said, "Turn over, Dave."

John stretched around to the bedside table and grabbed a condom from the drawer. It took him a moment longer to rummage and find the lubricant. He turned back to find David lying on his stomach, his head resting on his folded arms facing away from John. The bruises were fading, but still very obvious along the pale skin of David's lower back. The reality of it slowed John's need. *Not like this....* He stroked his hand softly over the blemished skin and said quietly, "On your side, Dave. I could hurt you this way."

David silently turned over.

John forced his breathing to slow and leaned down; he tenderly kissed David's shoulder and whispered, "Lift your hips a bit," while he pushed David's track pants the rest of the way. John quickly discarded his own pants and shuffled close along the bare back. His hand cupped protectively over David's hip bone, just holding him while John gently nuzzled into the already damp hairline.

"You have to let me know if this is okay," John breathed into David's ear. David gave a small nod and nothing more, because he knew better than to speak. But John hesitated. This wasn't going to be a quick shag just to get off; he wanted more and needed to hear David wanted it too.

"You have to tell me, Dave. I have to hear you."

David had learned that sex was something to be done in silence; either rough in a public toilet or fast by his own hand before he was seen. But under John's gentle touch he started to feel safe enough to find his voice. "Yes," he murmured and reinforced the single word with a slight push back against the hot skin behind him. "Yes," John repeated before he squeezed lubricant on his fingers and gently eased one finger into David.

When David emitted a small grunt, John slowed his progress and watched carefully as he slid the finger to its full length. With slight twists of his finger the initial resistance soon dissipated quickly and John added a second and then a third, his eyes moving from what he could see of David's face to the hand that was now bunching the sheet between clenched fingers.

John carefully slid his fingers out and was surprised when David let go of the sheet, gripped his wrist, and said breathlessly, "Condom, John. I might not be safe."

"It's okay, Dave. I've got one," John assured him, trying to put aside the fear that suddenly constricted his chest. *Deal with that later. David will be okay.*

John rolled on the condom and stroked himself a couple of times, more out of habit than need. He was already so hard it hurt. He smoothed his hand along the clear skin of David's hip and down his thigh, urging him to bend his knee and move his leg forward.

John wanted this so badly and could see the tremors of his hand as he guided his cock between David's cheeks. Sex was usually something done with little thought for the other person, but not this time. John was in new territory here. He pushed carefully but deliberately, taking his time to force the swell of the head past the muscle noting David's small moan when he finally slipped in. John paused to exhale and take another breath before sliding in the rest of the way.

Buried deep in David, John was momentarily overwhelmed by the swirl of thoughts and emotions fighting for supremacy over his desire to simply thrust his way to release. He tucked his chin over David's shoulder and kissed the tender skin below his ear before asking, "What do you need, David?"

David groaned at the unexpected question, laid his head back against John, and whispered, "Move… please."

John pulled back slowly and curled his hip to push in with a little more force; David gasped and clenched around him. "Oh fuck, you feel good," John muttered. "So good." He stretched his arm up along the pillow and found David's hand twining their fingers together as he began an easy rocking motion.

It was not what David had come to expect of sex; there was no pain or regret. In its place was the heat and sensation of desire. His head fell back against their arms as he was barely able to resist moaning as lips and tongue marked a path up his throat.

With each push John knew his resolve was weakening and he wouldn't be able to hold off much longer. "Need to come, Dave," he gasped in warning before wrapping his fingers around David's hipbone to begin a faster rhythm of deep, but not brutal, thrusts.

David's legs twitched restlessly against the sheets as he rocked back into John, his own cock dripping onto the bed and aching to be touched. He knew he was close. He wanted John's hand on him, but dropped his own between his legs instead. He moaned as his fingers began to squeeze and slide along the ridges of his shaft in time with John's thrusts, then hesitated at the feel of fingers enclosing his. This touch was enough and he gasped what might have been John's name before coming in his hand.

"Oh fuck, David…," was all John managed to moan before he crushed his face into David's neck and let go with a series of shuddering grunts.

They lay together in silence, John's arm wrapped tightly around David's chest, their fingers still entwined. He knew it had been more than lust; he'd needed it to be good for David too. He'd needed him to know that he… that he what? John instantly shied away from that train of thought, released David, and pulled out carefully, gripping the rim of the condom. He tugged it off before leaving the bed and going into the bathroom.

When he returned, David had barely moved. John sat on the bed behind him and gently wiped off the remnants of lube and come with a damp washcloth. When they were both clean John threw the cloth on the floor and snuggled down behind David, pulling the bedclothes up around them both.

Neither spoke.

JOHN'S arm held him and he could feel the steady breath of peaceful sleep against his neck, but David lay awake. He couldn't remember a time when he'd felt such intense pleasure and joy as under John's touch, but now there was that small seed of doubt building in his chest.

John murmured in his sleep and rubbed his face absently along David's neck. *Oh God.* He knew he loved this man and it was too much. David suddenly found it difficult to breathe. His lungs had no room to expand. He had to sit, get away from John's touch.

He carefully, but quickly, slid from under John's arm and sat on the edge of the bed. His hands and forearms were numb as he compulsively rubbed them. The need to stand up, to move, became overwhelming.

David stood away from the bed and looked at John; he knew he couldn't stay only to hear John say that he didn't love him.

It was in the early hours of the morning when David quietly closed the door as he left.

CHAPTER 9

"COME on, old man. Profits wait for no one." Jamie banged on the door with one hand while fiddling through his bundle of keys with the other. He knew he still had a key for the apartment, but he had so many keepsakes and "found objects" weighing down the key ring, finding it was another story.

John sat in the chair and looked at the empty bed. The sheets were rumpled and one of the corners had been pulled away from the mattress. The evidence of sex was clear... but the bed was very empty.

The banging on the door finally penetrated John's thoughts and he could hear Jamie's impatient calls. *Not today, Jamie. Please not today.* John ran his hand through his hair, let his head fall back against the chair, and exhaled a shaky breath.

Jamie was just about to start on another round of impatient knocks when he heard the latch being thrown on the other side of the door. *Fuck! What's wrong?* was the first thought that hit him when he looked at John.

John opened the door and instantly turned back into the apartment; Jamie followed him, anxious to find out what was going on. He glanced around the room to see if he could spot David and asked, "John? What's wrong, man? Where's David?"

"I fucked up, Jamie. Literally." John shook his head, gave a small bitter laugh, and flopped down on the couch.

A sense of dread filled Jamie as he sat next to John. "What happened?"

"I kissed him. We made love." John blushed and avoided looking at Jamie. *This is all too fucking hard.*

The wording "made love" didn't escape Jamie's notice; neither did the fact that John kissed David, whereas he didn't kiss Jamie once the night they fucked. He put his hand on John's shoulder and squeezed enough to let him know that it was okay to continue.

"I don't know what went wrong, what I did wrong, but he was gone when I woke up. Shit, he even left behind the clothes I bought for him. He only took his bloody sketchbook." John rolled his eyes and stared at the ceiling. "It was my fault; I obviously pushed him too hard. When will I learn to keep my cock in my fucking pants?"

"Maybe you did nothing wrong, John? He left his things, which could mean he's coming back," Jamie offered, trying to sound more hopeful than he actually felt.

"I don't know why he left, but I doubt very much that he's coming back," John said, his voice rough and defeated. Jamie didn't know what else to say so he just sat in what he hoped was a companionable silence.

After a few minutes John pushed out another heavy breath, rubbed his hand across his mouth, and said abruptly, "Fuck this! I'll go change and we can get the store open."

JAMIE tried very hard to stay out of John's way and be patient as he watched John spend the morning vacillating between obsessive organizing and snapping at him for no particular reason. But by the time Jamie brought the sandwiches John had run out of things to occupy his mind and was sitting silently at the small table in the kitchen. He gave a slight twitch of his lips as Jamie put the brown paper bag containing his sandwich in front of him. He looked at the bag, but made no move to open it. Jamie sat down quietly at the table and pulled his own sandwich out of its bag. He folded back the greaseproof paper and looked at the two triangles. *This is wrong.*

He sighed and picked one up, while saying quietly, "Eat your lunch, John." John gave a disgusted grimace and pushed the bag away. Jamie sat silently and chewed on his sandwich, not tasting any of it, until both triangles were gone. By the last mouthful he felt sick to his stomach.

Eventually John broke the silence and groaned, "I can't believe I fucked up like that."

"Shit, John!" Jamie exclaimed in an exasperated voice. "Stop bloody saying that."

John just lowered his head, closed his eyes, and pinched the bridge of his nose. Jamie leaned forward and asked slowly, "*Did* you force him, John?"

John quickly looked up and glared at Jamie. "Of course I didn't force him!"

"I know that… but I think you needed to say it out loud," Jamie countered.

John was about to answer, but stopped himself. *When did Jamie get so fucking smart?* Instead he simply gave a small nod. Jamie rubbed his hand over John's shoulder and suggested, "How about I go and ask around, yeah? Someone might have seen him."

"You couldn't find him last time," John said softly. "And what makes you think he would come back with you anyway?"

Jamie frowned and narrowed his eyes at John, understanding that that was the real reason John didn't want to look for David. He thought carefully for a moment and then said, "Think about it, John. After he was bashed, it was the middle of the night, he was frightened and in pain, where did he go? He went to you. Even after what had happened before, he still turned up on your doorstep."

John could feel the tightness in his chest increase and the heat behind his eyes threatening to turn into tears. *Not gonna happen.* He stood up abruptly, fished his car keys out of his pocket, and growled, "I'm going for a drive."

Jamie watched his retreating back and called after him, "Try the shelter, John."

JOHN wandered around the dining room of the shelter as they cleared the lunch plates from the rows of trestle tables. *So many empty plates.* The last of the men were shuffling out as John approached a middle-aged woman stacking plates on a well-worn trolley. "Excuse me?"

She looked at him with vague suspicion before answering. "Yes, what can I do for you?"

John suddenly felt nervous and fidgeted as he asked if she'd seen David. She shook her head and said curtly, "Sorry, I don't know a lot of names. Best not to ask."

"Please, um… he is about my age and height, he has light brown shoulder-length hair. Um, pale blue-gray eyes." John was starting to feel desperate; she had to have noticed David. "He has a scar near his lip… and… and a sketchbook. He always has his sketchbook with him."

She smiled briefly at the mention of the book. "I know who you mean. Keeps to himself as much as you can in these places. I didn't ever see him talking to anyone. A lot of them are like that." She paused, squinted slightly in thought, and then added, "He's sometimes here at night, I think, but not a regular. Rarely here during the day."

John nodded. Even though David wasn't there he felt inexplicably relieved that this person remembered him. "Can I leave my number? In case he comes in… you could call me?"

"Listen, love, if you have a problem it may be best to report it to the police," she said, still trying to understand what someone like John was doing looking for that man.

"No, no, it's nothing like that. I'm just worried; that's all," John said quickly.

She looked at him for a moment and then said in a sympathetic voice, "These men can be very good at disappearing when they want to, but try again tonight… or try over at Saint Mark's around eight. We sometimes serve soup from the back of a station wagon there, although the authorities often move us on because the locals don't want the homeless in their neighborhood. Brings down property values, you know." She gave a disgusted shake of her head and then added, "I hope you find him."

John thanked her and headed back to his car. *I'll drive around a bit longer. Just a bit longer.*

JOHN slammed the drawer of the register shut; he just couldn't get the takings to balance tonight. The last customer had left an hour earlier and the door had been locked for nearly that long, but neither John nor Jamie seemed willing to leave the store and go home. Jamie looked at him from a shelf he had already tidied, sighed and called over to the counter, "I think it's time we went home, John."

John glanced at his watch. Another hour until eight, but he knew it was past time to finish up. He closed the ledger and was about to answer Jamie when he heard the distinctive and annoying ring tone of Jamie's phone.

With an apologetic look, Jamie fished his phone out of his pocket and looked at the display; he didn't recognize the number but put it to his ear and said "Hello?" He paused for a while, obviously listening, and then replied, "Yeah, I remember."

John went to walk past him to start turning off the lights when Jamie grabbed his arm and continued talking into the phone. "When was that? Yeah, I know where that is." John gave him a look, but Jamie simply gripped tighter and said in an excited voice, "Listen, thanks, man.... Yeah, look, come round to the store sometime.... The bookstore on Bellevue Street. Yeah, that's the one, and I'll shout you a meal. Thanks again, man." He flipped the phone and grinned at John. "They didn't all just spend the ten dollars, John. Someone spotted David at the central bus station!"

When John didn't move, Jamie gave him a shove and said in an urgent voice, "Go, John! I'll lock up, but make sure you call me... either way, yeah?"

John's fingers fumbled numbly around his car keys. He stood and looked at the car door. S*hit. What if David refuses to come back?* John leaned his hand on the roof and ran that scenario around and around his head until he slammed his palm down on the car and walked back to his apartment. He unlocked the front door, but only made it as far as the couch, where he picked up the white bag and jogged back to the car.

By the time he had parked at the bus station John's head was thumping and he'd convinced himself that David would be gone. Most of the travelers were leaving the building, heading home after their day's work, as John entered the main transit area. His eyes darted around the room for any sign of David until they finally settled on a figure sitting alone in one of the corners well away from the ticketing area.

David sat on the uncomfortable molded plastic seat, his sketchbook shoved inside his jacket so that only a tattered corner peeped out, and his head resting wearily in his hand. He knew it was getting late and the transit police would move him on soon but right then he didn't have the energy to move. The row of connected chairs shuddered slightly as someone sat down next to him. A softly spoken voice said, "Hey, Dave. Where're you going?"

David's heart slammed in his chest. He didn't know what to do so he simply opened his hand and showed John the few coins he'd been clutching and said in a small tired voice, "Nowhere, I guess."

John leaned forward, forearms on his knees, eyes staring down at his shoes, and asked, "Why did you leave last night?"

David winced before whispering, "Scared."

John turned quickly at the single word and looked at David; he frowned at its implication. "Scared of me?"

David refused to look at him; he gave a barely visible shrug and answered shakily. "Everything."

John had no idea how to take that comment or why it felt like a slap. He was confused and more than a little hurt. Reaching into his pocket, John pulled out his wallet. His hand shook as he shoved several notes into David's palm and said, "You can go now if you need to."

David stared at the money in his hand and slowly closed his fingers around it. He looked at John and noticed the bag of things that had been bought for him. His sense of exhaustion was crushing as he admitted, "I'm lost, John. I don't know where to go."

"Then don't go anywhere," John murmured and lowered his eyes, not able to look at the expression on David's face. "Come back with me, David. We can work something out." He rubbed his thumb compulsively across his palm as if trying to relieve a nonexistent itch, closely focusing on its movement.

Neither broke the new silence. But as it drew on, desperation took hold of John until his eyes closed and he whispered, "Please, David."

He felt movement and then several notes and coins, still hot from being so tightly held, fell into his hand. John opened his eyes and saw both his and David's money. He swallowed hard, hoping like hell he was right in his assumption of what that meant. He stood up, and when David stood beside him John handed him the bag.

John smiled when David took the bag from him, but the smile wasn't returned. David looked confused and unsure.

"Come on, David," John said gently and gave him the briefest touch on the shoulder. "Let's get to the car before the rain starts." David glanced toward the window overlooking the car park, but the darkness outside created a mirror and he was faced with the dim image of his own reflection. He quickly looked away and clutched tighter onto the raffia handles of the bag.

David's reaction didn't go unnoticed and, not for the first time, John wondered what could instill such self-loathing. Was it there before he became homeless or a product of what he had to do to survive on the streets? With clenched teeth, John began to walk to the door. It seemed an eternity before David took the first steps to follow him.

The drive home was spent in silence; David either stared out the window or at the white bag sitting between his feet. John ached to talk to him, but had no clue what could be said. How could he tell David all the things he felt without scaring the man off again? John's knuckles were white around the steering wheel by the time they reached his parking spot; he was sure David would leave again. He killed the engine and sat still in his seat. Words tumbled through his head, but with David sitting quietly beside him, none seemed right.

Finally John huffed out a frustrated breath and pulled the keys out of the ignition. He got out of the car and stood and waited for David to do the same before walking briskly to the apartment. When they walked through the front door David stood awkwardly holding the paper bag, unsure of what was expected of him. *Fuck. Just like the first time,* John thought miserably as he motioned for David to sit down. He said apologetically, "I have to make a call."

David nodded and said quietly, "Please tell Jamie I'm okay."

An unexpected chuckle escaped John's lips and he nodded before picking up the phone and walking into the kitchen. David listened to the few words John managed to get into the conversation and knew he was being pumped for answers. He sighed and looked around the room; it was so familiar to him now but at the same time everything had changed. He pulled the sketchbook out of his jacket and put it back on the coffee table. It was the early hours of this morning when he'd lifted the book, but it seemed so long ago. He'd replayed the previous night in his head so many times that David had begun to doubt that it had really happened, that John had actually wanted him. Yet here he was back again.

David heard John's gruff goodbye to Jamie and then the sound of the kettle being filled with water; he smiled briefly at John's automatic response of making tea. However, the smile disappeared when he heard what he thought was a cup shattering on the floor. When David walked into the kitchen he found John leaning against the sink with the ruin of a cup on the floor at his feet. Even with John's back to him, David could see that John was distressed.

With little hesitation, David quickly moved behind him, and after a moment of indecision rested his hand lightly between John's shoulder blades. John's breath caught in his lungs at the gentle touch and he dropped his head. David could feel John's warmth seeping through the cotton shirt. He didn't make any sound as he moved closer and pressed his body against John's back, just leaning against him with his cheek resting on John's neck.

The tears that had been threatening for so long began to fall and, for the first time in years, John made no attempt to hold them back. He reached blindly at his side until he found David's hand and clutched it desperately, needing the extra contact, the confirmation. David closed his eyes and whispered, "It's okay, John."

Those quiet words gave John permission he'd not had since he was a small child. He pulled David's hand around to his chest and wept; it was as if he cried for both of them although he wasn't sure why. David raised his other hand to the side of John's head and gently stroked his hair.

"We make a bloody hopeless pair, don't we?" John eventually mumbled. He gave a small hitching laugh and tried to stop his tears as he turned around to face David.

David smiled and nodded, passing his hand across John's face in an attempt to wipe his damp cheek. An embarrassed flush crept across John's face and he tried to turn his head away from the comfort offered, but David gently held him in place and whispered, "I wanted you to touch me last night, John. I still do."

I still do. John tentatively slid a hand up through David's hair, pushing it off his face, and said in a very shaky voice, "So I guess dinner can wait then?"

David's lips twitched into a grin and he shrugged. "Guess so."

John held tight to David's hand, the blood thrumming in his ears as he led him into the bedroom. Once in the darkened room he released the hand, smiled briefly to check it was okay, and started to undress. David glanced at John. He was suddenly nervous, but followed John's lead by pulling off his jacket and self-consciously unbuttoning his shirt. Even though he wanted this he didn't dare look at John while he removed his jeans. He left them on the crumpled heap created by his other clothes and stood feeling exposed and ashamed.

While undressing, John had surreptitiously watched David and even in the dim light he could see the embarrassment of the other man. He wanted to tell David how beautiful he was—even so thin and marked he was still beautiful—but that wasn't something men said to each other. Instead, he moved closer and leaned in to softly kiss him.

David couldn't hold back a small moan at the touch of John's lips and raised both hands to cradle his head, deepening the kiss with a passion that took John by surprise. He wanted John so much it hurt and that want was evident in the kiss. John gasped breathlessly into David's parted lips. Suddenly he felt the desperate need to have as much of his body against David's as possible and he backed onto the bed, pulling David with him.

"Oh God," John groaned as David tumbled on top of him; the press of skin to skin seemed to burn. David experienced the briefest moment of panic when he lost his balance and sprawled on top of John, but it was short-lived when he felt John's growing arousal. He closed his eyes and gently moved his hips against John as if to reassure himself that John would tolerate his touch. John raised his lips to David's temple, kissed him tenderly, and whispered, "Feels good."

David squeezed his eyes tightly before opening them and looking at John. He knew then that he needed to touch John, to taste him. He knew how to do this for him and started a trail of hot kisses down his throat. John's head was spinning at the heat of David's mouth and tongue inching along his chest, but he tried to keep his eyes open and focused, moaning quietly at the sight of David's tongue rasping over his nipple before continuing its journey down to his belly.

When he reached the fine line of hair below John's belly button, David hesitated and sat back on his heels.

Oh God, don't stop. Please don't stop. John held his breath, silently urging David to keep going, but afraid to push.

David placed his hand carefully on the milky skin of John's thigh. His thumb moved in a slow caress while he looked up at John for permission to continue. Although John didn't say anything, trembling fingers followed the line of David's cheekbone until they closed around his hair and encouraged him down. The action was familiar to David, but the touch was not rough and there was no cold concrete to make his knees ache. He took a steadying breath and nuzzled the skin he'd been stroking. John's musky smell filled his nostrils and David raised his head, allowing John's cock to slide against the stubble on his cheek before his tongue made fleeting contact with the tip. He flicked it briefly over the slit, testing and tasting. John grunted and twitched under David's almost teasing touch.

Tightening his grip on John's thigh, David lowered his mouth over the purpled head. John gasped at the combination of gentle suction and fingers now gliding along his shaft. David knew how to bring men off as quickly as possible and fight their hold on him as they came, but this was different. He wanted John cradled in his mouth.

His own cock hung heavy between his legs as he set up a steady motion of licking and sucking but resisted the desire to touch himself, giving all his attention to John.

John propped himself up on his elbows to watch David, but the shaking in his arms forced him back against the bed. He groaned loudly as David's hand increased its pace on his aching flesh and his hips involuntarily rose off the bed.

David fought the urge to gag at John's unintentional thrust into his mouth. He could do this for John, and he'd taken rougher treatment for bus fare or pencils. But John pulled his hair firmly and cried out, "Stop, Dave. Stop. Too close."

David instantly let go and backed off with a quiet, "I'm sorry, John."

John shook his head, trying to catch his breath. "Too close, that's all.... Come up here."

He reached down and pulled David up to him. John held David in his arms and pressed his forehead to the other man's. It took him a couple of minutes to regain his composure enough to slide his cheek against David's and gently part David's lips with his tongue. David closed his eyes and fell into the kiss, his own tongue sliding against John's.

At David's soft murmur John gently broke the kiss, his eyes dark and his breathing shallow. He ran his tongue across his lip, still tasting David while his thumb mirrored the movement passing gently over David's bottom lip. John's voice was rough as he said something he doubted he ever would again. "I need you, Dave.... I need you *inside* me."

John could feel the wave of panic that passed through David at his words and mentally kicked himself for pushing too fast. He dropped his hand down David's side and stroked small circles on his back. "It's okay, David. You don't have to do this if you don't want to."

David pulled away from John; he visibly struggled for a moment before seeming to reach a decision and meeting those green eyes. "I want this. I want you, John... but I am so fucking scared."

Reaching into the drawer, John gave him what he hoped was a reassuring smile while squeezing a large amount of lube onto David's hand. "So am I, but we can deal with it together, okay?" David's fingers were trembling as John lay back on the bed and tentatively guided them inside him.

John wasn't sure who was more nervous as David's fingers slowly worked at preparing him. He forced himself to keep his eyes open so he could watch David's face. *So serious.* The expression bothered him. He wanted—no, *needed*—David to enjoy this with him. John stretched his hand toward David. Not quite able to reach his face, he gently stroked David's arm and said, "So good.... You feel so good."

David looked at the hand. The look of stressed concentration eased and he gave John the smallest smile. Such a simple thing, but John suddenly felt overwhelmed by his love for this man and that scared him more than anything else. He pleaded in little more than a whisper, "Now, David, please.... I need you."

David carefully withdrew his fingers and reached for the condom, but John had already picked it up and said quietly, "Here, let me." David nodded and held his breath as John sat up and rolled the condom down over his aching erection. The caressing touch of John's fingers made him exhale a shivering whisper. "Not sure I can do this...."

"It's okay," John reassured as he lay back on the bed, gently pulling David with him.

Crawling closer between John's parted thighs, David carefully lifted them over his hips, his eyes never leaving John's face. John crossed his ankles behind David, smiled, and gave him a little squeeze.

David's breathing became shallow. He wrapped his fingers around his cock and began a slow push. However, when John grunted and winced David instantly stopped his movement and ran a soothing hand over John's belly. Opening his eyes, John shot him a small sheepish grin. "I'm all right. It's just been a while since I've done this... a long *long* while." Although the smile remained, his expression became a little more serious as he lifted his hand to stroke David's cheek. "I trust you, Dave."

The heat of tears suddenly threatened behind David's eyes, but it was not the time for that. Taking a deep breath to still the last of his fears, he pushed until he was buried deep into the man so willing to accept him. He closed his eyes, feeling every contact point between them, not yet daring to move.

John watched him for a moment, wanting to understand what was going through his head, but he couldn't endure the stillness any longer. He urged David on with a gentle roll of his hips. David looked down at him, his hair falling over his face as pulled back and rocked forward slowly, watching, making sure John was all right with his movements.

John gasped and arched at the solid glide of David inside him. He reached up and gripped David's shoulder, pulling him down, needing him closer. He puffed out breaths near David's ear until he was able to form the word "Harder...."

David lifted his head enough to look John in the face. *Different,* John thought as he saw the briefest glimpse of strength and confidence in David's eyes. *There you are, Dave.... I know what you really look like now*. However, all thought soon gave way to the demands of his body when David braced himself on his elbows and thrust hard and deep. John lifted off the bed to meet the force of the thrust and wrapped his legs tighter around David's hips.

David's mouth came down over John's and his tongue pushed firmly between his lips. David's kiss was hot and wet with an abandon that both surprised and excited John. He met the kiss with equal passion and knew he would give this man anything to see that look in his eyes again.

The kiss was finally broken, but David's mouth wasn't still; he buried his face against John's neck, sucking and licking the soft skin below his ear.

"Oh fuck, Dave. Gonna come...." John gasped, rotating his hips to increase the friction of skin and hair against his weeping cock.

When John came, the words *I love you* almost escaped. But he clenched his teeth so hard they ached and all he could utter was a guttural cry.

David's fingers compulsively flexed and clenched in John's hair as he felt the first wave of his own climax roll over him. He made no sound when he came, but clung to John until the tremors of his orgasm subsided.

His face was flushed as he raised his weight off John's body on trembling arms, but John had never seen him look more beautiful. That was the word that he whispered softly before raising himself up to give David a gentle kiss.

David's fingertips traced the curve of John's lips before he carefully sat back and eased out. His eyes flickered shut for a moment when he left John's body. With a small sigh, he stripped off the condom and looked uncertainly around the room.

"Here, David. Give it to me," John said, reaching for the soiled condom.

But David shook his head and got off the bed. "No, I can do it."

When he walked back in from the bathroom, he carried a small towel to gently clean them. John smiled at the quiet man who tenderly wiped the come from his belly and waited patiently until David was ready to get back into bed.

John lay on his side and pulled David into a slow and relaxed kiss, after which he whispered the words, "Stay with me."

David caressed John's cheek with the back of his hand and replied, "I'm here."

John wasn't sure if he meant just for the night or longer, but for tonight it would do.

CHAPTER 10

PERHAPS it was the shift in the weighting of the mattress or the cool air on his back where there had recently been a warm body, but John woke up knowing that David was no longer next to him. But the bed wasn't empty because he could *feel* David sitting quietly on the edge of the bed. John wanted to ask, but waited silently, holding his breath. The bed moved fractionally when he carefully stood up and John heard the soft pad of his bare feet crossing the bedroom floor. When the door closed John turned over and looked at the now vacant space on the other side of the bed. *He's not gone,* John reasoned and sat up to rub a hand wearily over his face. He willed that to be true but still needed reassurance. Leaning over the edge of the bed, John peered into the gloom beyond the mattress and gave a relieved sigh. *His clothes are still there....*

The thought had just passed when John heard the toilet flush; he quickly lay back down, facing David's side of the bed and feigned sleep. Through his eyelashes, John could just make out the bedroom door slowly open. David stepped in and stopped in the doorway; John had changed position. He waited and listened, hoping he hadn't woken him.

David walked quietly to the bed, carefully sat down, and slowly slid his legs under the covers. He settled on his side near the edge of the bed.

John could barely make him out in the shadows of the bedclothes, but *knew* David was watching him. He let his eyes close and tried to lay still; a near impossible task while being watched. After a couple of minutes John faked a sleepy stretch to cover the twitches starting in his legs and, with a slight groan, turned onto his other side. He knew he could have just admitted he was awake, but when he felt David follow him across the bed and tentatively settle against his back John knew he'd been right.

THE gray light was already creeping through the partially open curtains when John reached over and switched off the alarm clock before it reached the set time. He rubbed the heel of his palm sleepily across his eyes.

"It's almost spring," David said quietly. John blinked a couple of times and turned toward the voice. David faced the window. "Spring's a kinder season."

John almost said he didn't want him to worry about that anymore, but simply nodded and commented, "The mornings are getting lighter."

David's gaze shifted from the window to John, unsure of what to say now. John simply gave him a gentle smile and asked, "You sleep okay?"

When David nodded and returned the smile, something tightened in John's chest and, before he even realized it was happening, his fingers lifted and traced the curve of David's mouth, lingering briefly on the scarred lip. David closed his eyes, allowing the touch to turn into a caress.

John watched his fingers drag over David's bottom lip, pulling his mouth slightly open. He leaned in, their mouths near but not quite meeting as his fingers slid down the new growth of beard to rest lightly on David's throat. Soft lips had only just touched his when David's stomach gave a loud grumble.

David let out a small embarrassed laugh, but John leaned back and asked quietly, "When did you last eat?"

Embarrassment deepened to shame at the question and David tried to shrug it off. "With Jamie."

"Shit, David, that was half a bloody sandwich the day before yesterday." John's anger wasn't directed at David, but he quickly softened his voice when he saw the stricken expression on the other man's face. "Come on. We both need breakfast."

THE scene in the kitchen made David smile. John never stopped talking while busying himself frying bacon and eggs, buttering toast, and filling the coffeemaker. It was as if David left too many gaps in the conversation and John felt the need to fill them. Even though he wanted to ask if he could help, John had told him to sit at the table, so David contented himself with watching John fuss over the preparations.

"How do you like your eggs?" John asked, peering over his shoulder.

"I don't know. Anyway I can get them," David replied honestly.

The answer sobered John and he paused, his hand hovering over the fry pan as he watched the white become opaque over the yolk. He carefully slid the egg onto the plate next to the crisp bacon strips and carried it over to the table.

The smell of the bacon cooking had set David's stomach grumbling and twisting, but he waited until John sat down.

"Dig in, Dave," John said, trying not to be bothered by David's constant need for permission. "I'm not the best cook, but I *can* manage a bloody good fry-up."

"And soup," David added, giving John a slight smile before taking a mouthful of bacon.

A faint flush crept across John's face that David remembered that, but it was the delighted grin that was most evident as he echoed David's words. "And soup."

THE sensation of being clean and well fed was still unfamiliar. After John had gone downstairs to open the store, David showered and pulled on the sweatpants John had given him. He didn't know what else to do; this was out of his usual routine. He'd spent time in the small apartment before, but it seemed different now. *John was just trying to help,* David reasoned, *but last night... he brought me back here.* He shook his head at the turn his thoughts had taken and the fears they stirred.

After several minutes of standing at the bathroom door, David ventured over to the heavy bookcase that almost filled the main wall of the lounge room. Glancing along the titles, it was obvious that most, if not all, the volumes belonged to Maggie. There was nothing of John until he came to the end of the row. David paused at two small plain silver frames, each housing an old photograph. He carefully picked one up. The black-and-white picture showed a young woman with fair hair tied up in what looked like a heavily lacquered beehive. She was sitting on an old wooden swing, one hand on the weathered rope, the other supporting the little boy on her knee. The child looked barely more than two years old; both were caught mid-laugh. David ran a fingertip over the happy child. The other photograph was newer, color, but still had the faded pinkish tint of a print from the seventies. *Sunday best.* David smiled at a teenage John in a crisp white shirt and tie. He stood with an elderly couple, obviously uncomfortable having his photo taken. *He loved them very much,* David mused, noticing that John was holding on tightly to his grandmother's hand. *Private photos.* He suddenly felt that this was an invasion of John's privacy and put the picture down.

His hand had just let go of the frame when he was startled by a knock on the door. David's heart began to race and he instinctively took a step backward away from the bookcase. *This is wrong. I shouldn't be here.*

The knock was repeated a little more firmly.

"Hey, Dave. It's me, man. Um, me, Jamie."

David felt some of the tension drain from his shoulders; he quickly unlocked and opened the door.

Jamie gave David a beaming smile and pulled him into a hug. "Oh man, it's good to see you. Fuck, Dave, you scared us." He let David escape his grip and said with a grin, "Well, you look all right," but immediately regretted the flippant comment when he saw David's discomfort at being seen in only his sweatpants.

Jamie didn't give the embarrassment a chance to set in and grabbed his hand to lead him to the couch. "How are you *really,* Dave?" he asked, forcing direct but not threatening eye contact.

"I'm okay," he replied in an attempt to give his usual dismissive answer. Jamie didn't respond. He knew to sit and wait David out on this one. Eventually David sighed and mumbled, "I don't know.... Confused, I guess."

"Confused about what exactly?" Jamie asked gently.

David shrugged and indicated vaguely around the room with a wave of his hand. When the hand came to rest, Jamie enclosed it in both of his and said quietly, "John was really upset when you left. Okay, I haven't known him long, but it was bloody obvious he wanted you back. He wants you here."

David frowned, wanting but not willing to accept what Jamie was trying to tell him. Jamie squeezed his hand and asked, "Are you going to stay?"

"I don't know.... I want to." David sat and looked at Jamie's hands holding his. "I'll try."

"Try hard, Dave. Please."

Try hard. Of course he would try if it meant being with John, but David knew that ultimately trying might not be enough. His stomach clenched and he shook his head. "I don't know how to do this anymore, Jamie."

"What do you mean, Dave? What can't you do?"

David shook his head again and rubbed his free hand compulsively over the back of his neck; he couldn't explain.

Jamie watched David struggle. *Fuck. He has to know that John loves him by now.* "You need to trust him, Dave. Take the risk. Although, to be honest, I don't think it's much of a risk."

David didn't answer. Jamie couldn't understand how much he was asking. It had taken a lot of physical and emotional bruises before the "walls" were in place, and loving John would leave him vulnerable all over again. He could already feel it happening—and it terrified him. On the streets he had his routine: he ate and slept when he could, escaped into the books as often as possible, and saw Adam... although that *always* came at a cost.

Sitting up, Jamie gave an encouraging smile. "You'll be okay, Dave. Better get back before the boss notices I'm gone. I sneaked out while he was cornered by the pensioners. See you downstairs. Put on your new clothes, yeah?"

David watched Jamie leave and let out a shaky breath. He went through to the bedroom and looked at the white paper bag still full of the neatly folded clothes. *They smell clean,* David decided as he carefully lifted them out. He smiled at the sight of the simple white underwear.

THE bell on the store door jingled, causing both John and Jamie to look up. David entered looking very sheepish. He was dressed in the new jeans and a black long-sleeved T-shirt; it was only his tatty old boots that spoiled the picture.

"Hey, Dave! Love the new wardrobe," Jamie beamed. "Looks great. Doesn't he, John?" Jamie turned to John and groaned. "Oh fuck... googly eyes! You two are gonna be painful, aren't you!"

Embarrassed, John shot Jamie a withering look that was totally lost on him as he grabbed David's arm and dragged him to help rummage through a large cardboard box of secondhand novels.

The day passed easily and quickly although John seemed to find a lot of reasons to go to the back of the store. He tried very hard to give David his space and didn't interfere with Jamie and David's lunch routine even though he took every opportunity to glance in David's direction. By mid-afternoon John had become quite disgusted with his need to see David... *just to make sure he was all right,* he told himself... and focused his energy and thoughts toward reconciling the ordering system.

He was barely aware of Jamie ushering the last of the evening's customers out the door and was startled when a jubilant voice broke his concentration. "Home time!"

"Shite, Jamie! Stop sneaking up on me. You are being a total pain in the arse today."

Jamie gave a cheeky grin and replied, "Suffer, old man. I'm happy."

John stood up with some menace and took delight in Jamie's rapid backward step. He walked past him into the store and growled, "Don't push it, Jamie. I'm still your boss." But John's frown quickly disappeared when he saw David standing at the front counter.

David gave him a little half-smile. Although he was waiting for John he still didn't take anything for granted; he was ready to say good night and leave if he read any doubt in John's face.

Jamie followed John through the door and held his hand out. "Give me the keys, John. You two head upstairs and I'll lock up." He gave John a look that could only be interpreted as *Take him home, John.*

John thanked him and turned to David. "Come on, Dave. How about I shout you dinner out?"

David looked slightly panicked until Jamie butted in with, "You have the orders to finish, boss, and David looks knackered. I made him sort all those books this afternoon."

John started to answer but remembered an earlier time he'd suggested a meal out and said quietly, "Yeah, you're right. I'm pretty tired myself. Night, Jamie."

David gave Jamie a gentle smile as they walked past him and out of the store.

DINNER was quiet with just the two men, fish and chips and very little conversation. When they finished, John cleared the table and said, "I'm sorry, Dave. I really have to finish the ordering, but the TV is there, or grab a book from the shelf." David nodded and started scanning the bookshelf.

John settled to work, his eyes flicking between the neatly written figures and his old calculator. David had picked up a hardback novel and sat, legs tucked under him, at one end of the couch, where all he had to do was look up to see John at the table. It was a luxury to be able to read a hardback, but David soon regretted his choice when he was overcome by his weariness and the book became too heavy to hold. He desperately fought sleep, wanting to go to bed, but needing to wait for John.

By the time John looked up, David's eyes had drifted closed and the book lay open on his lap. John watched him for a while and realized how tired he always seemed even though he frequently dozed in his chair in the store. When David's hand slipped off the edge of the book for a second time, John said gently, "You look tired, Dave. Head off to bed and I'll be through in a minute."

David's head came up and he looked a little embarrassed at having drifted off, but he nodded, closed the book, and slowly made his way to the bedroom.

Determined to make the orders tally John continued to fiddle with the paperwork, but no matter how much he cursed them he just couldn't seem to get the figures to make sense. Eventually he had to admit defeat;

his mind was elsewhere. Closing the ledger he stood and switched off the light.

The bedside lamp was already off when John entered the bedroom and David was snuggled down under the quilt. John undressed as quietly as he could and slid into his side of the bed. The sheets were cold on his bare skin so he scooted closer to David, immediately feeling the heat radiating from his body. John stopped short of actual contact and lay for a while listening to the steady breathing of the other man.

When David gave a gentle sigh, John leaned forward and brushed his lips lightly against the back of David's neck and whispered, "It's just me."

Sleep safely, Dave.

CHAPTER 11

SUNDAY, John contemplated as he stretched and turned to look at the sleeping form beside him. *Sunday with David.* The thought both excited and unnerved him. *Nothing planned, nothing to fill the time to distract us.* The now familiar nervous flutter hit his stomach with the knowledge that they'd never actually spent that much time alone together.

John also realized that he hadn't had the chance to *really* look at David at length in the daylight. David was always so uncomfortable when under scrutiny that John's attention was usually fleeting, but here David lay unguarded in the morning light. His hair fell slightly over his face, but John could see the creases at his eyes were relaxed and the tension in his jaw was gone. David's soft lips were slightly open, enabling a steady, but quiet, snore to escape. The flutter in his belly stilled only to be replaced by a tickling warmth. John groaned at the change. *Fuck, McCann, since when did you find snoring a turn-on? Get a grip and stop acting like bloody Bridget Jones.* He told himself off but its effect was negated by the grin that spread across his face. He reached over and pushed the hair gently off David's face, well aware that the touch would wake him.

"Morning, Dave," he said, trying to sound a little more casual than his broad smile indicated.

David blinked a couple of times to clear away the last of his sleep and grunted back a passable greeting. He turned onto his back and pressed his hand to his eyes. John waited until he was sure David was fully awake and asked quietly, "What do you usually do on Sunday?"

David frowned at the unexpected question and gave it serious thought before he answered in a sleep-roughened voice. "Depends on the weather, I guess."

John nodded even though David was looking at the ceiling and not him. After a short silence, David cleared his throat and continued, "On a good day I go to the park, try to catch up on sleep. It's safer to sleep during the day."

On a good day. John wondered about the possibility of "good days", but asked, "What about on a bad day?"

David gave a little shrug. "Try to find somewhere dry. Bus stops or train stations sometimes. You get moved on a lot. Some days I just walk; others I'm too tired."

John frowned. "What about the shelter? Isn't that there to help?"

"Others need it more than me. I have Margins six days. Books, drawings… good company. If I can I go to the shelter at night sometimes, get a bowl of soup, somewhere warm to sleep, that's enough."

John thought David had finished speaking, but he added quietly, "Some men cry at night or call out to people they don't have anymore."

Pain twisted through John's chest at the very real possibility that David could be one of those men, but before he could respond David continued. "It's okay most of the time. You get used to the snoring and farting… a bit like here actually." He turned and grinned at John.

"You cheeky bastard," John laughed.

"So what do *you* do, John?" David asked carefully, still unsure of his boundaries when it came to John's personal life.

The question threw John a bit but he tried to answer it honestly. "I don't know anymore. I used to spend the day working, you know, meeting clients. Now… now I want to spend it with you."

David could easily see the color rise on John's face and didn't quite know how to react to that. He looked away and said softly, "Jamie might be more fun."

"Oh God, I get enough of him during the week." John chuckled but suddenly realized that David knew about him and Jamie.

"You know we got together once, but that's all it was… a bit of fun."

David wondered why John felt the need to explain that to him and said simply, "I know. Jamie told me."

John looked at him, concerned that David would think this was the same thing, but David gave him a reassuring smile. John fought the reemergence of the butterflies and leaned in to gently kiss him. When the kiss was returned his hand closed around the top of the quilt and slowly began to pull it down.

David's horror at being so exposed was instant and he grabbed at the quilt, but John covered David's hand with his own and gently loosened his grip. "It's okay, Dave." David let go of the fabric and closed his eyes. John recognized the action as one of embarrassment rather than fear and ran his fingertips slowly over David's chest, laying a soft kiss just behind his fingers. John's hand flattened so that the warmth of his palm spread through David's flesh and traveled down until it rested on David's belly.

"So beautiful," John murmured and kissed just below his belly button.

David opened his eyes at the unexpected words and frowned when he caught John's eyes.

"Believe me, David," he grinned. "A bit thin but that'll change."

The heat built under the palm and David mumbled, "Too hairy."

"Okay, hairy and beautiful," John laughed before pulling gently at a curl.

David's eyes locked on John's fingers as they stroked the trail of dark hair descending from his naval. John watched the rapid rise and fall of David's belly as the rate of his breathing increased.

Slightly embarrassed by his response to the attention, David shifted his leg in a vain attempt to hide the thickening of his cock. Noticing this, John slid his hand down the pale skin of David's thigh, opening him up again. "*That* is not something to be ashamed of." To prove his point he kicked the quilt off the bed, revealing his own burgeoning erection.

David smiled and lifted his hand to John's arm, running his fingers up and over the smooth skin of his shoulder. *So fair….* He looked up into those green eyes before his hand slipped to the back of John's neck and carefully pushed his fingers into the hairline. John shuffled closer until he could feel the length of David's body aligned against his own. Despite David's physical response, John still felt the need to say, "You know you don't have to do any of this if you don't want to." David didn't answer other than to kiss him.

Although their bodies ached for more, neither let their hands drift down. John concentrated on the slow and intimate kiss until it was as if he was melting into David. The merging scared him and he pulled away. "Oh God." He chuckled breathlessly in an attempt to cover up his true reaction. "You're gonna make me come just from that kiss."

John's head dropped and rested on David's shoulder so he could catch his breath and steady his nerves. He could smell the heat rising from David's skin and couldn't resist a gentle kiss and nuzzle. Without raising his head, John lifted his hand to caress David's face until he felt lips and then a tongue on his fingertips.

"Oh fuck," he groaned and moved up to capture that mouth in another kiss.

It was only then that John's hand moved down to David's cock. As he wrapped his fingers around the silky skin he whispered, "Touch me, Dave. Please."

David slipped his hand cautiously between their bodies and followed the rhythm started by John. Both men struggled to keep their movements slow as their bodies strained against each other reaching for impossibly closer contact. It was mere minutes before they were breathing raggedly into each other's open mouths, desperately trying not to lose the momentum.

Through the white haze of his approaching orgasm, John realized that David's raspy breaths contained his name… over and over. It was too much, and John gave a strangled cry before spilling into the other man's hand.

When John caught his breath he knew David had come with him.

With a breathless laugh, John's head fell back against the pillow. "Fuck, that was just… *fuck!*"

David nodded and managed a grinned, "Yeah."

John went to wipe his hand across his face until he realized it was sticky with David's come. He leaned back and pulled several tissues from the box on his nightstand and wiped both himself and David. "It's about now I wish I hadn't decided to quit smoking yet again," he chuckled. "I think caffeine is in order."

He swung his legs over the edge of the bed and ran a hand along his midriff; it was still slightly sticky. John grimaced and said, "I think I need a shower first."

David watched John leave the room and rolled over onto his back. He was still not used to being naked other than behind a locked door in a small shower cubicle on the rare occasion he was able to beat the queue before the hot water ran out. It felt good to stretch out on the bed and feel the air cooling his overheated body. He extended his toes to the end of the bed and his arms above his head and inhaled deeply. It had been a long time since he'd felt some control over his own body. He smiled and sat up. *Coffee.*

After pulling on his track pants, David padded through to the kitchen; he wanted to have the coffee made ready for John. The coffeemaker was already plugged in and David looked at it for a few minutes to figure out where to put the water. He filled the jug and poured it into the machine, carefully watching the level rise. He smiled and fitted the now empty jug back into place. *Coffee.* David glanced around the room trying to figure out where John would keep the coffee. It wasn't on any of the benches. He stood in front of the closed cupboards for a long time, wishing he'd paid more attention.

When John walked into the kitchen, dressed and toweling his hair, he was met with the sight of David sitting at the table, not willing to meet his eyes. John put the towel over the back of the chair and sat down. "What's wrong, Dave?"

"I wanted to make coffee," David mumbled.

John couldn't fathom what the problem was but could see that the water had been put in the machine and nothing else. He smiled and said, "Thanks. Here, I'll show you where things are."

David got up and followed John to the cupboard. "I keep the coffee here. Some people keep it in the fridge, but you don't have to. The cups are here… sugar here." The whole time he was talking, John was handing things to David. "You get the machine going and I'll get some toast on."

John sliced the bread and loaded the toaster while keeping an eye on David. It made him smile that David could finally take pleasure from the success of such a simple task.

WINTER sun was a glorious thing, John had decided. It was a bright cloudless day where all the colors seemed to be heightened by air that was so cold it took your breath away only to return in puffs of white. It had been an age since John had taken the time off to wander around a Sunday market and he was enjoying himself. He moved from stall to stall, picking up various items, noticing that David didn't touch anything and made sure to avoid eye contact with stallholders and shoppers alike.

After a while it became obvious to John that David was cold; his arms were pressed tightly against his body and both hands were jammed into his pockets. He looked tense and chilled. It made John realize that this was the reality of winter for David and others like him: being bitterly cold and not able to do anything about it.

They walked past a stall with a large assortment of coats and jackets. John stopped and looked through a rack of sheepskin-lined jackets. He held one up in front of David and said, "Here, try this on."

David looked at him and shook his head.

"Come on, Dave. You're cold and you need a coat." John knew it was difficult for David to accept "handouts", but he couldn't see why he couldn't buy him a coat.

"I'm okay," he replied in a tone that clearly meant don't push it. John looked at him a little surprised but said, "All right. How about we go and grab a drink in the café to warm us up."

The café was full of people chatting excitedly and pulling bargains out of plastic bags, but John managed to find them a small table in a back corner. John sighed to himself. The day seemed to be a whole series of small steps forward followed by missteps and setbacks. He passed David a menu and said quietly, "I just wanted to buy you a coat because you were cold."

David stared down at the laminated menu; he wasn't reading but needed somewhere to look other than at John while he collected his thoughts. Finally he said in a soft but clear voice, "I know, John, and I do appreciate that you want to do these things for me, that you want to take care of me. It's just...." He broke off and sat quietly for a while. John could see the tension in his clenched jaw and when the waitress came over he smiled and said, "Can you give us a few minutes, please?"

David waited until she left to continue. "I don't know how to explain the way I feel. How can someone who is willing to sell himself in a public toilet have trouble accepting a handout?"

John sat and thought about what David had just said; Jamie had kept trying to tell him that despite his situation David was a proud man. He said he understood but still kept doing these things. *Fuck. Jamie was right again.*

John took the menu from David and smiled. "Mind sharing a sandwich?"

CHAPTER 12

THE small plastic button snapped in half as fingers clutched and wrenched the linen shirt. The fabric strained and tore, leaving pale skin to bare the marks of purpled fingerprints. The hands hurt, turning to fists, punching to the point where knuckles bled. They unclenched and pushed, cheek grazed and bleeding against the rough concrete of the rendered wall. But the real pain was lower. This can't happen.... Please stop.

John tried to make sense of the small sounds in his head; pained and frightened murmurs. *David.* The muffled noises of distress continued. John sat up and tried to focus in the gloom of the darkened bedroom. "Dave?" he whispered. No reply. *Still asleep, still asleep.* He reached out and gently placed his hand on David's shoulder. "Wake up, Dave. You're just dreaming."

John wasn't sure whether it was his touch or words that startled David awake but he quickly pulled away from the hand with a strained, "No... please...."

David's reaction initially shocked John, but he quickly reasoned it was probably a residual of the dream. He said slowly and quietly, "It's okay, Dave. You were dreaming, that's all." David looked at him but his expression was one of confusion. He glanced around the room as if unsure of his surroundings and carefully edged to the side of the bed until he was able to slide his legs out and sit on the side.

Sitting up, John looked at David's hunched form; it was so hard not knowing what to do to help. He leaned over and carefully rubbed his hand over David's back, but David cringed away from John and quickly stood up to avoid any further touch.

John reached over and flicked on the bedside lamp. Squinting a little at the sudden light, he said in a soft but worried voice, "David?"

After starting to turn toward John, David shook his head and walked out of the bedroom. He stood in the kitchen feeling lost and disconnected from his surroundings. David desperately wanted the comfort John offered, but couldn't face him. The other touch was still too clear in his mind. *Too damaged for John.*

He took a glass from the draining rack and turned on the tap, but the liquid threatened to spill over the rim of the glass with the constant tremors of his hand. The water was tipped back into the sink untouched.

David stood and watched the water slowly drain through the old and ineffective plumbing until he heard a quiet voice behind him. "Come back to bed, Dave."

Not knowing what to say, how to explain, David simply nodded and accepted the gentle hand resting on his arm that guided him back to the bedroom.

John hadn't been sure if the touch would be welcome when he saw David silently staring into the sink, but he simply didn't know what else to do. He purposely kept his touch light, guiding rather than gripping.

When they reached the bedroom David got into the bed without any further words of encouragement and carefully pulled the covers up, facing away from John. A wave of helplessness swept over John as he looked at David's back. He crawled into bed as carefully as he could and made sure he was close but not touching. "Try to get some sleep, Dave," John said in a deceptively calm voice. He was met with silence.

It hurt that he couldn't touch him, that he couldn't hold him. Not for the first time John felt in over his head. He didn't know how to deal with this. *How do I tell him it's all right when I don't know what the fuck is wrong?*

JOHN went straight into the back room of the store, leaving David to wander up to his chair among the used books. Jamie leaned against the counter and watched the two men. He frowned and walked to the door of the kitchen. "What's happened, John? What's up with Dave?"

John stood at the sink with his back to Jamie and muttered, "Leave it, Jamie. Okay? David had a bad night is all."

The tone of John's voice and the shape of his back convinced Jamie to try elsewhere for answers. He quietly walked to the secondhand book alcove where he knew David was sitting, legs folded beneath him, staring into space. Jamie sat in "his" chair, like he had done so many times before, and waited until David turned to look at him.

"What happened, Dave?"

David returned his gaze to the bookshelf and said softly with a shrug of inevitability, "Ghosts."

Jamie nodded, even though he had no idea what David meant. David sighed, turned back, and said, "I'm okay, Jamie. Just a dream is all."

"Wanna tell me about it?" Jamie asked, but David just shook his head. "You know you can, Dave. Talk to me about stuff, I mean. Man, you know every possible thing there is to know about me."

David gave a little smile and said, "Yeah, I think I do."

Jamie grinned. "Yeah yeah, I like to talk and you *are* a great listener." His smile slipped a little as he added more seriously, "You never judge me, Dave. I'm sure John will listen, too, if you give him a chance."

John will listen, but he won't understand what it was like. David didn't voice his thoughts.

Jamie watched David carefully and knew he'd pushed enough for now. He leaned over and gave David a little kiss on the shoulder, knowing it would be barely felt through the fabric of the shirt and said, "Okay, Dave, I'll give you peace, yeah? We still on for lunch?"

David smiled and nodded as Jamie got up and left him to settle in the safety of his books.

WHILE Jamie sat with David quietly eating their lunch, John took the opportunity to slip out of the store with the excuse of grocery shopping. He needed the air, needed to get away for a few minutes to clear his head. The previous night had scared John more than he cared to admit.

Trying to decide between the red and green peppers gave John the relief of something mundane to think about. The supermarket was always quieter at this time of day and it gave him a chance to wander through the food aisles and pretend his life was still normal.

He looked up from the produce when a woman walked past and commented on the ever-escalating prices. They made eye contact briefly and John recognized her from the shelter.

She smiled at him. "Hello again. Did you find the man with the sketchbook?"

"David. Yes, I found him, thanks," John replied, a little surprised that she remembered.

"Good. I'm pleased to hear it." She gave a single nod and turned back to the tutting at the price of the broccoli.

John hesitated for a second, absently rubbing his thumb over the waxy skin of the pepper in his hand then asked, "Um… would you mind joining me for a coffee? I really would appreciate some advice."

The woman gave John a searching look before answering. "Sure. Meet you next door after the checkout."

JOHN looked at the plastic-coated red-and-white-check tablecloth while she gave the waitress her order. He ran the edge of his fingernail along the line of the intersections and watched the indentation slowly smooth out again. She noticed how unsure John seemed and said cheerily, "I'm Barbara, and thank you for the invite. It's not often I get picked up in the market these days."

John broke into a relieved smile. "I'm John."

"Hello, John. Lovely to meet you," she replied, giving him the chance to control the conversation.

His smile dissolved as he said quietly, "I'm not sure how to do this or even what to ask, but I…."

"Is David doing all right?" Barbara interrupted.

"If you'd asked me that yesterday I would have said yes, but today… I don't know."

Barbara gave John a long look, trying to fathom how to broach the subject; in the end she decided to opt for blunt honesty. "Tell me one thing, John; what kind of relationship do you want with David?"

John's cheeks colored, but he answered. "I want... I want us to be, um... together."

"Okay, now I have to ask; do you really know what you are in for here?"

The question startled John and he tortured the tablecloth for a moment longer before answering. "I thought I did, but now I have to admit no and that's why I am talking to you, I guess." He hated the admission that he couldn't control the situation. Asking for help simply wasn't in his nature.

She nodded, understanding how difficult this conversation was for John, and softened her tone. "So what happened to change your opinion since yesterday?"

John rolled his eyes and gave a small frustrated chuckle. "Seems daft in daylight, but he, David, had a dream last night that, um... upset him. He didn't want me to touch him and wouldn't talk. I didn't know what to do."

Barbara gave him a sad look. "I don't know how long David has been on the streets or what drove him there, but he's going to need a lot of patience, John. Things can happen out there that we would have trouble understanding."

John nodded thoughtfully. "He was beaten pretty badly a while back, but this seemed different."

"Some things are more difficult to get over than others. John, you have to understand that I believe David falls into the unfortunate category of the chronic homeless, and they are often there for reasons other than economic." John felt his stomach clench at the labeling of David, but he nodded for her to continue. "Many of these people, particularly the men, have trouble dealing with their situation as well as their reason for being there. Okay, I know I'm generalizing, but most men would hate being seen as a victim and that's what many of these men have become. To compensate they can adopt a fight-or-flight mentality."

John frowned and interrupted. "I can't see David fighting."

Barbara smiled at John's instant defense of David. "I know. From what I remember he was often withdrawn and tried to avoid any contact when he visited the shelter. So what I mean is he falls into 'flight' because he withdraws into himself."

"Or runs," John said softly.

Barbara looked at him for a moment before repeating, "Or runs. Either way, John, try to talk to him. You need to be honest and up front about things so he knows where he stands. Ask him questions if you want to know what's wrong. Let him know you don't expect an answer straight away, but you are there if he wants to talk. Give him space and time."

She hesitated for a minute, unsure whether to ask the next question, but she knew it was important for John's sake. "I am assuming you have a sexual relationship with David?"

John did *not* want to have that conversation, but he nodded and nervously gulped a mouthful of tea.

Tread carefully, Barbara told herself. "As I said before, John, things happen on the street that we might not understand, and safe sex is not always an option." She paused and watched John's reaction before saying, "You have to make sure *you* are safe, John."

The muscles in John's jaw tightened at her words and he thought back to his first time with David. *I might not be safe.* He closed his eyes briefly, exhaled a slow breath, and said quietly, "David was worried about that the first time we…." He let the sentence trail off.

Barbara gave him a smile and said, "He sounds like a good man, John. Don't hold it against him; he might not have had any choice. Try to get him to a doctor if you can."

John wanted to answer, but his throat closed and he just nodded instead. Barbara gave him time to take in what she'd said and perused the display of cakes and slices.

After a drink and a breather John was able to say, "He's tired all the time. He doesn't say anything, but he frequently dozes off during the day and I know sometimes he aches."

"Oh John, that doesn't have to mean there is anything wrong. Could very well be the result of poor nutrition and disrupted sleep patterns. Life can be pretty brutal on the body when there's never enough to eat and the warmest place to sleep is under a bridge. Get him on a vitamin and mineral supplement and if he needs to sleep, don't worry. It's either his body or his mind needing to shut down for a little while."

Tears prickled the back of John's eyes and, embarrassed, he looked back at the tablecloth.

Barbara could see he was overwhelmed and struggling to keep control. "So how are *you* doing?"

John rubbed his fingers over his eyes and took a deep breath. He picked up his cup and gave a small shaky laugh. "I suddenly wish it was more than tea in here."

Barbara laughed a little and ran her hand over John's arm. "I'm not going to kid you, John. It's not going to be easy, and it may not work out. So you need to decide if he is worth all this. If he is, I'm around to talk to."

THE store was relatively quiet when John pushed the door open, but he could hear Jamie babbling away about something at the back of the store. "Just me!" he called out and walked toward the voice.

Jamie was in the middle of a very animated monologue about a bicycle mishap he had when he was nine while David sat eating his half of an apple. John smiled at David's intense expression as he listened about scraped knees and dented pride.

He's worth it.

CHAPTER 13

"HE'S getting worse, isn't he?" Jamie said quietly, handing John his mug of tea.

John looked up toward the back of the store and although he couldn't see what David was doing he knew the pattern would be the same as it had been for the past few days: agitated, not settling, not talking. John took a sip of the tea and murmured, "I don't know. The other day after his dream he seemed to settle once he got into the store, and then... then *this* started."

Jamie nodded. David had listened quietly to him that afternoon and by closing time he was talking and helping unpack boxes. He shrugged. "I don't get it. He was so much better by the time you got back from the market."

"Yeah, we talked a bit after work and he fell asleep on the couch," John said and remembered how exhausted David had been. "So what went wrong?" He frowned and rubbed his hand wearily over his eyes; he could feel a headache starting to build. Jamie watched and recognized the gesture. He leaned over and rested his hand on John's shoulder, rubbing just a little. "I dunno, man, but we'll figure it out."

The two men sat in silence for a few minutes until Jamie huffed and said, "It started the next morning, didn't it? We'd finished the unpacking from the day before *and* gone through the invoices, so we started flicking through the calendars. Aussie beaches, cute puppies... even cuter film stars, you know, and he found an art one. Not really my taste, but David seemed to like it so I gave it to him to put up in the kitchen." Jamie hesitated and asked, "That was okay, yeah?"

John gave a little smile and said, "Yeah, that was okay. So he was happy. What changed?"

"Dunno." Jamie frowned, thinking back. "He opened it on this month and asked me what day it was. I told him, drew a smiley face on the day, and wrote 'David's calendar'. Maybe that was wrong because he went all quiet. I hung it up in the kitchen and when I got back he was in his chair." *Like when he first came to the store. Shit, maybe even worse,* Jamie thought but didn't want to make John worry any more than he already was. Instead he asked, "What's he like at home?"

"The same. He won't talk to me. He cringes if I try to touch him." John blushed at the mention of their physicality. "He alternates between sleeping too much and not sleeping at all. I woke up last night and he was standing at the bedroom window, just staring out." The sight of David looking down at the empty street had hurt John more than he'd admit to Jamie; something had gone wrong. *I obviously can't be doing enough.*

Jamie didn't say anything, but rubbed his hand over John's back just to let him know he wasn't alone in this.

JAMIE split the sandwich in half and put David's share on the arm of his chair. "Have your lunch, David," Jamie said quietly, watching carefully as the pencil continued its unceasing motion over the already creased and smudged page. He put his hand gently on David's arm to still its movement. "Come on; leave that for now." Jamie's touch took a moment to register, but David stopped and sat looking at the sketchbook.

"Dave, what's happening right now? John and I are worried about you," Jamie said just loud enough to be heard in the quiet store.

David looked at Jamie's hand and then closed his eyes. "I don't want to do this."

The unexpected words confused Jamie; he wanted to ask what David didn't want to do, but whispered, "You don't have to do anything you don't want to."

David didn't answer, but the thought was clear in his mind. *Maybe in your world, Jamie.*

Jamie sat back in the chair and let David return to his drawing, watching his hand skitter across the page in rapid and, at times, seemingly uncontrolled movements. The picture didn't make sense to

Jamie; it was dark and abstract, not the usual delicate renderings elsewhere in the sketchbook. The pencil lines created deep indentations in the soft cartridge paper and the graphite was so dense in places the paper's texture was flattened and shining.

Jamie chewed his sandwich triangle slowly and tried to make small talk between bites. David didn't touch his share.

THE excited babble of the five-year-old faded as the young mother held her hand and led her through the store door. The purchase of a first reader was always recognizable, but it also signaled late afternoon. The schools were empty, parents had picked up their children, and they were heading home to start tentative explorations of the written word and dinner.

David had put the sketchbook down, his fingers aching, and now sat curled in his chair. He glanced up at the polished wood store clock and his stomach cramped. *It's time to go.*

He unfolded his legs, not really surprised at how they trembled while he pulled his boots on over the socks John had bought for him. He took a deep shuddering breath and stood up. His sketchbook lay on the floor beside his chair and he looked at it, uncertain what to do. David knew he didn't want to take it with him, but... *John will keep it safe.* He bent down and picked it up, holding it close for a moment, fighting the urge to simply sit in his chair again, *safe with John.* He shook his head, his jaws clenched tight as he walked down the store.

John looked up and smiled when he heard David approach, but the smile faded when the sketchbook was pushed across the counter toward him.

"What is it, Dave? Do you need a new one?" John asked hopefully, but not really believing that's all it was.

David shook his head and kept his eyes on the book. "I need to go out, John."

A bolt of nausea hit him at David's words and he just stood and stared for a few seconds before he realized he needed to answer. "Um, okay. Will you be long?"

David's fingers rubbed over the cover of the sketchbook, mentally warring whether or not to lie to John. He swallowed and said quietly, "I don't think so. I don't know."

John frowned. He really felt sick now. "Okay, Dave. I'll put your book upstairs and wait for you." He went to put his hand over David's, but the fingers were quickly withdrawn and David whispered, "I have to go."

John listened to the bell on the store door jingle as David left.

THE early evening weather was still mild but David already felt cold and sick to his stomach. He quickly walked away from the store, pushing down the memory of John's face as he left. *Can't think of that, can't think of John.* It was already dusk by the time he reached the toilet block on the perimeter of the park and he recognized some of the men already there.

David leaned against the cracked concrete wall and watched the dust of the gravel creep over his boots until they almost disappeared in the gray. The younger men always got picked first but he knew he wouldn't be here much longer. A pair of clean leather shoes appeared in front of his. David didn't look up as the man opened his wallet and shoved a twenty toward him. He didn't move. Jamie's words came back to him. *You don't have to do anything you don't want to.* He knew it wasn't true.

"Well, do you want it or not?"

David felt like he was moving through molasses as he lifted his hand to take the money.

"ARE you going to close up, John? Or do you want me to?" Jamie asked, well aware that it was already half an hour past their usual time.

John looked up from the messy ledger page. "I keep thinking about dragging this place into the computer age, but I haven't managed to do it yet." He paused and added quietly, "It's okay, Jamie. You go home I'll wait a little longer."

Jamie nodded and lifted his fingers to the back of John's neck. "Call me, yeah? You know... when he gets home."

"Yeah, he shouldn't be too long now." John smiled without any real conviction. Something felt very wrong this time, but he knew that he *would* wait for David to come home.

THE concrete was cold and hard through the knees of David's jeans. Water from the leaking toilet had soaked through the fabric; his knees ached.

The man had left without a word.

David sank back onto his heels and rubbed the palms of his hands on his jeans. He'd told the man to stop before he came. He'd never had the courage to say that before. But this time he told him before they started. The problem was when David tried to pull away the man had wrapped his fingers in David's hair, reminding him he had no choice in this and fucked his mouth hard before coming down his throat.

David looked down at the state he was in. His new clothes were soiled and wet. He thought of John choosing these clothes for him; picking them up in the store, maybe holding them against himself and deciding between colors. Now in the blue glow of the "junkie" light they looked old and used.

Tears stung his eyes and he swallowed them back only to be reminded of the taste still in his mouth.

David's stomach lurched and he scrambled for the edge of the toilet bowl and vomited until his empty stomach cramped and convulsed over air and bile. A young hustler pushed the door open and leaned against the wall. "You okay?" David's white-knuckled fingers gripped the edge while his other hand still clutched the crumpled twenty. He nodded and waited until the youth closed the door.

He pushed himself back, wiped his mouth with the back of his hand, and stood up, not sure what to do other than get out of the toilet block. The hustler was still outside when David opened the door; he moved out of the way to let David get to the sink and said quietly, "You need a hit? I got some if you need it."

David spat the water into the sink and grimaced at the metallic taste. He shook his head and walked out. He hovered outside the toilet block, not sure which direction to head. The only one *not* possible now was Margins and John.

IT had been dark for a few hours, but the "open" sign hadn't been flipped and the door remained unlocked. John sat at the counter unmoving, the sickness in his stomach growing. When a group of youths walked noisily past the front window John looked up at the clock and sighed. *A bit longer.*

Another hour had passed before the front door opened, but it was Jamie who walked in and stood beside John. "I got worried when you didn't call," he said a little apologetically. "I went upstairs first, but there was no one there…."

John glanced at the door again and said quietly, "I couldn't face it yet."

Jamie nodded, not sure what to do or say now that he was here, so he settled on his mother's favorite "cure-all". "Want me to make a pot of tea?"

John tried to answer, but the words wouldn't form. He looked away from Jamie, his fingers clenched as tightly as his jaw while he blinked away the tears he didn't dare allow to start. Jamie watched John and although his first instinct was to hug the man, he was wise enough to know that was the last thing John could deal with right now. Instead he slid open the drawer at the counter, grabbed the store keys, and said, "Come on. Let's go look for him."

John took a shaky breath and gave Jamie a silent but grateful look. Jamie smiled and threw him the keys while he scribbled a note for the door of the store. *David, if you get home before us call John's cell phone. Love, Jamie xx.* He then taped a couple of coins to the back of the note.

John smiled over his shoulder and said quietly, "Thanks, mate."

By the time they reached the shelter, Jamie was sure they would find David inside and jumped out of the car almost bouncing on the balls of his feet while John locked up. He quickly disappeared into the foyer of the old building. John followed, less convinced, but a tingle of hope started in his belly. The foyer of the old building smelled vaguely of disinfectant and stale cigarette smoke; it housed notice boards covered in leaflets detailing rehab clinics and counseling for the long-term unemployed, and tattered pages of photocopied or handwritten pleas for missing persons. John glanced at them briefly and quickly looked away.

Jamie was already at the reception desk trying to get someone's attention when John called to a man handing over a blanket to a wary-looking youth. "Is Barbara on duty tonight?"

He turned to John and shook his head. "No. Sorry, man. Only male staff in here at night. Can I help with something?"

John tried to explain as best he could with regular interjections from Jamie, but the shelter worker just shook his head again and suggested they have a look around. The large hall was full of small beds, each one becoming home for a single night. The first thing that struck John, other than the overcrowding, was the smell, and it hurt John to remember how he had complained that David stank when he first took over the store.

As he scanned the room, many avoided his eyes, retreating to the safety of their own thoughts, while others met him with open defiance. The memory of David's words about nighttime in the shelter suddenly hit him. *Some men cry at night or call out to people they don't have anymore.* He had to leave. Jamie saw him turn and walk out the door. He thanked the shelter helper, smiled gently at a few faces, and hurried after him.

John was already outside leaning against the wall lighting up a cigarette. He glanced up at Jamie and shook his head. "He's gone back to *that,* hasn't he?"

Jamie wanted to lie and say no, but couldn't. He leaned beside John and watched an old man pushing a battered shopping cart filled with bags, paper and plastic, through the narrow opening of the door. Jamie hoped there would be room for him even though he doubted it. He sighed and said quietly, "I don't know, John, but something was really upsetting him. So there has to be a good reason, yeah?"

John tipped his head back against the wall and exhaled a long stream of smoke before saying, "I thought he would be able to talk to me about his *reasons* by now."

Jamie nodded. "He still has a lot to work through, I guess. I can't even imagine what his life has been like."

So many images flooded John: David hurt and bleeding in his stairwell, his shame at not being able to stay clean, the tentative nature of their lovemaking. John wanted to make it *all* right for him so he could lead a normal life, but Barbara's words of warning were only just starting to become real.

After stubbing his cigarette out on the graffiti-covered wall, John straightened his back with a weary roll of his shoulders and said, "Let's go, Jamie. He's not here."

Jamie nodded and said a little too quietly, "Yeah, maybe he's at home already… and didn't see the note."

John didn't answer.

They drove home the long way past the park, both looking at every person they passed, but neither said a word. By the time they reached the store it was well after eleven and the note was still stuck to the door untouched. John reached out to rip it off, but Jamie stilled his hand. "Leave it please, John. Just in case."

John looked at Jamie, ready to argue, but left the note with a small nod of his head. "Just in case."

CHAPTER 14

THE two young mothers stopped talking when they alighted from the bus and looked at the quiet man sitting in the corner of the bus shelter. One made a hushed comment, to which the other shook her head, and they tugged their children away a little faster. David lowered his head and closed his eyes. *Not long now.*

He ached and his head thumped, but none of that mattered now. He was here and would see him soon. It would be worth it.

A group of teenage boys spilled out of an old car and laughed as they shoved one another toward the low brick wall in front of the school where they quickly took up residence. David shrank back into the shadow of the shelter. He'd learned from experience to avoid teenagers in large numbers. He heard another car pull up. The boys started cheering and he could make out a shout of, "Hey, Robinson!" He leaned forward enough to see Adam getting out of the driver's seat of a new car sporting learner driver plates. From his hiding place, David watched the boys surround his son, who proudly showed off the little blue car until the school bell sounded.

When the boys dispersed and disappeared into the school building, David whispered sadly, "Happy birthday, Adam."

A SOFT breath on the back of his neck was the first thing John registered as his uneasy sleep receded. *David.* But the reality of the night before soon invaded that thought and an empty nausea overtook him. He reached out to the nightstand and lifted his cell phone. John knew there'd been no call, but he still felt compelled to check. *No messages.* He turned onto his back and pinched the bridge of his nose; his eyes stung and the small amount of sleep he'd managed had done nothing to ease his headache.

It was still early, but John knew he couldn't stay in bed any longer. It felt wrong. But at the same time he didn't have the energy to get up.

The movement in the bed woke Jamie and he sat up, momentarily thrown by his surroundings; it had been a long time since he'd crawled into bed with his parents in this room. He looked down at John and, although both men were still fully clothed, he felt a little awkward and unsure of what to say. John acknowledged Jamie with a brief nod, but escaped further conversation by sitting up and swinging his legs over the side of the mattress. When Jamie started to speak a simple good morning, John held up his hand to silence him, got up, and walked through to the kitchen.

After a visit to the bathroom, Jamie braced himself and entered the kitchen where John was stacking dishes in the cupboard. Jamie watched for a little while before getting the courage to ask, "You okay?"

"I'm fine," John replied in a manner that told him not to pursue it any further. But Jamie ignored the tone, understanding John's defense mechanisms, and suggested, "We can look for him again."

"He's gone, Jamie," John snapped, determined not to allow the emotions bubbling so close to the surface to break through.

"You found him last time," Jamie said quietly.

John slammed the cupboard door and spun around to face Jamie. "How many times do I have to *keep finding* him? Tell me that."

That surprised Jamie; the answer seemed so obvious. "Until he stays."

John's resolve crumbled and he sat heavily at the table. Barbara's words ran through his head. *I'm not going to kid you, John. It's not going to be easy, and it may not work out. So you need to decide is he worth all this?* He pushed his hand through his hair and looked toward the window away from Jamie.

"I can open Margins if you want," Jamie offered and sat opposite John, fiddling with the handle of the empty mug left on the table.

John shook his head and sighed. "Leave it today...."

"But what if he comes to the store? We have to have it open. I'll stay at the store if you want to go look again. Maybe that lady from the shelter can help this morning?"

John took the mug gently from Jamie and turned it over in his hands. He focused on the authors' names repeated several times in what looked like copperplate—obviously a publisher's promotion. He placed the mug carefully on the table and looked up at Jamie, his voice soft but determined. "You're right. I can't give up that easily."

"Of course I'm right. I'm always right, yeah?" Jamie grinned and was instantly up out of his chair and heading for the door. "Come on then. Go find him." John couldn't help but smile back at the young man literally pushing him out the door.

JOHN scratched absently at the beard of stubble on his jawline as he drove down the main street. He felt dirty and uncomfortable in yesterday's clothes, the same ones he'd slept in. *One fucking night and I'm complaining.* He turned the car into a side street next to the shelter and shut off the engine. Jamie's optimism had stayed with him for the first part of the drive, but now John sat in the driver's seat reluctant to leave the confines of the car. His head fell back against the headrest and he closed his eyes. *What if he's not there? What then?* The impending sense of loss was so powerful that it virtually immobilized him. He couldn't do this, couldn't go in there again and not find him among all the other lost souls.

A tap on the window roused him and John opened his eyes to see Barbara standing on the edge of the sidewalk. He wound down the window and gave her a not very convincing smile.

"John, isn't it? What brings you here?"

John got out of the car and told her as briefly as he could what had happened since their last chat. Barbara simply stood and listened with the occasional nod. When he finished she said, "To be honest, John, I don't know what to say to you. But let's start by going inside to see if he's there and we can talk properly over a coffee."

Barbara locked her handbag in a drawer in her office and quickly checked through the roster for the day. John waited patiently as she frowned over her paperwork and sighed. "Never enough willing hands. Okay, let's see if we can find...." She looked at him for a reminder.

"David," John said quietly, his stomach already churning. Barbara gave him an apologetic smile and put a hand on his arm while she called out to a young man in the next room. "Brian, let John check around a bit. He's looking for the 'sketchbook' guy."

"Sure thing," Brian said. "But I haven't seen him around here for quite a while." He turned to John and after giving him a quick once-over suggested, "There are still a few in there, but its mainly old guys sleeping it off until chucking out time."

Barbara was already waiting at the table in the kitchen when John finally gave up his search of both the sleeping area and dining room. "Come and sit down, luv," Barbara said gently, taking note of John's miserable expression. "As I said before, I don't really know what went wrong, but from what you said it seemed that in *his* mind it was very important to go, even though he obviously didn't want to."

John nodded. "It was tearing him up for days before...." He hesitated for a minute before asking, "He left his sketchbook with me. Is that good or bad?"

"I don't really know; I think you know him better than I do, but it does tell me that he cared enough to entrust it to you," Barbara said softly, taking hold of John's hand. "I've *never* seen him without it."

John looked away. It took him several uncomfortable minutes before he managed to suggest, "Maybe I could call the police?"

This is so hard. Barbara watched him carefully as she said, "It's too early for that, hon. Maybe tomorrow. But to be honest I don't think they'll follow it up; he's an adult who left of his own accord and... and I'm sorry to say, would still be regarded as a transient."

John closed his eyes, but knew what she said was true. He took a deep breath and nodded. Barbara squeezed his hand. "I'll keep an eye open for him here and ask around. Look, I've got a map of the park and can show you the most popular places. Plus we can check out where the soup wagon is going to be tonight."

IT was already late afternoon by the time John sank back into the driver's seat. He'd wandered through the park hopeful at first, but gradually became more dejected as he witnessed many dirty faces that either avoided his curiosity or were simply lost in their own survival.

None of them were David. He checked his cell phone again, but he hadn't missed any calls.

John sat in the car for a long time. He watched the gray smoke of his cigarette slowly drift out the open window. *I didn't manage to give these up for long,* he mused as the long line of ash finally fell onto his trouser leg. It was afternoon and John knew he needed to head back to relieve Jamie, even though it felt a lot like giving up. He butted what was left of the cigarette into the ashtray and turned the keys in the ignition.

The news on the car radio was heading into the expected "feel good" human interest story as John pulled away from the red light at the intersection near the store. He glanced briefly at Margins, more out of habit than anything else, and caught sight of a figure sitting on the sidewalk just out of sight of the storefront. He was past it before he could see clearly, but by the time he'd parked the car his heart was like a jack-hammer in his chest. He shoved the keys in his pocket and jogged to the corner, slowing to a stop as he reached its edge. *Take it easy, Mac.*

He took a deep breath and calmly stepped around the brickwork to stop at the figure. When David didn't move John asked quietly, "Dave? Why are you outside?"

David didn't look at him, but stood up slowly. John could see his fingers twitching and flexing as he fought to hold himself together enough to answer. "I just came to get my book." It was said softly, but with the finality of a door slamming in John's face. He looked at David, waiting for more, but David continued to stand with his arms now defensively wrapped around his body and his eyes on the ground between them.

Something clenched inside John. "It's upstairs." He turned his back on David and walked to the door of the apartment. Without further comment John opened the door and stood aside for David to walk up the stairs.

On entering the living room John's eyes flicked to the sketchbook and he said, "It's on the coffee table." He watched David walk across the room, eyes down, and pick up the book.

John didn't understand any of this. *What the fuck did I do wrong?*

"I looked for you," he said, trying unsuccessfully to keep the anger and bitterness out of his voice. "Half the bloody night I looked for you, David."

David hesitated, his fingers tightening reflexively around the spiral binding of the book. He couldn't explain. There was no way to make John understand. He knew it was no excuse for what he'd done but said tentatively, "I had to see Adam."

"Okay, you had to see your son. I can understand that, but I don't get what's been going on with you and why you didn't...." John stopped speaking. It suddenly struck him what it all meant and why David hadn't come home. He stood and glared, not wanting to believe it.

John slowly shook his head and said with a quiet bitterness to his voice. "Bus fare. Is that right, David? Is that right?" His hands clenched into fists as his voice rose to a choked shout. "Still acting like a fucking whore for a few fucking dollars?"

John's words battered him; he stared down at the dirty fingers that clutched tightly at his sketchbook. David wanted to run, to get away from the accusations, *the truth,* but he simply didn't have the strength anymore. He felt numb, heart and soul. Only every other word registered and he closed his eyes.

All the anger and frustration John had bottled up since the night before poured from him onto David, with John only pausing to take a breath when he saw David's book hit the floor. David staggered, his grip on the back of the chair the only thing holding him on his feet.

The room was suddenly silent as John stood and watched David sway slightly before crumpling to his knees. The air left John's lungs, taking all his anger with it, to be replaced by the sickening realization that he was the one hurting David now. Forgotten keys previously gripped tight enough to make sharp indentations in John's palm fell to the carpet and he rushed over to David. "Oh fuck, Dave. I'm sorry. I'm so sorry," John gasped and dropped to where he could wrap strong arms around him to support and hold him close.

David was unresponsive and simply let himself be held, only vaguely aware of John's hand moving over his face and through his hair. The warmth of John's breath against his neck went unnoticed. He barely heard John's breathless, desperate words. "Please, Dave. I didn't mean it like that…. I was angry."

John lifted his face and pressed his forehead against David's. "Oh God. I can't stand the thought of someone else touching you, using you like that."

David didn't answer.

"Come on, Davey," he said, trying to calm himself more than anything else. "You're cold. Let's get you in a bath."

With some effort, John managed to get both David and himself to their feet and guided him slowly to the bathroom. John pushed the pile of towels stacked on the chair onto the floor and got David to sit down.

The rolling sickness in his stomach increased as John watched how David simply allowed himself to be maneuvered without any acknowledgment or comment. He was at a loss what to do and considered calling Barbara for help. *Fuck,* he even considered calling Jamie but wanted, needed to be there for David himself. John started the water running and turned back to David.

With shaking hands John crouched and pulled David's boots off. He kept waiting to be told to stop, that he could manage himself, but it didn't come. He rolled off the socks he'd bought; David's feet were cold. "Your feet are like ice, Dave," John said quietly and rubbed one between his hands. He looked up. David was watching at him, but not really looking. John pulled one of the fallen towels under David's feet to keep them off the cold tiles and stood up to carefully tug the T-shirt over David's head before undoing the button of his jeans.

He checked the bath and stilled the taps. "Come on, Dave. I need you to stand up," John said quietly, watching for a response. When there was none he put his hand on David's back and with a little pressure repeated the instruction. "Up, Dave, so we can get you into the bath."

David turned, looked at John, and then wearily stood and stepped into the bath. John sat on the edge of the porcelain lip, not caring that the warm water soaked his trousers. He lifted the flannel and gently wiped it over David's shoulders.

"It's going to be okay," John said, trying to convince himself. "You're home now. It'll be all right after a good night's sleep." He squeezed the flannel tight and dropped his face into his hand for a moment. It had been a long time since he'd been in a situation that couldn't be solved with rosters, meetings, and simple hard work.

He straightened, exhaled a deep breath, and stood up.

John calmly removed his clothes and stepped into the bath behind David. He pulled him back against his chest and whispered, "You'll see. We can do this if you help me," not caring that the water lapped onto the floor.

CHAPTER 15

THE vague mint of his shampoo and the underlying scent of David were the first things John consciously registered as he drifted toward waking. He slowly became aware of the light press of his skin against the warmth of David's back; his arm wrapped protectively around him and his nose buried in David's hair. They'd stayed together in the bath until the water had cooled, John speaking softly at first, David not at all.

John tightened his hold slightly and listened to the gentle snore, the night before still playing through his mind.

DAVID had fallen asleep as soon as he'd crawled under the security of the quilt despite the light still filtering in through the window. John lay with him for a while before he carefully slid out of bed and padded through to the living room, where he dialed the store number.

"Hello, Margins Bookstore."

"It's John. I'm home. David's here."

Jamie hesitated. John sounded exhausted. "Is everything okay, John?"

"Yeah," he said, and then added quietly, "I don't know. I was angry, Jamie. I reacted badly and said things... called him things I shouldn't have."

Jamie frowned, knowing it would just make things worse if he called John on it. He sighed softly and said, "You were upset, John. He'll understand. David's a good person. Just talk to him, be honest with him."

"He's asleep. I think he...." John's jaw clenched as he fought through his emotions. "He's asleep."

"I'm about to close the store. I can come up if you want. You know, just for a drink or chat.... Yeah?"

John relaxed a little even though he wasn't going to take Jamie up on his offer. "Thanks, mate, but I'm tired. I think I'll just get some sleep."

"Okay. Sleep's good, John. Mum always said that it gives us a chance to heal," Jamie soothed. *"He's strong, you know, John. Despite everything...."*

HE'S strong, you know, John. Despite everything.... John rested his face carefully against the crook of David's neck. He knew David wasn't a child, knew he was a grown man and contained a strength that he doubted existed in many men, including himself, yet he brought out every protective instinct in John. He gently nuzzled the nape of David's neck, smiling a little when David moaned lightly in his sleep and leaned back into the touch without waking. He kissed the soft skin below David's ear, lips just brushing the heat of the pulse point, and whispered, "What brought you here, Dave? What brought you to this?"

John's eyes drifted shut and he just *breathed* David in while contemplating all the questions he wanted to ask. *What was your life like, David? Your wife and job.... What happened? Why did you end up out there on the street? How long did you live like that before Maggie gave you somewhere to feel safe? Safe.... What caused the nightmares? What happened, Dave?* John squeezed his eyes tight; it hurt to think of David out there knowing what could have happened to him.

Taking a shaky breath John gently pulled David's hair off his face. "You've changed me too, you know?" he whispered, wishing he could say these things when David was awake. "I'd never actually stayed the night with anyone before you...." John gave a sad laugh at how fast he usually exited a bedroom. "Now the thought of my bed without you...." He watched his fingers slowly thread through David's hair. "I don't think I can go back to my 'old' life, Dave. It seems like a world for a different person now. But I need to know, are you still going to be here at the end of my year?"

The seed of fear had started to grow. All the "what ifs" appeared in rapid succession. What if David left again? What if David was really sick? *Stop it, Mac.... Stop it.* John let his arm drop down again and encircled David's waist, his fingers tickled through the hair on David's belly comforted by the small murmur David made in his sleep. He pressed himself tightly against David's back and lie like that, simply listening to David sleep.

It was almost an hour before David began to stir. He didn't say anything, but the subtle change in body language told John he was awake.

"I'm sorry, David; I shouldn't have lost it like that," John said very quietly while he flexed his fingers over David's warm skin. "It's just the thought of someone else touching you."

David winced and a wave of self-loathing threatened to engulf him. What could he say to that? It had been his choice even though he felt like he had no choice at all.

The silence lingered in the room. Both men wanted to speak, but neither felt able to start.

David was tense in John's embrace and his panic started to rise that David would run again. *Talk to him. Jamie said to talk to him,* John thought, grasping at anything to make this work. His voice was low and soft as he told David how he'd felt, trying not to lay blame, but explained the emptiness and fear when David didn't come home. The more he spoke the easier the words flowed until John reached what he really needed to say. "I can't do this without you. Can you let me love you, David? Can you do that?"

The words stopped and absolute terror took over. John could barely breathe. The blood pounded in his ears while he waited for a response. Any response.

David didn't answer but a gentle shudder shook his body and John realized that even though he made no sound, David had begun to cry. John tightened his hold, moving his arms up around the other man's chest. He buried his face in David's neck all the while talking in a hushed panicked tone. "It's okay, David. We can work something out. Jamie's been getting you to help.... I guess... I guess I've been using you as unpaid labor.... We can work it out so you can stay... we can always work it out. *Oh fuck, Dave,* we can always work it out."

John knew he was babbling as the tears streamed down his face, but he was afraid to stop until David lifted his hand and reached blindly for him.

It was only when his fingers were tangled tightly in John's hair that David allowed himself to pour out a lot of the grief and pain he'd held onto.

John knew now to let David cry. He simply held him pressed against his chest until David's grip loosened and he lay exhausted in John's arms.

John wiped his hand over his face, for once not embarrassed by the tears still rolling down his cheeks. He clasped David's hand in his own and rested them lightly on the rumpled sheet in front of David's chest. "I meant it... before... what I said."

David closed his eyes and twined his fingers a little tighter through John's. He desperately wanted to believe him.

"It's not something I've said to many people in my life," John continued. "Men just *don't* where I come from. We *love* a pint or our football team, but we don't say it when it really means something." David felt John's chest rise and fall as he sighed. "Actually I've had little cause to use it at all. I loved my mam and grandparents... I think I loved my da. But other than that I only ever said it to one person. Jean McMullan." It surprised John that this was actually leaving his mouth. He *never* talked like this; even as a child he kept things to himself.

Despite the softness of John's voice, David could feel it rumble lightly in his chest. Its gentle cadence soothed and made him feel safe... at least for a while. When John paused, David opened his eyes just a little and murmured, "Tell me."

John gave a breathy chuckle and started. "I was barely into my twenties when I finally got the courage to ask Jean McMullan out to the pictures. She worked in the same office and had been the object of my desires, and quite a few wet dreams, for an eternity." David smiled, but didn't make a sound in case John stopped. "Anyway... I have no idea what the film was, but the night went well and we ended up an item. I remember a while after I told her how much I loved her, certain that I would spend the rest of my life with this girl. She told me she loved me back, but the next week she broke it off to go out with Mark Lynch. I was devastated and couldn't understand what I'd done wrong. Then she told me. Mark had a car and money to take her better places than the cheap seats at the local cinema. I left Bradford after that and vowed to change my life. I guess I did in ways I didn't quite expect."

David tensed against John and said quietly, "I told my wife I loved her."

John waited for more, but when there was none he leaned forward, kissed David softly on the neck, and murmured, "Hey, I lied. There was another love in my life. Do you want to know about it?"

David nodded against John, took a deep breath, and exhaled slowly.

"I must have been all of seven or maybe eight at the time," John started, relaxing back into his pillows while his fingers made slow circles on David's shoulder. "I had just been to the store for my gran and had her old string bag full of tatties; fuck, that bag was heavy. I put it down for a breather and heard a noise. It was tiny little sound that I could barely make out." David turned over and propped his head on his hand so he could watch John's face as he drifted back to the little boy. "There was an old flour sack at the edge of the drain. I remember I bent over it to see if I heard the noise again and it moved." A broad smile lit up John's face and he laughed. "I nearly shit myself! But in the sack were two kittens. One had already died and the other wasn't far behind. It was this little black thing, all wet and smelly. It barely had its eyes open, but I know it looked at me and mewed."

John stopped, rubbed his hand over his mouth, and shook his head. "I struggled home with the bag of potatoes over one arm, the dead kitten in the other and the live one up my jumper. My gran raised hell at the state of my clothes when I got home, but toweled the little one dry and gave it some warm milk while Granddad and I buried the other one on the allotment where he grew the biggest yellow dahlias I'd ever seen. Like giant suns. Sooty lived another sixteen years before he ended up in the allotment. I loved that little cat."

David lifted his hand to gently caress John's face. "Still bringing home strays."

"Only if you stay until we both end up under the yellow dahlias." John smiled under David's touch. When David returned the smile John leaned up so their lips could meet briefly before he groaned and said reluctantly, "We'd better get up and go down to the store before Jamie thinks he's in charge."

DAVID closed the bathroom door and turned to look at himself in the mirror. His eyes were still red, he needed to shave, and his hair was a mess. He tried to see what John saw; he easily saw the bedraggled stray, but someone John could love enough to spend the rest of his life with just wasn't in the reflection.

CHAPTER 16

BACON. Eggs. Bread for toast. Coffee for the machine. John checked and double checked all the items that lay out on the bench. He nodded to himself and opened the cupboard door so the crockery was in plain view.

The tiled floor of the kitchen was cold and he absently rubbed the top of his foot against the flannel-covered calf of the other leg. He knew he could get his slippers but cringed at the thought, not quite ready to let David see him in what Marian had called his "old man slippers". *Shit, I really need to call Marian,* John cursed silently but was cut short when he heard the bathroom door open. "Okay, what else?" he murmured and quickly scanned his preparations.

David wandered across the living room to lean against the door frame of the kitchen. John couldn't help but smile at the site of a still slightly damp David in his old track pants and T-shirt and seriously messy towel-dried hair.

John turned back to the stove and made a show of fiddling with the frying pan. He said in what he hoped was a convincing voice, "I was gonna make us some breakfast, but I think I might grab a quick shower first."

David grinned at John's very unsubtle comment. "I'll do it." He walked over and carefully took the pan from John's hands. John gave him a sheepish look, knowing he hadn't fooled anyone. "Everything is here…. Milk for the coffee is in the fridge…."

With a slight tilt of his head David attempted a frown. "Oh, okay. I wouldn't have thought to look there." He then gave a John a small smile that clearly read "thank you" but said, "I'll get started on breakfast."

John resisted the urge to run his fingers through the wayward hair and left the kitchen.

David stood and looked at the food for a long moment. He couldn't quite remember when he'd cooked for himself or anyone else, for that matter. *I need to do this,* he thought and was determined to prove he was still capable of such a simple task. He measured out the coffee according to the instructions on the jar, filled the jug with water, and poured it into the machine. After flicking the switch he stood with his arms folded and waited until the first dark drip hit the bottom of the jug.

He smiled to himself; it was more than he'd managed on his last attempt.

By the time John was out of the shower and toweling himself dry his stomach was churning. *Was it too much? He knew what I was doing. Did I set him up to fail?* He shaved as fast as he dared and by the time he turned off the extractor fan, he smelled the unmistakable scent of bacon frying.

The coffee jug gave its last gurgle when he walked into the kitchen. David was standing at the stove carefully turning one of the eggs. John noticed how slow and pedantic his movements were. He seemed to radiate concentration. With the egg safely flipped, David's shoulders relaxed a little and he turned to see John watching him. "I made us breakfast," he said with more than a little relief.

"So I see." John grinned and moved toward him. "Here… want me to dish?"

"No, I can manage," David replied quietly, but firmly.

"Okay." John laughed and raised his hands. "How about I set the table?"

"Yeah… please," David smiled and returned his attention to the bacon that was crisping nicely.

Within minutes both men were sitting at the table, cooked breakfast in front of them and freshly brewed coffee in their mugs. John reached for his bottle of HP sauce, poured it liberally on his food, and stuffed a forkful of egg-yolk-soaked toast into his mouth. "Mmmm…. Bloody good, Dave," he mumbled, his mouth still full of food.

"I know." David smiled around his own mouthful of bacon.

"FUCK!" The word seemed to vibrate around the bookshelves.

"Jamie," John growled and looked up to see the young man struggling in the front door carrying a large and somewhat battered cardboard box. He dumped the box noisily on the floor and gave one of the nearby pensioners from the Seniors Book Club an apologetic look. John watched as she just smiled indulgently at Jamie. *He gets away with blue bloody murder.*

Jamie strolled up to the counter after greeting the other ladies and threw John's car keys to him. "They had a lot of fiction to get rid of. There are a few more boxes in the car."

John nodded, threw the keys back at Jamie, and held back a smile as he said, "Excellent. Bring them in." Jamie groaned, but knew better than to argue. Although when David offered to help, Jamie jingled the keys at John with a playful smirk and led David out of the store.

David was a hard worker and matched Jamie's energy in short bursts, yet John noticed how quickly physical exertion tired him out. But John trusted Jamie with him and knew that despite his playful nature he always kept a careful eye on David, never letting him take on more than he thought he could handle.

There were four large boxes in total; John usually bought secondhand books in large quantities from people who were moving or deceased estates. He smiled at the sight of David sitting cross-legged on the floor, surrounded by piles of books, digging into a new box, not caring that it was dusty and covered in cobwebs.

Jamie emerged from behind John carrying two mugs; he handed one to David and was about to take a sip from the other when John took it out of his hand with a cheeky grin. "Thanks, Jamie, but you should have made one for yourself too."

"I live to serve you, boss." He smiled and gave a low bow, just managing to stay out of reach when John took a swipe at him. David sat back and watched the interaction, a happy smile on his face.

Jamie bent to pick up a pile of books deemed suitable for resale and stacked them on the book trolley. He was pleased there were some good ones; novels that would complete trilogies or series. It wasn't the resale value that pleased him; it was the understanding that some people couldn't afford the rising price of a paperback and were always overjoyed to find the conclusion to a much loved story or follow the lives of characters who had become like friends or family.

"Put the others back in the boxes and I'll drop them in the Dumpster after work," John said as he took another mouthful and raised the mug at Jamie before walking back to the counter.

David frowned at the stack of novels to be discarded. He grabbed an armful of torn and tatty books and followed John to the front of the store.

"I'll take those out later, Dave," John said as he saw David approach. But David put the books on the counter and looked from them to John before asking, "Can I have them?"

John laughed, but stopped when he saw the serious expression remain on David's face. "Of course you can. But they're old and dirty and you know you can help yourself to anything on the shelf."

David glanced back at the books a little embarrassed. "They're not for me."

John almost asked what David had in mind, but simply reiterated in a gentle voice, "Of course you can have them."

David kept his eyes on the ripped cover of an old classic without making a move. John knew there was more to be said so he waited. Eventually, when David had found the right words, he looked up and stated, "We need more than food, John. A dry place to sleep is important, but we also need to be treated as *thinking* human beings. Maggie did that for me. Letting me in the store to read kept me...." He shrugged, not sure how to end the sentence. John nodded and encouraged him to continue.

David stood a little straighter and said, "Being able to read gave me an escape, but it also kept me thinking on a level higher than survival and allowed me a little dignity. So I was hoping I could take these books down to the shelter."

"Great idea." John beamed. He couldn't stop smiling as he scooped the books from the counter and headed to the back of the store to help David fill the box.

JOHN resisted the urge to take the heavy box from David as he pushed open the shelter doors. David had been through this foyer many times under very different circumstances. Today, however, he felt mixed emotions as he followed John to the front desk, hanging back when Barbara appeared.

"John, how are you?" she welcomed as she walked around the counter to give him a hug and then, without waiting for his reply, looked past him to David. Her voice changed to a calmer, gentler tone. "Hello, David." She made no attempt to touch him, but held steady eye contact until he gave her a little smile and a hesitant "Hi."

Better, much better, she thought and turned back to John. "So what brings you here today?"

"Well, David actually," John grinned. "I was going to throw out this box of old paperbacks and Dave suggested we bring them here."

"Maybe some of the others would appreciate a book to read," David said softly, keeping his eyes on the box in his arms.

John nodded and raised his eyebrows at Barbara.

"That's a wonderful thought, David," she acknowledged. "I'm sure you're right." She called to one of the volunteers to show David where to set up a space for the books and suggested that John join her in the kitchen to make them all coffee.

John checked over his shoulder, reassuring himself that David was okay before following her through the door. Barbara signaled for John to sit while she lifted three mismatched mugs off the draining rack and flicked the switch on the well-used electric kettle. "It's only instant, I'm afraid," she apologized as she spooned the granules into the mugs.

"That's fine," John replied, waiting for the real conversation to begin. He didn't have long to wait.

After putting the little sugar bowl in the middle of the table Barbara sat and looked at him. "I'm impressed with the change in him, John. I actually suspected that he was gone for good when you were here last."

John leaned forward on the table. *Where to start?* "I know I nearly lost him then, Barbara. He was so ashamed, so...." John raised his hands in a helpless shrug and shook his head.

"But he's here, John," she reassured. "And suggesting coming to the shelter today is a huge step for him. I'm really quite amazed."John hadn't actually considered that and slowly nodded while she continued. "You know, he's been coming here on and off for quite a while, but today is the first time I've heard him speak. I was beginning to think he couldn't."

"Yeah, he doesn't say much," John agreed.

Barbara laughed and got up to pour the boiling water. "He's looking good too, John. But I have to ask: has he seen a doctor yet?"

Fuck! John felt his stomach plummet and he glanced over to the doorway.

"I can talk to him about it if you want, John," she said quietly, recognizing the look that had settled on John's features. "I do this as part of my job and he might find it easier to hear it come from me."

It felt wrong to John. He should be the one talking to David, but he also knew Barbara was right. She had all the contacts and knew the procedures. With teeth clenched, John nodded.

"Go and ask him to come in please, John." Barbara smiled gently. "Stay out for a little bit, okay?"

John stirred an extra sugar into his coffee and left to get David.

Barbara was right when she said this was part of her job, but it didn't make it any easier. She pried open the lid of the cookie tin and chewed nervously on the edge of an oatmeal cookie while she waited. The opening of the conversation had run through her head at least three times by the time David stepped through the door.

"Come in, David. Grab a seat," Barbara smiled and tilted the tin toward him. David took a cookie and put it next to his mug. He waited quietly.

"You're looking a lot better these days," she said, trying unsuccessfully to settle him with small talk. "I hardly recognized you without your sketchbook." David merely sat and looked at a point somewhere near the sugar bowl, making it clear that no amount of idle chit-chat would make him feel comfortable.

"Okay, I'll get straight to the point, David." She took a breath and sighed. "Part of what I do here is counsel people on health issues, and a big part of that is sexual health." Barbara watched him closely before continuing. "Have you been tested for HIV and other sexually transmitted diseases?"

David picked at the edge of the cookie for a moment before he looked away and shook his head. It was very obvious to Barbara that there could be a problem here so she took a risk she normally wouldn't and carefully put her hand on David's arm. She felt him tense, but didn't remove it. "What is it, David? Can you tell me what's wrong?"

He glanced at her briefly, but didn't say anything.

"Do you need to be tested, hon, or do you already know?" Barbara asked, her apprehension starting to build.

David nodded, then frowned and gave an agitated shrug.

"I don't understand, David. What do you mean?"

He concentrated on the rough texture of the cookie while he tried to formulate a reasonable answer. "I don't know how I *can't* be positive."

Barbara sighed; she hated this part of the job. "But you don't know for sure?"

He shook his head and finally looked up at her. "I tried to be safe, but sometimes I just…."

"It's okay, hon. I understand that sometimes you had no choice," she said calmly. "I also understand how scary it is, but you need to know for sure. For your sake *and* for John's."

David sat still and thought that through for what seemed like several minutes before he nodded and asked, "Can you organize it for me?"

"Of course I can." She smiled at him. "Now stop dissecting that cookie and eat it. And one more thing." Barbara's smile became a little sad. "One day can I see what you draw?"

"Yeah," David replied in a low emotionless voice.

She got up and walked over to the door to give David some breathing space. He sat at the table and quietly took in the reality that the tests would be set up and within the next few days he would know for sure. Up until then the only thing that mattered was staying alive to watch Adam grow for a few more years to be independent, but now... *now* there was John.

Soft footsteps behind him alerted David to John's presence so he wasn't surprised when a hand gently squeezed his shoulder. He put his own hand over John's and said, "It's okay, John. Barbara's gonna book me in."

John's grip tightened when his voice eluded him.

Other than the bustle of the reception area next door the kitchen was silent until David stood up. Still holding John's hand, he turned to face him and said, "It's okay, John. No matter what the results are, it's okay."

He put his arms around John and pulled him close. David's embrace felt solid and John leaned into it, accepting the comfort offered, well aware that *he* should be the one offering.

"I can go with you," John whispered, but David shook his head.

"No; I need to do this on my own, John." With that he pulled back and gave John a reassuring smile that didn't match the cold fear that had settled in his gut.

BUSINESS is always too good here. Barbara sighed as she looked over the men who were already gathering for the evening meal. An old man with a walking cane and threadbare hand-knitted cardigan stopped at the pile of books and started to browse through the titles. He glanced up at Barbara, who smiled and told him to take whatever he wanted and just return them when he was finished. A surprised and delighted smile lit his face for a moment and he quickly put two of the tattered paperbacks into his plastic bag.

CHAPTER 17

DAVID'S heels pushed deep into the mattress, pulling the ripples they'd created in the white base sheet into sharp creases. His thigh muscles strained and trembled as he struggled to keep some semblance of control. John had braced himself at arm's length; his palms flat on the pillow on either side of his lover so he could look down on David's face as he approached his orgasm. He wanted to speak, to tell David how beautiful he looked flushed and sweating in the shadow of his raised body, but John was too close.

David pushed his head back into the pillow; his eyes squeezed shut as a strangled gasp escaped his open mouth. It may have contained John's name, but the sound was too raw for him to be sure. John's head dropped between his already aching shoulders when he both saw and felt the stripes of David's come hit his belly.

"Oh God, Dave," was all he was able to groan before he thrust hard into his own release. Finally his elbows gave way and he inelegantly slumped heavily onto David's breathless body.

John managed to get his arms back under him and eased himself back a little with an apology. "Sorry, Dave. I kind of lost it there."

"Yeah," David answered with sex-roughened hoarseness. "I noticed."

John chuckled and started to pull out.

"Careful!" David exclaimed sharply, obviously distressed, and quickly reached down to make sure John had a firm hold on the rim of the condom.

"It's all right, Dave. I've got it," he said quietly, trying to reassure David the condom was still on and intact. He carefully pulled it off and tied the end before getting out of the bed to throw it in the waste bin. He grabbed a facecloth and hand towel from the bathroom and lay back on the bed.

David was still on his back, but his hand covered his face. When John gently rubbed the damp cloth over David's flushed skin, a quiet voice came from behind the hand. "I'm sorry, John."

The cloth barely hesitated in its task as John winced but quickly banished the building fear. He swiped the cloth over himself, dried them both with the towel, and then tossed it on the floor so he could take his place on the bed beside David. John lifted the hand and gently kissed the lips below. "You have nothing to be sorry for, David. Do you hear me? *Nothing.*"

"HE'S quiet this morning," Jamie said while he watched David sort the children's books.

"He's always quiet, Jamie," John replied wearily, without looking up from the invoices.

Jamie frowned. "You know what I mean…. Quieter than usual."

John almost pointed out that David rarely spoke at the best of times, but wasn't really in the mood to discuss it. Unfortunately for John it wasn't in Jamie's nature to let things go that easily. He leaned closer and said, "Maybe I should go and talk to him and…."

By this stage John had had enough and snapped irritably, "Let it go, Jamie… please."

Jamie was a little taken aback by John's angry response. He stepped away and said quietly, "I'm sorry, John; I can't help worrying about him."

John instantly felt guilty at his lack of patience and said, "No, *I'm* sorry. He'll be okay. We just need to give him a little space this morning."

With a reluctant nod, Jamie wandered through to the stock table to start pricing the new arrivals. He'd barely started when the phone rang.

David knew his response earlier that morning had been irrational. It certainly wasn't the first time they'd made love, but now the risk to John seemed more real and he'd panicked. He knew Barbara was right. He had to be tested, but suddenly it was a possibility he had to face up to.

The book between his fingers slipped and almost fell to the ground. His hands had begun to tremble again and his limbs were numb. David closed his eyes and tried to breathe through it. He felt like he needed to move, to do something, anything to stop thinking… but if he moved he was sure he would shatter into a thousand pieces….

David focused all his energy on the feel of the thin hardback book and concentrated on its texture. It was cool and smooth under his touch; there was a slight wrinkle in the glossy cardboard near the top of the spine. *Better. What else?* He opened his eyes and looked at the cover of the illustrated book. A wolf looked back. He ran his fingertips over the yellow eyes of the watercolor animal, turned the cover, and began to read. "The wolves looked out with hungry eyes but no one else could see them…."

He had almost finished the children's book when he looked up to see Jamie in front of him. "Phone call for you, Dave."

It took David a moment to realize what it was Jamie had said. It must have shown on his face because Jamie put his hand over David's and gently closed the book. "Come on, Dave. Come and take the call."

He put the book back on the display shelf and led David to the front of the store where he picked up the receiver and handed it to him. Jamie gave David a reassuring smile before giving him some privacy.

"Hello, David. It's Barbara," the voice on the other end of the line said. "I've managed to get you booked in today if that's okay."

David glanced across to the door to see John hovering, desperately trying to look like he was busy sorting through the same invoices he'd completed half an hour earlier.

"David?" Barbara queried softly when he didn't reply.

David rubbed his hand over the back of his neck and sighed. "Yeah, it's okay. What time?"

"I'll pick you up in about twenty minutes. There's no charge. The clinic bulk bills and the shelter signs for you so you don't have to worry about that, but the doctor will probably want to do a full check-up, so let John know we might be a while."

David nodded and then remembered Barbara couldn't actually see him. He said in a resigned voice, "I'll be ready." David held onto the phone for several moments after she'd hung up, trying to calm his nerves before he faced John.

By the time he replaced the receiver, Jamie had joined John at the counter and they were making a poor attempt at a conversation. When David walked through and stood beside them, Jamie stopped midsentence and said, "That was the lady from the shelter, yeah? What did she say?"

"Jamie!" John warned and glared at the young man.

"It's all right," David said with a smile for Jamie. "It *was* Barbara; she's picking me up soon." He tried very hard to make his voice sound calm, but when he felt John's hand on his back rubbing gently in silent support he knew he hadn't succeeded.

"Want me to make you a cuppa before she gets here?" Jamie offered, not sure what else to suggest.

David shook his head. "No thanks. I think I might go upstairs and clean myself up a bit if that's okay?"

"Of course it is," John answered, well aware that David had already showered that morning. "I'll give you a call when she gets here."

Upstairs, David sat on the edge of the couch with eyes closed and willed himself to stay still and wait.

When Barbara walked into the store she smiled at the two men, who both gave her an anxious look. "You have a beautiful store here; very welcoming," she said as she reached the counter.

"Thank you," John said and turned to Jamie. "Can you go and let David know Barbara's here?"

"Sure," Jamie replied and, with a quick smile at Barbara, he headed out of the store. Barbara waited until Jamie was through the door before she asked, "How're you holding up, John?"

John rolled his eyes and shook his head. "Scared shitless, if you want the honest truth."

"That's understandable." She smiled and patted his arm. "But it needs to be done for both your sakes."

"Yeah, I know," John said. "Although sometimes I have to wonder if denial isn't a hell of a lot easier."

"Has he spoken to you about it?" she asked, indicating the flat above the store with a tilt of her head.

"No, not really," John said. "He's bloody terrified, but trying really hard not to let me see it."

"Try to get him to talk if you can, John. His kind struggle if the results aren't good."

"His kind?" John repeated and looked at her through narrowed eyes.

"It's okay, John." She smiled gently, realizing her mistake. "I just meant the quiet ones. David seems a very insular person and will try to deal with it all himself. Believe me, that's *not* a good thing."

John nodded, knowing she was right while doubting his ability to get David to talk. But he would try. He looked up at the sound of the store bell and smiled at David. "Are you sure you don't want me to come with you? We both know Jamie would love the chance to run this place."

David stood with his hands shoved deep in the pockets of his old jacket and shook his head. John was about to push it, but Barbara held her hand up behind David, signaling for John to back off a bit. He understood David needed to do this without him, but it was still hard to see him leave the store and stay behind. John stood quietly until the door closed then turned to Jamie and clapped him on the shoulder. "Come on. I think we deserve a tea break."

BARBARA indicated for David to grab a seat while she went to register him with the receptionist. He sat on the white plastic seat and watched as she talked and laughed with the young woman behind the counter. David tentatively glanced around the waiting room; it was too easy to recognize the despair and resignation of the others isolating themselves on their own chairs. It was full of people just like him. *No, not like me,* he thought desperately. *I don't want to be that anymore.* The thought made him feel guilty because despite everything he was one of the lucky ones.

"Robinson."

David flinched at his surname and looked up. The receptionist repeated his name and added, "Room two and take this with you." He took a breath and stood up ignoring the urge to walk out the front door. Barbara gave him an encouraging smile as he took the thin manila folder and made his way into the second room down the corridor.

He hesitated just inside the doorway, unsure whether to walk in or wait until the doctor acknowledged him. Eventually the doctor said, "Take a seat," and took the folder from him. He didn't really look up from the checklist while he reeled off a series of questions about David's *lifestyle,* as he put it. David answered each devoid of emotion, somehow feeling disconnected from the words that described his life. The doctor finished by listing the next few procedures and said, "Do you have somewhere you can be contacted? Or will I just list the shelter?"

David frowned and quietly said that his address was already on the paperwork. The doctor read the form silently for a minute and then looked at David for the first time. "Good. Let's get started then."

IT'S done, David thought as he sat in the car and stared out the window, avoiding the sight of the little swatch of cotton and tape on his arm. It had started to rain while he was in the clinic; not the bone-chilling rain of winter he used to dread, but spring rain. He'd noticed the trees in the planters outside the storefronts already had buds waiting to bloom. But today his vision of the world outside the car blurred as he focused on the raindrops skidding across the side window. It was always easier to dwell on smaller things than acknowledge a "big picture" that threatened to overwhelm him. Sometimes it worked; others it didn't.

"You okay?" Barbara asked gently.

"I don't know," he answered truthfully.

Barbara accepted the answer as an honest one and said with similar candor, "You usually get the results in a couple of days. Have you got the number for the results line?"

David gave a single nod.

"You know that even if you *are* positive it doesn't mean you have AIDS, hon. With the medications around now, having HIV is not necessarily the death sentence it used to be."

"Will John be all right?" David asked softly.

"So long as you're careful and always use condoms."

He nodded again but David had already decided to slip away quietly if there was any chance that he was a risk to John.

"Hey, I meant to say earlier; those books you dropped in yesterday were a big hit." Barbara smiled, hoping to give David something else to think about. "Any chance you could do that on a regular basis?"

"I don't know," he said with a slight frown, but the idea was implanted and Barbara had managed to divert some of his thoughts.

CHAPTER 18

JOHN frowned and tried to force his clothes to fit the drawer, but still they bulged out and stopped it from closing. He pulled at the handle in frustration and hauled out a fawn cable knit sweater. *Shit, I don't even remember buying this.* He threw it on the bed and sifted through the drawer until he found another couple of items to remove. With a small pile of clothes on the bed he was finally able to close three of the four drawers.

He looked at the empty bottom drawer and smiled. *Perfect.*

John lifted the white paper shopping bag that held David's few belongings. Not meant for such long-term use, it was torn at one of the corners and the glue on the seam was starting to give way. John carefully placed it next to the dresser beside the empty drawer.

DAVID had retreated to his chair fairly early. He'd already rearranged the entire science fiction section, washing down the shelves as he went, but had hit a point where he simply "lost" what he was doing. David stood and looked at the tidy shelves, feeling agitated and not sure what to do next. When a customer reached past him, David shrank back and headed for the safety of the battered leather chair.

It didn't surprise Jamie to see David curled into his chair, face all but buried in a novel. He picked up the cookie tin and wandered into the secondhand book section.

"You got sci-fi done fast," Jamie said as he flopped down in the chair next to him and pried off the lid of the tin. David simply nodded without looking up from the book.

"Cookie?" Jamie asked. He grabbed one out for himself and waited. When David didn't acknowledge the offer Jamie sighed and asked, "So when do you get the results?"

"Tomorrow," David answered a little too quickly. He closed the book and put it on the floor slightly under his chair. "I have to call after eleven."

Jamie put his hand gently on David's arm and lied, "I'm sure it'll be okay, Dave."

David's breathing faltered slightly and he looked away, holding on tightly to the denial he couldn't speak. It was hard for Jamie to watch. He knew David was worried, but for the first time he understood just how genuinely frightened David was. His hand slipped down David's arm and threaded through fingers drawn into a loose fist. The squeeze of his fingers was returned and David gave him a little smile. Jamie smiled back but had to ask, "Have you talked to John about it?"

David looked down at their clasped hands and shook his head.

"You can't go through this on your own, Dave, you know... if things aren't okay. Even though I think they will be."

"I'll know soon and John's worried enough," David said in a firm monotone. He hesitated, then added as he looked down the store to the front counter, "You'll help John, won't you, Jamie?"

You'll help John, won't you? Jamie was about to answer that of course he would, until it hit him what David was actually asking. "Don't you even think about it, David. Don't you fucking dare!" Jamie growled in an angry but hushed voice.

When David didn't answer Jamie pushed the point. "He loves you, David, and don't think you'll be doing him any favors by not including him. John needs to go through this with you. Don't shut him out." Jamie stood up and kissed David lightly on the temple before saying, "Don't shut either of us out, okay?"

As Jamie walked to the front counter his hand swiped across his eyes to rub away an imaginary irritation. John looked up at him and frowned, unsure if he should ask what was wrong, but Jamie shook his head and said quietly, "Leave him for a while, John."

THE brown paper bag tossed on the counter in front of him startled John until he realized it was just Jamie back with the lunches. He pulled out his sandwich and watched Jamie's daily ritual of heading to the back of the store to split his lunch with David. John had suggested that they buy David his own sandwich, but both men had looked at him as if he'd said something particularly daft.

"Lunch, Davey." Jamie grinned and sat beside him. David had his sketchbook out but was writing rather than drawing. He looked up at Jamie and said, "I might skip it today. I was thinking I could take a walk to the library instead."

"What've you been planning?" Jamie asked, trying to read the scrawled list written on the corner of a page full of words.

"I'm not sure." David shrugged and made a point of closing the book. "But I've been doing some thinking since yesterday and Barbara said something I want to check out."

Jamie's curiosity was definitely piqued, but experience told him that he'd have to wait until David was ready to volunteer his plans. He shot David a cheeky look and said, "Okay, keep your secret... but take some lunch with you, yeah?" Before David had a chance to answer, Jamie put both sandwiches back in the bag and securely twisted the corners. David took the bag and smiled his thanks.

WITH his sandwich safely in his jacket pocket, David walked the streets he had walked so many times before. But it was different this time; he had food, money, a place to live, and most important of all, the suggestion of a purpose. He hadn't thought it all through. This was just a beginning, and that in itself was a big enough step.

Although it was still cold, the sun shone and warmed David's back as he approached the somewhat imposing façade of the City Library. He was glad they'd resisted changing its name to Community Resource Center like so many others; there was something solid and permanent about the word *library*. He smiled at the solid columns and decided not to go in quite yet.

Pulling the brown paper bag out of his pocket, David sat on the concrete base of one of the statues at the bottom of the stairs. He looked up at the discolored bronze military man on his horse. The front hoof was raised in a noble and defiant gesture. David chewed thoughtfully on one of the triangles and splayed his fingers under the hoof, feeling the realistic indentations in the sole. His fingertips barely reached the edges of the hoof. *Larger than life,* he mused, and again glanced up at the hero on horseback. He pulled the other half of the sandwich out and smiled. *Jamie's half.*

With the last of the sandwich finished, David carefully folded the paper bag and put it back in his pocket. He absently patted the horse's fetlock and walked up the steps into the library entrance.

Like all large libraries, it provided plenty of reading space ranging from lounge chairs to student carrels. It brought back memories. At the start David had tried to find refuge here. It was quiet and he'd needed the "stillness". He'd managed for a while, hiding away in the tall shelves or among the elderly who frequented the library to escape the loneliness of their own four walls. But as David got dirtier and more desperate it was made clear that he wasn't welcome anymore. It seemed that even a daytime haven for scholars and the lonely had limits.

The reference librarian smiled at him as he approached and waited patiently while he collected his thoughts. "I'm not sure if you can help me," he said quietly and looked at the neatly cut squares of paper piled on the desk ready for hurriedly written Dewey numbers.

The librarian smiled and raised an eyebrow.

David could feel the thump of his heart as he pushed himself to speak. "The homeless shelter… um, I'm trying to find some old books to give to the shelter." The woman looked at him for a moment while she considered his request.

"Okay." David glanced up briefly when she answered. "Just give me a minute and I'll ring through to the office. They might be able to help you." He took a breath, gave a barely visible nod, and waited.

After several minutes standing at the front desk, David hugged his jacket a little tighter around himself and decided to give up. He was only a couple of steps away when a different woman's voice called him back. "I'm sorry to keep you waiting, sir. How can I help you?"

David acknowledged her with a nervous smile and quietly told her his idea. She listened carefully to his request and nodded thoughtfully when he'd finished. "You know, this might be a solution to a problem

I've had for a while. Come with me." Without waiting for an answer, she turned and started a brisk walk through to the workroom. A little taken aback by her sudden departure, David needed to jog a couple of steps to catch up with her. The workroom was filled with the typical clutter of the overworked and understaffed; books sat in piles and on shelves in various stages of processing while the library staff ploughed on with only a curious look as he passed. He was taken to a tiny adjoining room with a very unofficial printout taped to the door stating *Purgatory.*

"Shelf weeding is a constant process and these books are to be pulped," she announced as she waved her hand in the direction of the shelves partially obscured by large boxes sealed with masking tape. "But I hate the thought of books being destroyed no matter how old they might be, so if you can put them to some use you are more than welcome to them."

He moved slowly into the little room and the smell of new print similar to the store gave way to one he was more familiar with; the once carefully chosen and read, now discarded to the secondhand bookshelf. It was a combination of dust, old binding glue and well-thumbed paper. He looked around at box stacked on box and knew this was bigger than his own little problems. He could do something with this.

When David finally emerged he had two big bags of books and, more importantly, an idea.

"YOU want the light off?" John asked gently as he climbed into his side of the bed. David had gone to bed an hour earlier, but was still awake, facing the far wall. He rolled onto his back, smiled at John, and nodded. John flicked off the lamp and settled beside him. Both men were silent while John struggled with how to ask what he needed to. Eventually he propped himself up on one elbow and lay his hand on David's chest. "We haven't talked much, Dave... about tomorrow, I mean."

David peered at him through the dim light of the room and said honestly, "Never been much good at that."

John laughed a little sadly at the irony of the comment. "We're a right pair, aren't we? I'm bloody useless at saying what I feel... always have been."

"You said a lot the other day," David whispered.

John's fingertip traced David's jawline and he grinned. "I did, didn't I?" He bent down, kissed the path of his fingers, and murmured, "I meant it." John settled back and whispered, "Sometimes I can't believe how lucky I am that I found you, that you let me be part of your life."

The words had barely left his lips when John felt David tense. A shadow seemed to pass between them and John knew it was time and asked the question. "You think you're positive, don't you?"

Icy fear gripped him when he heard the quiet "Yes."

Unsure if he wanted to know the answer to his next question, John watched his thumb slowly smooth over David's chest hair. "Can you tell me why?"

David fought to control the building anxiety and suddenly needed to stop John touching him. He slid out of John's reach and sat on the edge of the bed. His jaw clenched and unclenched, not wanting to speak the truth as he saw it. *I have to let him be part of this. John needs to know.* His voice was surprisingly devoid of emotion when he stated what he saw as a simple fact. "You were right the other day, John.... I *am* a whore."

The words impacted John with the force of a fist. He stayed on his side of the bed and stared at the back of the man he loved, devastated at hearing his own words and worse, that David *believed* them to be true. After one false start at speaking, John got up and crawled across the bed to kneel behind him. He tentatively placed his hand on David's back and murmured, "You did that to survive and see your son. That's not you. It *doesn't* define you as a person, David."

"I might have put you in danger, John," David said, his misery now obvious.

John's lips brushed the back of his neck and he moved his hands around to slowly stroke over David's chest. Settling behind David, John said, "I'm okay.... We're always careful, always safe."

David nodded and leaned back a little. He knew Jamie had been right; they needed to talk. His first words were hesitant. "A man... a *client*... refused to use a condom. I told him no, but he said he'd already paid and said it wasn't my choice anymore." David stopped. John thought he was finished and was surprised when David cleared his throat and continued. "While he fucked me, he laughed that he never used rubbers and was probably leaving me with a little something. Said he wanted to *spread the love*. His idea of a joke, I guess."

John lowered his head until his forehead rested lightly on David's shoulder. His voice was slightly muffled when he asked, "Is that what you dream about?"

David was determined to talk now that he'd started, but the words for this wouldn't come. He shook his head and remained silent. John felt the change and needed to be closer. He moved away just enough to sit on the bed behind David, then shuffled forward and pressed himself solidly against David's back with legs on either side of his hips. John held David against him, enveloped him, and asked, "Can you tell me?"

John's skin touched him everywhere; his breath warm on David's neck. He let himself drift in John's embrace.

I can say it. It can't hurt me here.

"The first time someone hurt me," David said softly, then corrected himself, "... *physically* hurt me."

John pushed his fingers through David's hair, kissed his neck lightly and whispered, "Tell me, Dave."

His voice sounded vaguely dislocated when David sank back against John and started to speak. "I don't really remember much about the first few weeks. I remember being confused. I didn't know where to go. I walked a lot. Was too afraid to sleep until I was so exhausted I had to...." David paused, eyes closed, and let John's breath warm him enough to go on. "They woke me up with a kick... punched and kicked me over and over. Then I was against a wall. It scraped my face." David frowned. The hands on him now were soft, not like then. John let out a shaky breath and brushed the back of his fingers over David's cheek while he listened. "I didn't understand, John.... I didn't understand why they did that to me."

John could do little more than nod and give him a gentle kiss because he didn't understand either.

"Someone helped me after. I was trying to pull my trousers on but the button was ripped off and they were bloody. No matter how hard I tried I couldn't seem to get them on and I was so ashamed." He stopped speaking and sat still in John's arms, only vaguely aware of the other man's tears. Then he whispered, "Still so ashamed."

Those quiet words shook John into action and he roughly wiped his hand over his face. His voice was low and a little rough when he spat out, "No, David. Fucking hell, no. Those bastards did that to you. You did nothing wrong... not a damn thing." He shuffled back a little awkwardly on the bed until he could swing his leg around and then crawled to the edge to sit next to David. He took David's hand, held it between his, and said, "They had no right to do that to you, none of them."

They sat like that for what seemed like a long time. John knew it had been a huge step for David to talk to him about the attack, about the rape, and he needed to respond with a clear head. Even in the darkened room John could see the strained twitch of David's leg muscles slowly subside and his shoulders slump forward. John leaned over and kissed David lightly on the back of his shoulder and said, "I can't fix any of that for you, but I need you to understand that no matter what happens tomorrow, please let me be with you."

David watched John's thumb gently caress the back of his hand and nodded slowly.

John's eyes held a weary determination when David met them; he nodded again and gave a shaky smile followed by a shrug. "Wanna hear what I've got planned for those books?"

John laughed and wiped his eyes again. "Yeah... I wanna hear."

CHAPTER 19

IT'S time. A shared thought as all three men checked clocks and watches from various parts of the store. Without saying anything, David pulled the card with the phone number out of his pocket and walked through to the kitchen. The others didn't follow. Instead they pretended to go about their daily duties, ignoring the fact that the numbers in the ledger didn't make sense or that the authors' names seemed to have disappeared from conscious memory.

"I'm sorry, Mr. Robinson; I don't have your results here. The doctor has put a note on your file asking you to come in to the clinic," the voice on the other end of the line explained with quiet efficiency.

David said thank you and hung up. He stood very still, his hand resting on the receiver in its cradle. When John appeared in the doorway David said in an expressionless voice, "I have to go to the clinic, John."

Without any hesitation, John grabbed his jacket off the back of the chair and stated, "Come on. I'll take you." David didn't argue and let John lead him through the store to the car.

"Is your friend okay? It looks like he had some bad news," an elderly customer asked. Jamie's stomach lurched as he watched them go.

THE drive to the clinic was done in silence.

When John finally switched off the ignition in the car park, he just sat and stared at the dense graffiti on the opposite wall. The jarring colors seemed to make more sense than the blur of scenarios and emotions vying for attention in his mind.

He couldn't move. The terror that enveloped him was broken only when a gentle hand covered his own, still gripping the steering wheel. "It's okay, John," David said softly. "I can go in."

Not sure if it was the touch or calm voice, maybe a combination of both, John was able to drop his eyes and take a deep breath. He smiled, shook his head, and reaffirmed his stance of the night before. "Together, Dave. We'll be all right together." He pulled out the keys, unclipped his seat belt with more bravado than he actually felt, and said, "Let's get this done."

The waiting room was as busy as it had been several days earlier, but instead of having Barbara there to organize his appointment David walked up to the receptionist, and gave his name and that of the doctor. He explained quietly why he was there and then sat in the same plastic chair as his last visit... only this time John was beside him.

Dr. Coulson eyed the two men with vague curiosity when they entered his room. He pulled out the required file and keyed the code into the computer. No one spoke while he scrolled through a few screens to remind himself why they were there. Eventually he stood up, opened a filing cabinet drawer, pulled out a few pamphlets and said to both of them—still unsure exactly who the patient was but guessing it was David—"It's good you came down today. That way we can get treatment underway immediately."

David nodded and resisted the urge to look at John, whose chair was placed beside but slightly behind his.

"Now first of all, here is some information on your condition and how we can treat it." He handed David a glossy piece of paper with the deep red heading "What Is Anemia?" The doctor continued speaking about the causes of anemia while he pulled a few more sheets out of the drawer, not noticing the look of utter confusion on David's face, who was trying to take in what was written on the sheet without actually understanding what was going on. John put his hand on David's shoulder and said with barely concealed anger. "Stop. What are you saying? What exactly are you telling us?"

The hand in the filing cabinet paused and Dr. Coulson turned and gave John an irritated glare. "I am trying to discuss your *friend's* treatment."

David could feel John start to rise from his seat; he held his hand out, but spoke directly to the doctor. "My blood test results. They wouldn't give them to me on the phone."

Coulson frowned at the question and returned to the computer screen. "According to your file you are anemic and have a mild parasitic infestation; both of which we'll treat. HIV negative, Hepatitis B and C both negative."

Negative. John's eyes drifted from the doctor to David, who was sitting staring as if he couldn't quite comprehend what he'd just been told. He gently rubbed David's back and tried to listen to what the doctor was saying, but all he could do was grin and keep his hand moving.

LUNCHTIME had come and gone and Jamie hadn't closed the store to go and buy the usual sandwiches. It felt wrong without David there to share. Instead he hovered over the kettle waiting for it to boil, more for something to do rather than actually needing a cup of tea. It had been a couple of hours since the others left for the clinic and thankfully Jamie had been kept busy, but the lull of early afternoon left him to think and worry.

When the doorbell finally tinkled his head shot up and he quickly stepped into the store to see John and David walking toward him. Both were smiling. He knew straight away that David was okay, but rather than returning the smiles Jamie stood with his arms wrapped around himself. His voice was very small as he said, "I was so scared, Dave."

Without any hesitation David left John's side and enveloped Jamie in a tight embrace. He whispered softly, "I'm know... but it's all gonna be all right." He gently stroked his hand over Jamie's hair and added with a little smile, "I've been wormed and given my shots."

Jamie slipped his arms around David's waist and let out a shaky laugh. "So I guess that means we can keep you."

John stood and watched David comfort his young friend and understood for the first time the effect all of this had had on Jamie. He'd known David for longer than John, helped Maggie bring him into the store and slowly won his trust. Become his friend. *Hell, if Jamie hadn't persisted I would have thrown David out that first morning,* John realized and felt more than a little ashamed that he'd not once considered Jamie as part of this. John quietly left David and Jamie and went into the kitchen. The past few days hit him. He slumped against the wall, pinched the bridge of his nose, and let the tears fall silently.

"LEAVE them 'til morning, Dave." John smiled as he looked at the greasy cardboard containers, bowls, and chopsticks strewn about the coffee table. The debris of a celebration of sorts could be left for another day. He shook his head, amazed that he could even contemplate such a thing. *Everything has a correct place and life must be routine and neatly labeled. Where did that John go, because he certainly doesn't live here anymore?* He looked up at David, who'd been standing near the armchair watching him, a slightly bemused look on his face. John chuckled. "Just lost in thought for a moment... thinking about the man I used to be and how he would have gotten up in the middle of the night to clean this away rather than let it sit." He shrugged, embarrassed at the admission. David simply nodded, but his smile was warm and open.

"Come on; it's been a tough day." John laughed, turned his back on the mess, and walked through to the bedroom.

The entire time they were undressing John chatted about anything and everything; even when his head touched the pillow he was laughing about his burgeoning relationship with the woman at the local Chinese restaurant. He felt high as a kite and couldn't seem to contain suddenly boundless energy.

David lay beside him, smiling at his obvious joy, but when it looked like John was about to launch into another tale, David lifted his hand and gently placed it over John's mouth. He could feel the curve of John's lips under his palm as he was silenced. David slowly removed his hand and leaned forward to kiss the still-curled lips, breaking into a broad smile himself. The attempted kiss became a giggling embrace as they held each other, neither able to fully comprehend that it was now possible for them to have a full future together..

As the laughter subsided, it was replaced by gentle touching; that same happy disbelief being expressed through fingers and lips.

John's mouth moved over David's skin, not quite kissing, more like sampling and exploring. There was nothing of his usual sense of urgency because he knew now that he had time to take it slow. When his tongue took a languid swipe at an already peaked nipple, he glanced up to see David's reaction. John paused briefly at the sight of David watching him through slitted eyes. As their gaze met, John felt David's fingers rest lightly on his head before threading through his hair. John smiled a little wickedly and let the tip of his tongue trail slowly down, stopping now and then to plant an open-mouthed kiss on random selections of skin.

David shifted his hips under John's touch, suddenly far too aware of his very obvious erection. John eased back and rested on his elbow. He gently stopped the hand that reached for the edge of the sheet with a quiet "Let me look at you, David, please?"

David hesitated, but released the material to fall back to the mattress, leaving him exposed in the warm light of the bedside lamp. At that moment, John's heart felt too big for his chest and he lifted David's hand briefly to his lips before placing it back on the sheet.

Leaning forward, John brushed his lips over a still prominent hipbone and spread his fingers through the dark hair beside it. Close but not yet ready to touch, John looked up and said with a slight flush of color, "You know, I've never actually paid any attention to another man's... um, penis, before."

David didn't answer, but raised his eyebrows and chuckled when John added, "I know my own well enough, but it never seemed important to, ah... *get to know* anyone else's."

Despite his heart hammering in his chest, David gave a little shrug and reached down to slowly edge John's hand closer.

John gently, almost tentatively, ran the flat of his fingers along the silky skin of David's shaft, paying close attention to the ripples and veins. A bead of pre-come grew and trickled down near John's fingers. He watched its path before curling the tip of his tongue to taste the fluid, *taste David*. John looked up to see David watching him intently, a slightly confused expression on his face. The act had taken on a whole different meaning for David and he found it difficult to understand the pleasure John was taking from this. John smiled, a little unsure, and asked, "You okay with this? I need you to tell me, Dave."

David gave a small nod and watched John crawl between his legs to settle in the cradle of his thighs. He wasn't ready for the sensation of John's lips closing over the head of his cock and let out an involuntary gasp. *Is this what it feels like to them, with me on my knees on the concrete?* The thought passed through his mind unbidden and he almost made John stop; it was wrong to let him do this, wrong for it to feel so good. But when he looked down at the fair head bobbing slowly, not forced or retching, he allowed himself to stop thinking.

John's mouth gradually took more of him in and began to increase the pace. He had no idea if what he was doing was right, but tried to mimic what *he* liked. It was a little more difficult than he thought it would be fighting his own gag reflex and he wished he could use his tongue more against the press of David's cock.

Stop trying so hard, he told himself and eased back to enjoy the experience.

John's fingers wrapped around the base of David's cock and began a careful squeeze and release, matching the rhythm of his mouth. He could feel David moving with him and heard his soft grunting breaths. John's own cock began pulsing at the sound and he pushed his hips hard against the bed, trying to get some friction. His legs were over the edge of the bed and the position was awkward, but he didn't care. This wasn't about him.

David's hand tensed in John's hair; his fingers tightened and pulled hard. "Close, John," he groaned and tried again to pull John off, afraid to come in his mouth. Reassuring fingers stroked along his hip and belly and when David looked down he met John's eyes. It was all he saw before the force of his orgasm closed his eyes.

John stilled both hand and lips while he concentrated on swallowing until he felt the spasms ease to a gentle shudder. With a last gentle lick, he released the softening cock and rested his face against David's thigh. Breathing in the scent of sweat and come, he reached down and gripped his own aching cock. It only took a couple of rapid twisting strokes before he came.

Gradually, John became aware of David's fingers moving through his hair in slow caresses. He looked up and, not knowing what to say, simply straightened enough to rest his cheek against David's belly. He could feel the strong beat of David's pulse through the warm skin and hear the quiet gurgles. John smiled sleepily at how *right* this all seemed and kissed him lightly before letting himself drift.

CHAPTER 20

WAKING was easier than it had been; there was no resentment of the morning at giving up the refuge of sleep. David leaned back into the steady rise and fall of John's chest against his back and the warm breath that barely ruffled his hair. The sun was already up and David realized they'd both slept in. *You fell asleep without setting the alarm.* He smiled. *What am I doing to you, John?*

David closed his eyes and his hand drifted slowly back until it rested lightly on John's hip. He smiled when John murmured a few unintelligible words in his sleep. The skin was smooth under his palm as he carefully explored the contours of John's hip bone. Delicate changes in temperature and texture all registered behind David's eyelids as his fingers continued their journey down John's thigh. He could feel the press of John against his buttocks and squeezed his eyes tighter, trying to etch every touch, smell, and sound in his memory. He needed this to last.

Soft lips brushed over the back of his neck before the low rumble of John's voice. "Morning, Dave."

"Hey," David answered quietly and withdrew his hand, embarrassed that he'd been caught touching.

"You don't have to stop." John grinned against his neck.

"Yes, I do." David sighed. "I think we've slept in."

John groaned, eased away from David, and craned his head to look back over his shoulder. "Shite. I can't remember the last time I slept through my alarm."

"I think you were too exhausted to set it," David mumbled with a small smile.

"Mmmm… oh yeah, I remember." John chuckled. "You know, maybe we should just leave the store closed today and spend the whole day right here?"

Although David smiled at John's suggestion, the intimacy of it made him hesitate. He appreciated how strange it was to feel this after all they'd been through, but a whole day with nothing to distract John from him seemed frightening, too revealing. "Maybe not, John," he said in a very small voice. "Or you'll end up out there in my home rather than me sharing yours."

The comment, or maybe the tone of voice, made John stop. He rested his forehead against the nape of David's neck, wanting to tell him this was his home too, but he knew it wasn't true. The bottom drawer remained empty despite the state of the once-white paper bag.

He sighed, gently rubbed his hand over David's shoulder, and said, "Yeah, time to get up." David felt the air cool against his back and the mattress shift as John got out of bed and headed for the bathroom.

Breakfast had already developed into a comfortable routine. David organized the coffee and set the table while John fussed around the frying pan, scrambling eggs and adding an assortment of unnecessary condiments. Full plates and steaming mugs were placed on the table and they settled to enjoy their food and quiet conversation.

John watched David get up to pour another coffee and couldn't help but wonder what his life was like before. How long had it been since he shared a simple breakfast with his son? When David handed him his mug and sat down, John asked cautiously, "Did you do this with Adam?"

David glanced briefly at John and then back to his plate. "Adam hates… hated eggs. He used to always try to convince me that he was allergic to them."

"Was he?" John said, hoping David would continue.

David huffed a small laugh and looked up. "Nah, but it was a good excuse to get me to make French toast."

"But doesn't that have eggs in it?" John frowned.

"Yes," David replied with a broad grin.

John laughed and shook his head. "You sound like a good dad."

David stopped cutting his toast and leaned back in his seat with a sigh. "I miss him."

John was at a loss what to say. He didn't know David's history, why he was no longer part of his son's life. He nodded sadly and suggested, "After yesterday I think you need to see him, Dave. You still have time to get the bus, take the whole day off if you want... even if that just means catching up on your reading."

David pushed his plate a little further onto the table and rubbed his thumb over a coffee mark on the lip of his mug. John patiently piled another mouthful of egg onto his fork while he waited. It actually took three forkfuls before David answered with a quiet, "Thanks, John. I better get going then."

DAVID stepped into the bus and pulled a couple of balled-up notes from his pocket. It took him a while to straighten and sort them, no different from every bus trip, but this time the driver gave him an irritated look and told him to hurry it up rather than looking past him until he could snatch the offered money, avoiding contact and conversation. David took his change, mumbled "thank you", and sat in a seat near the back of the bus.

He stared absently out the window and watched the world go by like he usually did, but this time it felt very different. He was clean, he'd eaten a real breakfast with someone he loved, and the money... well, he was almost proud of the work he'd done for the money.

When the bus pulled up at the stop, David stepped off. He still kept his head down and eyes on his feet while the other passengers moved away, but David took up his position in the corner of the bus shelter feeling more positive than he had in a long while. Although the morning sun warmed his legs he kept himself in the shadow where he could see out without being easily noticed.

David watched the usual parade of teenagers, some moving quickly from family wagons lest they be seen by their friends while others parked barely roadworthy but much-loved older-model cars covered in crude stickers and rust-retardant paint splotches.

A couple of kids skulked into the shelter and sat on the bench. They shot David a look, but quickly decided he was no threat to their plan to ditch school. David listened to their excited chatter and smiled at the possibilities of youth and a whole illicit day.

"Hey, Robinson, come here," the taller of the two boys called out when he noticed a blue car pull up. David's heart started to pound and it suddenly became difficult to breathe. He didn't dare look up when he heard the shouted reply of "What?" He tried to make himself as small as he could in the shadow of the corner.

"Wanna keep those 'L' plates on and drive us to the city?" the other boy yelled at the driver of the car, ignoring the man swapping seats with the teenager.

Adam looked over and shook his head. "Get the fucking bus, you losers." He laughed when they flipped him the bird and then gave the man now at the steering wheel a sheepish look as he reversed out of the parking space.

David didn't take in their derogatory remarks about his son or even their half-interest in whether he was all right or about to have a heart attack. He sat quietly with his head in his hands until the return bus pulled up.

The return ticket shook as he held it out to the driver and David quickly retreated to the backseat. He'd felt completely trapped in the little bus shelter. The thought of Adam seeing him, recognizing him, made him feel physically sick. *What could I have done if he'd come over? Could I speak to him or would he speak to me? Would he even know who I am?* Questions chased themselves around and around David's mind until he forced himself to stop. He narrowed his focus on the glass of the window, mapping each of the scratches and reading the backward lettering of the message intended for those outside the bus. His breathing gradually eased until he reached the point that he could look up and take in his wider surroundings. He was near his stop.

It was still early when David got off the bus and he debated whether or not to head straight back to the store. The two teenagers jumped down the steps and ran off along the sidewalk, laughing and arguing over what to actually do now they were there. He watched them push each other into oncoming pedestrians and then disappear into a music store. He turned in the other direction, hands shoved deep in his pockets, and started to walk toward Margins.

The midmorning sun was warm on his shoulders and helped dispel the cold sweat that had lingered since he first heard the boys call Adam's name, but the knot deep in the pit of his stomach was still there. Barely two blocks from the store, David stopped and sat on the edge of a concrete planter box. He picked up a couple of discarded cigarette butts and a chocolate wrapper and threw them in the trash can next to the planter, then looked up at the small tree. Its branches had shed the naked gray of winter and fresh tender leaves were already uncurling. David ran his fingertips over a patch of mottled bark that had obviously been picked at by another pedestrian seeking a quiet moment. But despite neglect and unintentional abuse, the tree still followed the seasons and grew. He leaned forward to rest his forearms on his knees. *It's okay. Let it go....*

After pushing his hand wearily through his hair, David stood up, took a breath, and started to walk.

His fingers fiddled idly with the money still in his jeans' pocket as he went to pass a small store with an assortment of backpacks hanging outside. David stopped and frowned at the range of colors, brands, and logos. He pulled the money out of his pocket and carefully counted out the change before lifting down a dark blue pack with several pockets, but no flashy brand name.

AS soon as David walked through the door of Margins, John knew something was wrong. David's body language always gave him away. "Did you see Adam?" he asked cautiously. David merely nodded without lifting his head and made his way through the store. John and Jamie gave each other a look.

Jamie started to move from behind the counter to follow him, but John quickly put his hand on Jamie's arm and shook his head. "I'll talk to him. How about you flip the door sign and go get us some food." Jamie sighed and watched John walk up the store before putting the kettle on a low heat, grabbing some money out of the cash register, and heading out to do his sandwich run.

David was sitting quietly, his boots already side by side on the floor. He knew one of them would soon arrive to check on him and steeled himself for the questions.

John sat quietly in the spare chair and picked up the bag. He turned it over in his hands and attempted unsuccessfully to suppress a sharp bout of queasiness. He tried very hard to keep the fear out of his voice when he asked, "You going somewhere, Dave?"

David looked at the bag and then John. With a slight frown, he shook his head and took the pack back. "It's just to put my things in, that's all."

It was on the tip of John's tongue to tell him he didn't need a cheap pack for that, but he left it. Instead he smiled, closed his hand over David's, and said with a humorless chuckle, "You had me worried there for a minute."

David gently pulled away so he could put the pack down beside his chair and then slowly twined his fingers in John's. "I'm sorry, John. I didn't mean to." He paused for a moment before adding quietly, "I saw Adam this morning."

John cocked his head and watched David's expression carefully as he asked, "I know, Dave. What's wrong?"

"He nearly saw me," was the near whispered answer.

"Would that have been so bad?"

David nodded and grimaced. "He can't see me like this."

"Like what, David? Have you looked at yourself lately?" John asked, a little surprised.

David ignored the reference to his appearance and muttered, "He's better off without me."

John remembered being told the same thing when *his* father left and felt his frustration rise. "Can't he be the one to decide that?"

Although he didn't answer, John could see the tension in David's expression and felt how unresponsive his hand had become. Pushing back his own issues, John squeezed David's fingers. "It's up to you, David. I know it's none of my business."

"I love him so much, John, that it hurts like hell to stay out of his life, but that's how it has to be. I know how it was today and I know I couldn't speak to him and explain where I've been... what I've done."

He frowned briefly and added, "I started writing him letters a while back."

John looked at him with genuine curiosity, but before he could ask, David shook his head and said, "No, I didn't send them."

"So you still have them?" John queried softly.

David looked down the aisle of books and gave a defeated shrug. "They were written in the blank bits of my sketchbooks... sometimes as part of the picture. I lost most of them when my stuff got taken."

John remembered how fiercely David had protected his sketchbooks when he was beaten. Even the one he saved had the spiral spine partly torn out and many of the pages were ripped. With a small sigh, John rested a comforting hand on the back of David's neck and said, "Keep writing them. Maybe one day he can see your pictures and read your words." David went to answer, but the thought of Adam seeing his book, his thoughts, was too much, and he was forced to gulp a breath. John pulled him closer with a light kiss to his hair and a whispered, "He'll get to read them.... It'll happen one day."

John glanced up to see Jamie standing hesitantly with their lunch tray, not wanting to interfere. Seeing John's small nod and smile, Jamie put on a grin and said, "Man, you two never miss an opportunity for a sneaky snog. Come on; take a lunch break."

David gave Jamie a slightly embarrassed look and straightened up with a shaky breath. Jamie simply put the tray on the floor and sat cross-legged at David's feet, stretching an arm over one of his knees.

The three men shared sandwiches, tea, and comfortable conversation until John checked his watch and said, "Better flip the sign again before we have the afternoon seniors knocking at the door." He looked briefly at the backpack and added, "Put your shopping upstairs, Dave, while I show Jamie what real work looks like."

David gave a little laugh and ran his hand over Jamie's hair before picking up the pack and wandering down the store. Both men watched David leave.

When he heard the store door close, Jamie turned to John and asked, "What happened?"

John rubbed his hand over the back of his neck in an attempt to ease the tension headache steadily building. He grimaced. "Adam almost saw him today. Scared the shit out of him."

Jamie shook his head; he couldn't even begin to imagine what David was going through. He fiddled with David's empty mug and muttered, "Poor Dave. It must hurt him so much to need to hide from his son."

"Yeah," John said quietly. "He bought a new backpack today."

The intent of John's words was obvious. Jamie looked up and frowned. "It doesn't have to mean he's gonna leave, John." He pulled himself up into David's chair. "Maybe he just needs to know he could if he had to, yeah?"

John knew Jamie was right, but slumped a little and said, "I just wish he didn't need to."

ON his own in the apartment, David sat on the edge of the bed and stared at the back-pack. Why did this little cheap bag seem safer than the life John offered him?

John said he loved him, but….

He unzipped the top and reached for the paper bag containing his belongings. One by one he pulled out the clothes John had bought for him, each item freshly laundered and folded. David laid them carefully out on the bed and ran his fingers over each one. He lifted his sketchbook and placed it beside them. Everything he owned.

It's enough. David gave himself a mental shake and packed his clothes into the bottom of the pack. He methodically emptied his pockets of small change, pencil stubs, and a couple of sweet cookies, putting them all down the side. The sketchbook was also slid down the side of his clothes and finally the tattered paper bag was folded and placed on top. David pulled the zip closed and put the pack on the floor next to the chest of drawers.

THE room was dark and quiet when David woke up. Even the seemingly ever-present street noises were silent. He turned carefully and could just make out the sleeping figure of John. One arm was under his pillow and the other folded in front of him so his fingers curled just out of reach of his open mouth. Listening, David could hear the slow soft breath that matched the steady rise and fall of John's chest.

Sliding his legs around until they reached the edge of the mattress, David cautiously moved off the bed. He stood and watched for a while longer to ensure he hadn't woken John, and then moved across the room to his pack.

David took hold of the shoulder strap and lifted it, desperately trying not to make a sound. By the time he reached the living room his footfall steadied and he walked quickly into the kitchen. The sudden flare of the florescent light stung his eyes as he flicked on the light and squinted while sorting through his belongings.

His fingers closed around the spiral spine on his sketchbook and he sat at the table. David spent several minutes looking through it and reading its content; some were simple lists while others were meant only for middle-of-the-night reading. He pulled out a pencil and in the dark shading behind the smiling face of a teenage boy he began to write. *I watched you do the right thing today, Adam. I wanted to stand up and tell you how proud I am of you instead of cowering in the shadows, but I couldn't do it. John said to me that one day you'll get to read this....*

CHAPTER 21

DAVID watched Jamie come into the kitchen for a third glass of water and grinned. Once again he strolled the long way around the table, craning his neck to see what David was doing. With a quiet giggle at how obvious Jamie was being, David made a show of covering the list he was writing. Finally it was too much for Jamie; his curiosity got the better of him and he leaned on the back of a vacant chair and groaned, "I give up. What *are* you doing?"

David chuckled at Jamie's pained expression and shrugged. "Just writing a list of where I can get some books."

"Um, David, look around," Jamie said with a flourish of his hand.

Rather than taking the bait, David just nodded and tapped his list. "These aren't for me; they're for the shelter."

With his curiosity piqued, Jamie pulled out the chair and sat down. He turned the sketchbook slightly askew so he could read David's scrawled list. There were single words, half-formed ideas, and the word "purgatory" traced over a few times next to what seemed to be business hours. Jamie frowned and gave David a quizzical look. "Purgatory?"

"It's a room in the library where they put the books ready for pulping," David explained. "The librarian said I could help myself. I sorted a couple of bags' worth, but that was all I could carry."

Jamie nodded and gave him a clearly delighted smile. "You went there and organized this with the librarians, yeah?"

"Yeah." David rolled his eyes, a little uncomfortable when Jamie continued to grin broadly at him. "I thought I might take them to the shelter tomorrow while John's at his meeting."

"With 'the suits'." Jamie groaned and grimaced. "I still remember the first time I met John in his designer suit, designer haircut, and designer attitude." He laughed and sat back in his chair. "Don't get me wrong. I thought he had definite potential, but...."

David thought back to his first meeting with John, John's look of disgust before he'd turned his back.

Jamie noticed the rapid change in David's expression and clearly remembered John's initial reaction to the store's "resident transient". He knew then that it still hurt and reminded him, "But we got him to look beyond the profit line, didn't we, Dave?"

"Yeah." David smiled and tried to shake off the memory. "Although seeing him take out his suit for tomorrow made me wonder."

Jamie frowned and said with undeniable certainty, "Nah, he can put the suit on, but it won't take him long to see it doesn't fit anymore. He's not the man he was."

David gave a moment's thought to Jamie's words and was about to query the logic, but Jamie had already switched topics. "I can help you sort them," he said, looking back at the list. "The books I mean. And we can get John to move them in his car, or I know this guy with a truck. Well, I met him once, but I think I still have his number."

He knew Jamie meant well, but David gave him a small apologetic smile and suggested, "Maybe... maybe later. But right now, I need to do this."

THE weight of the book bags made David's fingers ache. He stopped for a minute and shifted the handles out of the white ridges they'd created in his flesh before continuing down the path. Despite the discomfort, it felt good to be outside again and doing something worthwhile. Two weeks had passed since he'd seen Adam, and David hadn't dared to venture out of the store or John's apartment. He knew the others had noticed and seemed to take turns in making sure he was okay. As soon as John had something to do Jamie would appear. It crossed David's mind that they were actually keeping watch because the backpack definitely seemed to spook John. David shook his head. *Just because I need to know I can go if I need to doesn't mean I will....*

By the time he reached the shelter door, David's breathing was coming in short pained puffs; partly through the exertion of the long walk carrying the books, but also a reluctance to step up into the foyer. Even though he was on a mission today it was still a reminder of what he'd been and what he could so easily be again. With a deep breath and nervous swallow, he pushed open the door and stepped inside.

Hovering near the doorway, David watched the scene inside, very tempted to just leave the books, turn around, and walk back to Margins. But Barbara had other ideas. She'd seen him come through the door and had been watching him, gauging his reactions before approaching. With a pleased smile she waved him over. "David! It's good to see you." She glanced down at the bags and said, "Those look suspiciously like books."

David followed her line of sight and nodded. He held up one of the bags despite the strain on his fingers and told her, "I got them from the library. They have a lot more."

"Thank you, David. The last books you brought us were a huge success." She took the bags from him and put them on the reception desk. "Come on through to the kitchen. I'm due for a break and would love some company." Without waiting for a reply she headed in the direction of the kitchen, knowing given no choice he would follow.

As soon as they were seated at the table, Barbara gave him a gentle smile and asked, "So, David, how are you?"

David shrugged and said in a voice that made it clear he wasn't willing to give too much away to her, "Better, I guess."

Barbara nodded, but was well aware how he kept his eyes on his hands and picked nervously at a callous where his pencil usually rested. She left it there and asked instead, "How's John?"

"He's having lunch with his friends," David answered in a guarded manner.

"Uh-huh," Barbara said noncommittally and waited.

"His work friends. Or maybe they're not really friends but people he works with."

Barbara took note of how David used present tense when discussing John's business acquaintances. "So how is he, apart from having lunch?"

At that point, it became very clear to David that he wasn't going to get away with much with Barbara and he smiled. "John's good…. He worries about me too much, but he's good."

Barbara chuckled and stood up to pour the boiling water into the waiting mugs. David sat quietly while she carried the mugs to the table and took her seat. She pulled the lid off the cookie tin and frowned. "Not many left, I'm afraid. I raided the chocolate ones earlier." Barbara watched him carefully while he slowly reached into the tin, took a cookie, and placed it beside his mug. His actions were still of a man uncomfortable in his surroundings despite how far he'd come in the past few months. She took a bite of her cookie and said through the crumbs, "You know, it's okay that he worries. We all worry about people we care about, even when they don't need it."

With a nod and a hint of a grin, David picked up his own cookie and took a bite.

DAVID dropped his clothes on the floor and stepped into the shower. It wasn't that he felt dirty; it was more to reinforce the notion that he could stay clean.

He stood under the force of the shower, head dropped forward letting the jet hit the back of his neck and sluice down his back. For several minutes he just closed his eyes and gave in to the soothing sensation of the water. He'd talked to Barbara for a lot longer than he'd intended. They'd discussed the books, setting up some shelves, and somehow she also managed to get him to let slip the occasional comment about himself. *She's good at her job.* David smiled.

With a contented moan, he straightened and tilted his head back to let the water stream over his face. His open mouth soon filled with water and he grinned as it spilled over his lips and down his body. It felt good.

He reached for the shampoo and the smell of peppermint soon filled the misted bathroom. It brought back the first night he'd smelled that shampoo and what he was like then: dirty, frightened, and ashamed. Picking up the smooth white bar of soap, David turned it over and over in his hands while he slowly let the image wash away. It was only then that David allowed his soapy hand on his skin. There was a nearly forgotten familiarity to the body he felt beneath his fingers. Some of the sharp angles had softened, along with the revulsion of being touched by even his own hands.

Glancing down he watched the progress of his hand. Tiny bubbles were left in the trail of hair around his naval until they were rinsed away by the rivulets of water. The water ran warm over his belly and down his thighs. His hand hovered for a moment before returning to its path. Still soapy fingers slipped easily between his legs and settled just under his cock, holding barely tight enough to feel himself start to lengthen and swell. *Take your time,* he reminded himself, knowing there weren't a dozen other men waiting for their chance to remove some of the street from their skin.

But David pulled his hand away at the unbidden memory of rough and rushed release and stood with his open palms pressed against the tiles of the shower stall until all the soap was rinsed away.

With his hair toweled dry, he paused in the doorway of the bedroom. He'd been with John for almost six months, but still felt the compulsion to glance over his shoulder, expecting to be told he didn't belong there. David shook his head and looked back at the bed that John had made up with fresh linen that morning; every Sunday morning.

He walked over, brushed his fingers across John's pillow, and smiled briefly before turning his gaze to his own pillow. David moved slowly around to his side of the bed, carefully turned back the covers, and smoothed his palm over the fresh white sheet, cool and clean.

David unwrapped the towel from his waist and laid it purposefully within his reach on the edge of the bed.

Naked, he stretched out. Each muscle tensed to be slowly released until his body relaxed against the cool of the bed. His bed…. He rolled the thought over in his mind and reached his arm across the mattress to cover the space John would fill. David closed his eyes.

He could hear the faint stir of the curtain as the breeze, warm with the first hints of summer, blew softly through the open window. It caressed his bare skin and for the first time in what seemed an eternity David didn't feel at war with his body. There was no real ache of the ever-present fatigue and he didn't fight the stirrings of need.

Keeping his eyes closed, David's hand came to rest on his stomach. He let the heat of his palm seep through his skin before he moved it slowly down. His cock twitched at the nearness of touch, but he avoided direct contact, sliding instead along the crease of his thigh. Still slightly damp from the shower, his fingers explored the smooth skin, taking in the changes of texture of hairlines. The other hand mirrored the first, each making its own slow progress.

David exhaled a shaky breath and raised his hips enough to encourage further exploration. The breeze had picked up and, though still warm, it quickly cooled the path of pre-come that had begun to dribble down his hard flesh.

Finally David relented. The flat of his fingers skimmed the underside of his cock before encircling and tightening their grip. His hand moved deliberately, stroking himself in long, slow, downward sweeps so his fingers nudged against tightening balls. Images danced through his mind of John touching him, kissing him... all aberrant thoughts blocked and forgotten for now. His other hand lifted to his mouth and the faint trace of desire passed over his lips.

David's eyes remained firmly closed while he moaned around his fingers. His hips rose from the bed, urging his hand into a more determined rhythm. Harder, faster, squeezing around the swollen head. Breathing became more difficult. His breath came in grunted grasps until he felt it start. The tension in his belly and balls became a shockwave that rapidly built and rippled in ever-expanding waves. Fingers faltered and, with an uninhibited cry, David came.

A WHOLE different world. The phrase passed through John's mind for the umpteenth time that day as he parked his car in his spot near the store. When he turned the key in the ignition, killing the engine, he quickly reached up and loosened his tie.

Seeing his old friends had unnerved him a lot more than he'd anticipated. The brief lunch meeting had extended out to several hours and he'd slipped far too easily into his "executive" mind-set. Talk about closing files had morphed into discussions of his returning at the end of the year without him even noticing the shift in the conversation. It was all mapped out. He would complete his year in exile and return to the fold.

His stomach rolled, possibly from the rich food and midday alcohol, but more likely the thought of turning his back on the life he'd built, was building, with David.

John reached into the glove box and grabbed a discarded packet of cigarettes, lit one, and wound the window down. The year was half over and every time that realization dawned, John had managed to push it to the back of his mind. But he knew he needed to start making decisions. He inhaled deeply and leaned back against the seat before letting out the long stream of smoke. Up until that moment, his fear had been that David would leave, but now he had to consider that he might be the one to leave—let the lease run out on the store and pick up where he left off. John frowned and stabbed the cigarette butt into the ashtray.

He stepped out of the car and looked up at the building that housed his current life.

By the time his key was in the door to his apartment John's tie was in his hand and his stomach was full of now very familiar butterflies. He shook his head and told himself to settle down, but knew this time it was anticipation.

It was quiet when he entered. There was no sign of David so John left his keys on the coffee table and wandered through to his room. He stopped in the doorway. David was sitting cross-legged on the bed drawing in his sketchbook. John took the moment to just look at the man dressed in the same pair of old track pants he'd given him on that first night and a crumpled T-shirt. A grin spread across John's face at the sight of David barefoot and with definite bed head.

The butterflies increased their dance when David looked up at him and smiled.

CHAPTER 22

FORGET your planters filled with flowers, the sudden appearance of ice cream vendors and Christmas decorations appearing next to the tram lines on Melbourne streets; the one sure sign of summer is not having to turn people away before the doors are closed.

Barbara smiled as she looked around the main dormitory area of the shelter. The beds were freshly made and ready for the evening, but the nights were warm and many of those without their own beds chose to sleep outdoors. She didn't blame them; the shelter provided a refuge for some and safety for others, but when the beds were full and the lights were out the air hung with despair. She banished the thought; the sun was shining outside and she'd had a win.

Barbara picked up the tray of mugs and carried it through to the reception area. It had taken a couple of Sundays, but the shelves were almost done. She couldn't help but grin at David as he carefully measured the last of the wood while Jamie sat cross-legged on the floor beside him chattering, totally oblivious to the fact that David rarely answered. This had been the pattern for most of the morning; David quietly going about his business while Jamie flitted around the room handing him tools or supervising over his shoulder.

But she had already figured out that initial impressions of Jamie were deceptive. Many would have quickly written him off as a sweet but naive young man; however, Barbara's experienced eye saw a lot more. Yes, Jamie was sweet, but he was also perceptive and displayed an empathy that was quite rare.

Besides, it was very obvious that David liked him and it was a huge step that David felt comfortable enough to include him in this. Barbara watched their interactions and found it interesting, but she supposed not surprising that it was Jamie here and not John.

Jamie looked over and saw her cautious walk across the room, expertly balancing the laden tray while stepping over an assortment of books, wood off-cuts and discarded tools. He grinned and, with a gentle stroke to the back of David's hair, got up and lifted the tray from her.

"Tea break," he announced as he placed the tray on the floor. David stopped what he was doing, picked up a mug and leaned back against the wall. He was pleased with his morning's work and the sense of achievement showed in his face as he sipped at the hot tea.

"Looking good, David," Barbara announced, only partially referring to the shelf she ran her hand along.

"Getting there," he smiled quietly.

EVEN in his old apartment with its full housekeeping service, John had always made his own bed and organized his own laundry. He often wondered if that was one of the few things he allowed himself to carry out of Yorkshire; the need to take care of the basics and see to yourself. Kept him grounded, he supposed. He stuffed the last of the pillowcases into the laundry bag and wandered through to the bathroom in search of damp towels.

The first thing he noticed on entering the room was David's underwear and socks hanging on the rail of the shower stall. John looked at them and shook his head. Each night David would wash them out in the sink and hang them in the bathroom to dry. When John suggested he just throw them in with the other laundry he'd simply smiled and replied that he could manage.

John lifted them off the rail and neatly folded them. He left the laundry bag on the tiled floor and carried David's things to the bedroom. The bottom drawer was still empty and John was very tempted to put them in there, but he understood that had to be David's choice.

With a sigh, John squatted next to the backpack and unzipped the top. He could see next to the few articles of clothing, there were two sketchbooks now. John itched to look at David's latest drawings and even began to reach for them, but stopped when he saw two cookies stashed down the side of the pack. *Oh, Dave.... You don't have to do this anymore.*

He closed the pack and placed the underwear on top.

John straightened, sat on the edge of the bed, and looked at the pack. Things like that were little reminders that his life with David wasn't your typical relationship; there was always so much more to complicate things, things that threatened to unbalance them no matter how small and insignificant they might seem.

He sighed and pushed his fingers through his hair. *Did I really expect Dave to follow me back to my real life, perhaps to attend executive get-togethers as my "significant other"?* His sad chuckle became a groan because John knew that wasn't even a remote possibility. Apart from the fact open bisexuality wasn't an option once you reached the top floors, David wouldn't survive in that environment. And John wouldn't put him through it.

David was making progress. He understood that, and lately the backward steps seemed to be outnumbered by the forward ones. Although he hadn't said anything, John knew David's chats with Barbara had taken on a more formal structure. John didn't pry into what they talked about, but when he asked Barbara how David was doing she had replied a little cryptically, "I think you will be a better judge of that than me." He hoped so.

The folded underwear again drew his focus. *Maybe this is my real life now?*

BY the time he turned his key in the front door David was forced to give in to his exhaustion. The walk to and from the shelter, building the shelves, and talking to Barbara all took it out of him. David knew his sessions with Barbara were helping, but each little admission of information was hard fought and sapped his strength. There were so many issues and feelings twisted and tangled together that uncoiling them was slow and draining. David took a breath, straightened his shoulders, and pushed the door open.

David couldn't see John, but heard him speaking in another room. He followed the sound of John's voice into the kitchen where he found him leaning against the counter talking on his cell phone. The tone of his voice rather than the content of the conversation quickly alerted David that he was talking business.

"Look," John said with barely concealed frustration. "I told you that you can't tackle it that way unless you want the auditors on your arse and ultimately on mine."

David gave him a half-smile, not wanting to interrupt. John lifted his hand to wave, but was clearly distracted by the person on the other end of the line. With a small nod David walked back over to the lounge area and flopped down on the couch. It still annoyed him how quickly his body let him down; barely an afternoon's work and his muscles were complaining. He sighed and fell back against the cushions.

John moved away from the counter and watched David while he talked; his impatience with the caller increased by the second. Finally, he had had enough and barked into the receiver, "Listen, talk to Marian about it. No, she has all the details and will run you through them." He disconnected the call and rubbed his hand wearily over the back of his neck. *Even a fucking phone call makes my head thump.* He looked across to David, slumped, eyes closed on the couch, and asked, "You want tea, Dave?"

"Mmm… yeah, please," David answered in a voice that indicated he'd already started to drift off. He opened his eyes, blinked a few times and sat up.

He heard John turn on the tap to fill the kettle and leaned forward to pull off his boots. The leather was starting to wear through in a couple of places and the elastic had totally given up. He turned a boot over in his hands and looked at the sole; a small hole had started to form. *Cardboard will seal that well enough until winter,* he decided and put the boots side by side on the floor.

With a small grunt, David lifted his foot to rest on the other knee and started to knead some life back into it.

"You sound tired," John said gently as he placed both his and David's mugs on the coffee table.

"A bit," David lied.

John gave him a disbelieving smile and sat at the other end of the couch. "Here… give that to me." He patted his knee and encouraged David to swing his legs around and lie back. John rolled off each sock and rubbed his palm over the hot soles. "I still don't know why you won't let me drive you," he grumbled, starting to massage each of David's feet in turn.

"I can manage... and I like to walk." David smiled, watching John through heavy-lidded eyes.

Without stopping his ministrations, John huffed and mumbled half under his breath, "I know you can manage, but I might *want* to help."

David sighed and nodded. His voice was quiet and more than a little content when he said, "Someone donated a whole box of oranges today."

Even though it seemed like a change in topic, John knew better; this was David's way of letting him in.

"Yeah?" he said, not really asking a question but allowing David to continue if he wanted.

"Mmm.... When they were cut up, the smell filled the room and it reminded me of being a little kid. I remember my mum coming out to the garden with an orange cut into three pieces for my brothers and me. We sat in the sun and ate them. I was laughing because we were sticking the whole wedge in our mouths so that all you could see was an orange-rind smile. My mum told us off, but she wasn't really angry." He paused and said simply, "It was a good smell."

John's fingers barely moved while he listened to David speak. David had just told him he had brothers. When David stopped speaking and met John's eyes, John said one word. "Geraniums."

David gave him a quizzical look and laughed. "What?"

"That's the smell I remember," John clarified as if it was obvious and gave David's toes a squeeze. "The little plant pot of white flowers that sat on the dark green stoop; that's the step at the door."

David nodded and relaxed back into the story, easily picturing that little boy next to the flowers.

"I used to sit there and wait for my granddad to get home from work... or the pub if it was payday. Gran would growl at me for snapping the leaves, but I loved that smell. Not a smell I've really noticed as an adult."

"Smells are different when you grow up, but they still tell you things," David said, his voice becoming several shades darker. "I hated that I smelled bad, but there was nothing I could do...."

"I know, Dave," John whispered, understanding it was useless to deny it.

"It meant so much to me that you let me use your bathroom to clean up," David murmured. He paused and took a breath before asking, "Why did you, John?"

"I'm not really sure," John answered truthfully. "Maybe it was a mixture of concern and shame."

"Shame?" Coming from John the word seemed wrong, and it confused David.

"Yeah, Dave, shame. I judged you the minute I saw you. I wrote you off because of your clothes, the dirt on your skin, and yes, the smell." Saying the words hurt John more than he thought they could but it was right to finally admit it to David. "Thank God for Jamie, huh?"

David nodded.

"He pushed and niggled at me to look past that and see the person. He kept letting me know what it might be like for you; that you were often hungry and couldn't always get in the shelter on winter nights. I saw you trying to make a bed of cardboard in a doorway once, but when I went back for you the cops had moved you on." John hesitated just long enough to take a quick gulp of air before saying quietly, "It was as if you were suddenly very real to me."

"You went back for me?" David said more to himself than John, but John nodded and replied, "Yeah... I think I started to know even then that I was in trouble with you." He turned and gave David a slightly embarrassed grin. "That night was the start of it and each time after that it was worse. When you came here after being beaten up I was worried sick, but still so bloody relieved to see you. Shit, you should have seen Marian's face when I told her to leave. I sat and watched you most of the night. I kept telling myself it was just to make sure you didn't die on me, but as much as I wanted to I couldn't deny it any longer.... I knew I loved you."

David dropped his eyes and let the silence hang for a long minute or two. His voice was almost a mumble when he started to speak. "You'd been working on the accounts for most of the morning; I guess Maggie wasn't too good at balancing the books and you had that serious frown on your face the whole time. Except at one point your concentration wavered and you got this distant look in your eyes, almost sad. It didn't last long, but it was long enough for me to fall in love with you." His voice trailed off to be replaced by the rush of blood in his ears as he watched John's stunned expression.

Wrong, wrong. Shouldn't have said that. Panic rapidly built in David and he almost missed when John whispered, "Do you love me, David?"

With courage he didn't know he had, David carefully eased his feet off John's lap and turned to crawl closer. Every instinct told him not to risk this, but David nodded and leaned in to let his lips brush against John's.

John sat very still and let David kiss him, but when their lips parted his fingers found David's hair, pushing it back to see his eyes. The astonishment on John's face was replaced by a grin that almost split his face in two even though his voice still had an air of disbelief when he said, "I love you so fucking much."

David let the fear slide away and matched John's smile. He kissed John again, but this time—for the first time—it was equal. Neither led nor followed as they tasted and touched each other. John slowly slid down on the couch until he was almost on his back with David sprawled over him. The weight of David's body on his was solid and real as they gently rubbed against each other, hips rolling in an unhurried dance as if the cloth separating them didn't exist.

John's skin was under David's hands, his hair twined through his fingers. All else faded except for a nagging sound at the edge of his perception. Suddenly it registered: John's cell phone. David quickly pulled away, his breathing heavy as he moved to the end of the couch. The loss of touch was bewildering and John slowly sat up to where he could reach David and said, "Dave? It's just my phone. Ignore it. Let it ring out."

David glanced down at his now-clasped hands and said solemnly, "It might be important, John. It might be your work." John frowned and watched David's all too familiar emotional withdrawal. *Aren't we past this, Dave?,* he thought, getting more and more frustrated at the intrusion of the ring tone. "Fuck." John cursed under his breath, stood up, and flipped open his phone. "What is it?"

The metallic voice began to tell him about problems finalizing a contract, but John was only half-listening. The talk of numbers just didn't seem important and he realized he didn't actually care about the portfolio he'd spent almost the whole of the previous year courting and setting up. It just didn't matter. He looked at David sitting silently on the couch waiting for him and knew there was no real decision to make.

John let the caller finish his sentence and said in a surprisingly calm and sure voice, "I appreciate the call, Bob, but to be honest *that* is not my life anymore. I have something so much better."

CHAPTER 23

THE full summer sun was warm on the back of David's shoulders. People bustled past the courtyard café chattering happily and swapping postcard-size reproductions of the artworks they'd just viewed, but David was content to just watch the man sitting across from him.

John looked up from the exhibition catalogue to see David smiling; he could feel the blush creeping up his face and asked, "What?"

David just shrugged and kept smiling until John gave an embarrassed laugh and growled, "Don't give me that. Tell me!"

"Watching you pouring over the paintings; I guess I just didn't expect to see you like that... you know, totally engrossed. lost in the pictures. You don't seem the art type."

John squirmed a little in his seat and went to close the book, but David gently put his hand over John's and stopped him. "Why these pictures, John? As beautiful as the Pre-Raphaelites are, they're not what I imagined you liking."

"What did you imagine me liking?"

David grinned and said, "I dunno. Creative accounting?"

John pulled a face and made to swat him, but said, "When I was young, maybe seventeen, it was half-day closing and I caught the train to Birmingham for the afternoon. I'd just been paid and wanted to price new football boots or something. I can't really remember what. Anyway, I know I didn't have quite enough money and would have to wait at least another week." David watched John's eyes lose focus. This was always a good time, a chance to let go of recent histories and go back through tales of youth that gave glimpses of the journey.

"I'd taken a sandwich with me; Gran always packed me a lunch, and I sat in the park to eat. I'd just started and the heavens opened. Fuck, it started to absolutely piss down. I didn't have a coat with me and there was no shelter so I grabbed my things and ran to the nearest building." John stopped and shook his head, smiling at the memory. "It was a cathedral, a great bloody cathedral in the middle of the city. Not somewhere I'd usually venture." He raised his hands to the sky to emphasize his words, making David laugh.

"I remember standing there huddled in the doorway shoving my sandwich in my mouth watching the rain come down. It didn't look like it was going to stop anytime soon so I swallowed my last bite and decided to take a look inside." John looked at David with total awe in his eyes and tried to articulate the wonder he'd felt at his surroundings. "I'd never been in a place like that before and… and it took my breath away. The color from the windows… it touched everything. I remember looking down at my hand; my skin was reds and golds, and I couldn't believe how beautiful it looked." He looked up and saw David staring at the upturned palm as if the colors were still held there after all these years and murmured, "I didn't understand that the world could hold such beauty until then. I suppose I didn't expect it."

David met his eyes and smiled, making John clear his throat and look back at the book. "So… um, those windows I found out were by an artist called Burne-Jones."

The noise of a bored school group briefly interrupted him and he shot them a disgruntled look. David merely shrugged and said, "The pictures don't move and there are no shootouts or car chases, but you never know, John. Maybe one of them will find some *unexpected beauty* in the exhibition that they'll remember when they're all grown up. And if all else fails they'll remember running their fingers over the waterfall window and maybe decide galleries aren't too bad."

John listened to the softly spoken words and he was awed by the beauty of David; he could see it clearly, both physically and spiritually. John began to reply when he saw David's attention waver and it was obvious something behind John had caught his attention. The smile vanished from David's face. John watched as he gripped the edge of the table and pushed himself to his feet, still staring over John's shoulder.

"Dave? What is it?" John asked, looking around to see what had caused such a reaction.

David backed slowly away from the table and muttered what might have been, "I have to go."

"David?" John stood up and reached for him, but he'd turned and begun to walk rapidly toward the exit. John called after him as he pushed his way through the summer crowds.

He quickly gathered his belongings from the table to follow, but became aware of a figure standing at his shoulder. The young man just stood and stared at the retreating back before he turned to John, his expression a mixture of hurt and bewilderment.

John was torn between going after David and talking to the young man whose features were so familiar through the many portraits in David's sketchbook.

"That was my dad, wasn't it?" he asked quietly.

John looked in the direction David had disappeared. He sighed, turned back to Adam, and nodded.

Adam was at a loss of what to do or say and it took him a few false starts before he managed to spit out, "Why did he leave? What did I do?"

John shook his head and held his hand up. "You didn't do anything, Adam. Your dad has had some problems. Look, I really have to go after him and make sure he's okay." John pulled out his wallet and handed Adam a small cream business card with a new number penciled in above the neat typeface printing of the old one. He put his hand on Adam's arm and said, "Call me, please.... I'll do my best to explain." John could see the confusion on the teenager's face, but at that moment he couldn't deal with that because he needed to follow David.

Without waiting for an answer John made his way through the crowded thoroughfare and jogged out the exit toward the car park, only slowing to a walk when he rounded the corner and his car was in view. There was no sign of David.

John waited by the car for more than an hour, looking as each person entered the car park, occasionally pacing the length of the roadway to the entry ramp. He checked the male toilets both on this level and the one nearer the gallery, his nerves jumping as he approached the car again in anticipation, picturing David quietly waiting for him.

But David wasn't back.

John felt sick to his stomach when he finally turned the key in the ignition and backed the car out of the parking space. It felt wrong to leave, as if he was giving up and that David might still appear even though logically he knew he wouldn't. The drive home was spent watching pedestrians, peering through the windscreen into doorways, and missing the change of traffic lights while he scanned every face. By the time he parked near the store he had all but convinced himself that David had headed home... to *their* home.

The apartment was quiet when John pushed the door open, but that didn't necessarily mean David *wasn't* there. It had taken John quite a while to understand and appreciate the silence that often surrounded David. He moved from room to room, feeling his dread grow with each empty space.

He looked on the kitchen counter next to the stacked mail and paid bills for what he knew would still be there; a small silver cell phone. It had been several weeks since John had bought the phone for David. He'd smiled and said thank you, but had never taken it with him or even put it in his backpack. John doubted that he'd even turned it on. He pushed the phone to the back of the bench and whispered, *Help me here, Dave.*

THE sun had gone down and, other than the unrelenting tick of the wall clock, the apartment was silent. John sat in his armchair and stared into the darkened room. The stillness of his pose belied the agitation he was feeling. His head throbbed and every muscle threatened to twitch. He needed to do something. He just didn't know what. When the phone rang, John virtually flew out of the chair and clutched at the receiver. "Hello, David?" he said breathlessly, hoping rather than knowing who it was.

A hesitant voice spoke on the other end of the line. "Hi, um... John. Is my dad okay?"

John closed his eyes and took a deep breath. He knew he needed to answer the boy but found it extremely difficult to answer *that* particular question. In the end he replied quietly, "As far as I know, Adam."

There it is again, Adam thought. *He says my name as if he knows me....* "Has my d... has he ever spoken about me?"

John shook his head; the hint of a sad smile played on his lips. "David doesn't talk a lot, lad, but he has told me about you. He misses you very much."

Then why did he go? The question was there between them, neither giving it voice. John heard Adam sigh before he asked, "Can I talk to him? Will he talk to me?"

How the fuck do I answer that? What can I tell him? That his father had a full-blown panic attack in a bus shelter at the mere thought he'd see him? John rested the receiver against his forehead for a few seconds to compose himself, understanding that he couldn't tell the whole truth but not wanting to lie to the boy. He took a breath and said as calmly as he could, "I don't know.... Um, he's not here right now. I'm sorry."

Adam felt his throat close around a lump. *Please, John. He's my dad.* His voice was very small when he asked, "Will *you* talk to me about him?"

I want to, Adam... so much. I want to tell you how much he loves you. What he's put himself through to see you. The drawings and letters he's written. That David is a kind, gentle man who despite everything has a dignity that.... John could feel the burn of tears at the back of his eyes and cut the thought short. That wasn't helping. In a gentle voice, John said to David's son, "Adam, please understand that I need to speak to David first."

"What if he says no?"

What if he says no? Fuck! John rubbed his fingers over his eyes. It hurt to hear Adam's desperation.

When John didn't answer, Adam pleaded quietly. "Please, John."

"Give me your number, Adam," John replied softly, knowing he had to try.

John made no attempt to brush away the tears that rolled down his cheeks when he replaced the receiver. *You were doing so well, Dave. We were doing so well.* He leaned back against the kitchen counter, rubbed his hand over his face, and looked at his armchair. *I can't wait for you, David; I'm going to find you.* John shook his head and grabbed his car keys from the table.

BY now the streets were filled with people heading home to their own lives, leaving those without them behind to find something to fill their night. He'd tried several of David's usual haunts to no avail and could think of one more before heading home. John parked the car, silenced the engine, and turned off the lights. He sat behind the steering wheel and looked out the window. There was a bright moon so he could easily see the front gardens of the park. The flowers, red and yellow in the sunlight, shone bright and colorless along the edges of the path.

John looked at them as he stepped out of the car and walked into the park.

CHAPTER 24

JOHN'S feet stayed to the lit path of the park, but his mind wandered to places he prayed David hadn't ventured. *Don't go there,* he growled to himself and shook it off, somehow knowing that David had moved on from that. The night was still mild but John shoved his hands in his pockets as he walked the long path, constantly scanning the shadows and looking at the face of every lonely figure trying to find a quiet place to bed down. *I can't find you if you don't want to be found, Dave.* He sighed, but continued his determined walk.

Finally, he had to stop somewhere near the center of the park where a large round flower bed spiked off into a number of different paths. John stood and glanced down each as they disappeared around tree-lined corners. He sighed and out of desperation called David's name, only to be abused by a young couple seeking the solace of a private moment away from home and parents. He quickly apologized and moved away. That's when he heard the quiet reply. "I'm here, John."

John turned in the direction of the voice and squinted until he could just make out the hunched silhouette of David sitting on a family picnic table, his feet resting on the long wooden bench. David didn't make a move toward John, but simply sat and watched him.

Without a word, John walked over to sit on the bench next to David's feet. He leaned back against the table edge where, despite his need to throw accusations or simply ask questions, John sat quietly and stared out into the park. Together they sat in silence until slowly John felt the tension in the man next to him begin to ease. He sighed a little and lifted his arm to drape it across David's knee. John looked up and asked, "Are you okay?"

David gave the question serious thought before he nodded slowly and said, "He's grown a lot over the last few years."

David's face was impassive, but John knew better. He moved off the bench and onto the table next to David, where he sat close enough to feel David's body heat, but without actually touching. It was difficult to remain quiet. There were so many things he wanted to say to reassure David, but one lesson he'd learned over the past few months was to give David time.

After long minutes of silence, John slowly moved his hand around and placed it on David's back to gently rub between his shoulder blades while he whispered, "There's no hurry, Dave."

David just shook his head and looked away. "I was coming home, John. I just needed to get away for a while, but I *was* coming home."

"I know," John lied.

THE drive home was quiet, with David slumped in the passenger seat, his unfocused gaze aimed at the passing sidewalk. David looked tired and defeated when John stole a quick glance. "Almost home," he said softly and tightened his grip on the steering wheel when David repeated his words, "Almost home."

As soon as John turned the engine off David got out of the car and walked to the apartment, where he waited. "Do you want something to eat? Maybe something to drink?" John asked as he led him up the stairs and through the apartment door.

David shook his head with a flat "No." He hesitated in the middle of the room and looked at John. A small and somewhat apologetic smile fleeted over his features when he saw John watching him. "I'm sorry, John. No, thank you. I think I need to go to bed if that's okay."

"Of course it's okay," John said and cleared his throat. "You go through; I'll join you in a little while." He reached out to touch David's arm, but didn't quite make contact and stood back while David nodded and walked wearily through to the bedroom.

John sat on the couch and let his head fall back. His eyes closed, but he still threw his arm over his face as if to shield him from the light. *We don't need this now when things have been going so well.* He wanted to leave it, not mention the phone call and take the pressure off David, but John remembered the look on Adam's face and the desperate tone in his voice. *He's a teenage boy who wants to talk to his dad.* Thoughts about his own dad crept into the debate. He loved his granddad, but many times over the years he'd wondered not only what his dad was like, but perhaps more importantly, what he would think of the adult John. Would he be proud of how his son had turned out? There had been times in John's life when that question was vehemently denied but lurked in his thoughts nevertheless.

Not tonight, he decided. *Deal with it tomorrow.* He hauled himself off the couch, flicked the light switch, and walked into the bedroom. David was lying on his side so John couldn't make out if he was asleep. The room was silent. He quietly undressed and climbed into the bed, where he lay looking at David's back. As his breathing slowed and muscles began to settle against the mattress he heard the softly spoken question. "Did he talk to you, John?"

John's chest tightened, although he knew the only way to deal with this was honesty. "Yeah. He's very confused, Dave, but he wants to talk to you."

David didn't answer.

John shuffled closer and rested his chin lightly over David's shoulder so that his cheek rested against David's jawline. He took a small breath and said, "I gave him my cell phone number and he called me tonight." John could feel David tense and was tempted to pull David back against his chest, but reached up instead and ran his hand over the curve of David's shoulder; slow, soothing strokes.

David was torn between the need to know about his son and the desperate panic of Adam knowing what he'd become. "I can't do this, John," he whispered.

"He doesn't know where you are." John sighed, kissed the side of David's neck, and rested his forehead against his hair. "I told him I'd talk to you.... I told him you might not be ready to talk yet."

David's breathing became uneven and John knew he was struggling, but he also knew that he needed to continue. "He asked if I'd talk to him. Can I do that?"

No answer came except a shuddering breath.

"It's okay. You don't have to tell me now," John whispered, his lips making gentle contact with the man in front of him. David nodded and reached up for John's hand, pulling it around his chest. John wrapped him tightly against his body, pressed another kiss to his skin, and murmured, "I love you so fucking much."

"FUCK!" Jamie said a little too loudly.

John quickly shot him a withering looking and growled, "Keep your voice down, Jamie. I've warned you about that before."

Jamie glanced to the back of the store and held his hand up in way of apology. "So did Adam talk to him? Did David talk to Adam?" he asked at a more reasonable volume.

John shook his head and said sadly, "No, David panicked. I didn't understand what was happening until it was too late and he took off."

"Shit," Jamie said softly and leaned back against the counter. "Poor Dave. It must have scared the hell out him."

John's stance softened; Jamie understood. "Yeah, I haven't got much out of him about it." John glanced up to the back of the store where he could hear the faint shuffle of books as David reorganized the shelves. He sighed and said very quietly, "Adam wants to talk to him."

Jamie followed John's eyes and frowned. With a sad shake of his head he mumbled more to himself than John, "He's not ready."

"I know, Jamie," he said, pinching the bridge of his nose, trying to stave off the headache threatening behind his eyes. "It's so fucking hard because Adam's hurting too. I talked to him on the phone; he asked me to meet him."

"It's a funny thing, John," Jamie said softly. "I've worried and looked out for David for so long that it's almost hard for me to consider how Adam must be feeling. Except, I know I'd hate to not have David in my life now."

John looked up at Jamie and nodded with a quiet "Yeah." But in the back of his mind lurked the long repressed thought, *but I've been on the other side too.*

"Did you tell David?" Jamie asked.

John exhaled a long breath before saying, "I asked if it was all right; he hasn't given an answer yet."

"He will," Jamie said with a surety that almost made John smile. John admitted, "To be honest, I was tempted to just go ahead and do it without telling him...." John saw that Jamie was about to interrupt and held up his hand. "Don't worry. It was a fleeting thought. Just frustration, not one I'd act on."

"Trust is a hard thing to earn," Jamie said with a wisdom that would have surprised anyone who didn't know him well. "Especially with someone who's been through so much."

This time John did smile and gently ran his hand over Jamie's messy hair.

OXFORD Dictionary, Webster's Dictionary, Dictionary of Famous Quotes.... The reference collection was solid and tangible; real. Something David could move around and hold onto. Each time his mind strayed back to the café courtyard or the conversation with John, he lifted another book and reorganized another shelf.

"You've done a lot," John said quietly and placed a coffee mug on newly wiped shelving.

David stopped what he was doing and looked at the mug. He noticed it was one of the usual publisher's mugs with green and blue script. *The writing blurs a little in the sweep of the "T" as if the transfer slipped during printing. Not perfect, so maybe the hairline crack doesn't matter.... It might be all right that the letter is broken....*

"Drink your tea, Dave," John pushed softly.

David lifted the hot mug to his lips, but didn't drink. It hovered close while he whispered, "Please don't tell him what I did, John."

John blinked at the words. *Is that permission?* He stood and watched as David sipped the coffee, his hands clenched a little too tightly around the steaming mug. He carefully put his fingers through the handle and eased the mug away to place it on a nearby shelf. "I won't tell him anything you don't want me to," John said gently and wrapped David's hands in his own.

David stared at their joined hands and nodded, thankful of the contact to steady and ground him. They stood quietly until John dipped his head in an attempt to catch David's gaze and asked, "You sure you want me to do this?"

A frown twitched across David's brow and his lips tightened, but he nodded slowly and looked up. "Not sure about anything right now," he said, "but *he* needs this."

I think you both do, passed through John's thoughts.

JOHN found the number on his cell and waited until he heard a teenage voice on the other end. "What did he say?"

"Straight to the point, eh?" John chuckled nervously.

"Sorry… sorry, John," Adam apologized. "It's just when I saw your name, well…."

"It's okay, lad," John said quietly. "I understand." He took a breath and started. "I spoke to Dave… your dad. He's not ready yet, Adam… but you and I can have a talk."

There was silence on the other end for quite a while, but John knew there was nothing wrong with the line. Finally Adam asked, "This afternoon okay?"

John glanced up at the clock and said, "That would be good. Just tell me when and where."

Adam gave John the address of a café near his school and suggested they meet in an hour.

After John said his goodbyes he heard a quiet voice behind him. "Is he okay?"

John took a moment to compose himself before he turned around. One look at David's body language said it all. *Better than you are right now, Dave.* "He's disappointed, but he'll be all right," John said and then took the few steps to David and smiled. "I think he's skiving off school to meet me though."

David tried to smile, but his face contorted as he fought the tears that began a trail down his cheeks. John quickly pulled him close and whispered, "We'll forgive him one missed class though."

CHAPTER 25

JOHN looked at the menu board in the café. *What the fuck do teenagers drink?* He ordered himself a tea and sat down to wait for Adam. His fingers fiddled with the small salt shaker as he watched the fine grains shift within the glass confines. Several times he glanced up when customers came and went; he couldn't begin to imagine how David must be feeling. He'd been quiet since they'd talked, barely said half a dozen words. David had politely refused his half of the sandwich and gently fended off Jamie's chatter, but at least he hadn't retired to his chair. *That had to be a good sign, an improvement,* John thought, remembering the compulsive sketching and "hiding" in the battered leather chair.

His thoughts were interrupted when the waitress slid his cup of tea onto the table. "There you go," she smiled, recognizing his worried expression. "I put a couple of cookies on the saucer for you."

"Thank you," John answered and then frowned. "Actually, can I order a juice, too, please?"

IT had been easy enough to sneak out of his study period, grab his bag from his locker, and duck out through the side gate of the school. He'd asked his friends to cover for him if anyone looked for him, but rather than telling them where he was going he let them believe it was to meet a girl. They'd laughed at his agitation when he checked the time on his phone yet again until he could make his escape to whispered jibes and suggestions of how to "get some".

It was a relief to be away from his friends and finally walking toward the café. Watching his feet move rapidly over the cracked sidewalk, Adam wondered how he would cope if it was his dad meeting him instead of John. He pushed the thought out of his head, shoved his hands in his pockets, and set up a determined stride.

John was munching absently on one of the cookies when he saw the teenage boy walk through the door. Ignoring the nervous twist in his gut, John stood up and beckoned him over to the table. Adam gave a half-smile and sat down, pushing his school bag under his seat. "Thanks for talking to him for me, John," he said, trying very hard to sound adult.

John nodded and said, "I'm in a difficult situation here, Adam. I feel like I need to look out for David, but I can also understand why *you* need some contact with him."

"I just…," Adam started and then stopped to take a breath. "I want to know why he left us. Why he…." The question remained unfinished when the words simply wouldn't come. Adam quickly looked away from John and down to his hands.

"I can't answer that, Adam," John said sadly, wishing he had more to offer the boy. "All I know is that he was living between the street and a homeless shelter when I met him."

Adam stared at him with obvious confusion. "But my mum said he left us for another family."

"I don't think that's right," John said quickly, puzzled why Adam's mother would lie to him. "David won't really talk about any of it, but now and then he lets slip some information and I'm pretty sure he was alone when he left. He said he was confused and didn't know what was happening at the start."

John watched Adam as he spoke and the boy seemed to be struggling to sort through his recollections of his dad during their last days together.

"He wasn't too good before he left," Adam said, softly looking at the glass of juice in front of him.

"In what way?" John gently pushed.

"Dad always worked really hard. I mean, *really* hard, and I know he hated being away from me so much. I remember waking up one night and he was asleep in the chair in my room. I'd gone to sleep so angry with him because he'd had a meeting or something and missed… shit, I dunno, some school thing." Adam looked up at John to apologize for cursing, but John merely nodded for him to go on. "Anyway, he didn't get up one morning. I heard Mum yelling at him and she slammed the bedroom door. When I got home from school the door was still shut... and the next day too. I wanted to see how he was, but Mum told me he was sick and to leave him alone." He stopped and hesitated for several seconds to get it all straight in his head before he added, "I listened at the door, John... and I think I heard him crying."

The image of David hiding alone in his room crying made John's chest ache and the emotion played on his face for barely a second before he managed to suppress it, but it was long enough for Adam to see. "I didn't go in to see him and I think maybe I should have," he said quietly.

"You were young, Adam, and he was your dad," John said gently. "It's a bloody tough lesson to learn that your dad isn't perfect. Don't be too hard on yourself." He leaned forward and patted Adam on the shoulder, knowing exactly how he must be feeling.

"He had some kind of breakdown, didn't he, John?"

"I think so," John answered. "He's a bit better now, but he still has his bad days."

"That's why he left," Adam stated, confirming it to himself more than John. "I *hated* him for leaving us, leaving me without saying anything. For not caring enough to stick around. There were so many times I wanted to yell at him, and other times I just... I guess I wanted him to talk to. But he was never there."

"It hurt him not to be part of your life, Adam," John murmured. "But he was around. He went through a lot just to see you."

Adam frowned. "What do you mean? I *never* saw him after he left; not until the day at the art gallery."

John took a breath and thought through the best way to word this without giving away too much information. He started slowly and said, "David always made sure you were okay, Adam. He rarely had money, but the little he did have he spent on buses to see you; he's been around even though you didn't see him."

Adam shook his head and was about to argue when he stopped and paled. He stared at John as an unwelcome realization dawned. "The bus shelter near school; sometimes the kids used to joke about the old bum in there...." His voice trailed off and he quickly turned to look out the nearest window.

"It's okay, Adam," John whispered. "You didn't know because he didn't want you to know."

Adam blinked furiously, trying to keep the tears away. He kept his face turned toward the window as he said with a slight break in his voice, "They gave him a hard time, John."

John leaned forward, laid a hand on Adam's arm again, and said, "I did too, Adam; at the start."

"Fuck." Adam cursed half under his breath and angrily wiped away a stray tear with the back of his hand. John took a sip of his tea and let Adam have some privacy. He smiled and nodded at the watchful waitress to reassure her that things were okay.

Eventually Adam sucked in a shaky breath and turned to face John. "Can I ask when you met him?"

"Not that long ago, actually. Just the middle of the year," John answered, a little surprised that it had been such a short time. "He... was a regular at a store I took over."

Adam looked at him and frowned until John explained. "It was cold and the previous owner had let him read the secondhand books at the back of the store to stay out of the weather. It took her a while to convince him it was okay, but she was pretty persuasive."

When Adam merely replied with a small nod John felt the need to expand on the explanation. "He had an old leather chair among the books at the back. It's still there actually, and he used to spend his days sitting reading."

"Dad enjoyed reading," Adam confirmed with the slightest hint of a smile.

John returned the smile and added, "It was good for him to disappear into a book; he needed that."He paused and took a sip of his tea, not really wanting to admit what came next, but knew Adam needed to know the truth. "When I leased the store I didn't want him around," John said in an embarrassed and somewhat ashamed tone. "I thought he might scare the customers because he was a mess and smelled pretty bad. But I got to know him and ah, offered him somewhere to clean up." Seeing the miserable expression on Adam's face, John quickly said, "He's getting better, Adam... even if he still doesn't say much."

Adam took a few minutes to process the information and sat back in his seat, eyes following the condensation forming on his glass of orange juice. A lot of questions vied for attention in his thoughts; some he wasn't sure he wanted to be answered. Finally he looked up with a sigh and asked, "But he knows you're here with me?"

"Yeah, he does," John said softly. "Please understand that even *this* is a huge step for him, Adam. Even you talking to me has him terrified."

"Why? Why is he scared of me?" Adam scowled in confusion and John instantly tried to pacify him.

"I really don't think that's it. I think he's afraid of what you might say. No, that's not it. He's ashamed, Adam. Ashamed of leaving you, ashamed of how he's had to survive...." John shook his head, knowing he couldn't follow that path with David's son, and said instead, "Your dad never stopped loving you, Adam."

A tear made its way down Adam's cheek. "Will he ever talk to me, John?"

"I think so," John said with some confidence, because after meeting Adam he honestly believed it could happen.

Adam sat forward and took his first mouthful of juice and asked, "Can *we* talk again?"

"Yeah," John replied with a grin. "We can do that."

BY the time John parked his car, the store was already closed, yet he still peered through the front door to check it was empty. John briefly looked up at the front windows of the apartment. No sign of life. He walked to the doorway.

The living room was quiet; still no sign of David. He stood and listened. Somehow he knew David was around. At the barest sound of water moving, John turned to the bathroom and tapped lightly on the door before trying the knob. It was unlocked.

The bathroom was warm and steamy when John peered around the door and said quietly, "I'm home." David looked over at him with a small smile and nodded.

"Stating the obvious, I know." John returned the smile and wandered over to the bath to sit on the edge. He dipped his fingertips into the warm water and said softly, "Been some time since we did this." David sighed and nodded again while John dunked the sponge into the bath and squeezed the water over David's shoulder. The intimate moment gave them a chance to just be together before the conversation started.

David closed his eyes and waited.

"Adam's a good kid, Dave," John began quietly. "He misses you, but I think he understands." When the words started, David slumped forward and stared at the ripples he'd created in the water. John watched him carefully and whispered, "Mind if I join you in there?" David didn't look up or say anything, but slowly shuffled forward, creating a small wave that washed to the edge of the bath and enough room for John to settle behind him. With a small touch of acknowledgment on David's shoulder, John stood up and calmly removed his clothes, throwing them over the chair on top of David's.

The water threatened to spill onto the floor when he lowered himself into the warm tub, but it felt good against his tense muscles. John let out a low moan and settled back against the warm porcelain. "Come here," he murmured and slid his arms around David, pulling him gently between his legs. Without a word David leaned back into John's embrace to rest against his chest. They sat in near silence, the only sound being the occasional water ripple and John's lips as he kissed the wet hair clinging to David's temple.

When David turned his face and glanced up at him, John said, "He didn't understand why you left, Dave. Your wife told him you'd found someone else."

"No," David said quietly at first, but he repeated it with a slight edge of anger creeping into his voice.

"It's okay," John soothed him. "I told Adam that wasn't true."

"There was no one then," he whispered again.

"I know," John murmured and rested his cheek on David's hair. John knew this would be hard, but he wasn't quite prepared for how much *he* would hurt at David's distress. He exhaled slowly, understanding that this had to happen, and waited.

"I was scared. I couldn't figure things out and the more I tried the more confused I got. It... it was as if connections weren't in my head anymore. I knew they should be and they weren't there." The fear was evident in his voice as David tried to articulate how he felt, tried to work through it the way Barbara was teaching him. "I don't remember leaving. I knew I needed to.... Then I was cold and ...."

John felt the tension building in David's body and gently stroked his hair. "Adam knows something was wrong," John reassured and distracted him. "He asked me if you'd been ill. I told him that I thought so."

"I should have been stronger for him."

"Fuck, Dave." John sighed. "We all want to be stronger and better. Sometimes just to prove that we're good enough to be respected... or loved."

David quietly nodded and reached to find John's hand.

John took a long breath and said, "But in the meantime, my arse has gone to sleep and the water's getting cold." He kissed David and motioned for him to sit up. "I think we need to dry off, cook some dinner, and figure out what you want me to say to your son next time we meet."

CHAPTER 26

NAIL-BITTEN fingers touched the picture with a reverence usually reserved for a priceless treasure. They carefully turned the tattered-edged page to look at a montage of sketches; some finished, some roughly rendered, but all of John. Adam took in each sketch in turn, noting the fine detail in and around the eyes and the gentle curve of the lips. He looked up at John and asked the question that had been on his mind since the day at the gallery. "So you and my dad?" He left it hanging there and gave a single shrug, not knowing how to finish it.

John smiled and was able to say, "We're together, Adam, if that's what you're asking." He had discussed this with David, what to say and what to omit, but they'd both agreed they had to be up front with David's son about their relationship.

Adam nodded and looked back at the page. "I thought so," he said quietly. "That day at the gallery… you looked together."

"Looked together, huh?" John couldn't resist saying with a grin on his face.

"You know… comfortable with each other," Adam said and rolled his eyes at John. "I watched you two for a little while because I wasn't sure if it *was* my dad. His hair is a lot longer and he's so skinny."

John's eyes widened and he shook his head. "Dave's put so much weight on in the past few months."

"Nah, he's skinny," Adam said with a surety that made John laugh. "Not what he was like when I was a kid. Not that he was fat or anything; just more, um, solid."

"What *was* he like when you were young? Can you tell me that?" John asked, wanting to understand more about David before both depression and the street took hold of him.

"Dad? He was always a bit of a dag." Adam grinned and leaned back in his seat. "When I was just a kid we used to make up really sick jokes. You know, gross stuff, and Mum used to tell us off all the time. Of course that just made us do it even more."

John smiled and tried very hard to imagine David laughing and telling jokes; it saddened him that he couldn't quite do it.

"But I dunno, he did stuff different from a lot of dads. I mean, he played football with me, but he'd do other things too." Adam's smile took on an almost wistful shape as he remembered one particular thing. "Like my elf books."

Seeing the curious look, Adam quickly leaned forward as if he were telling John an important secret, but the light in his eyes told John it was a good memory. "Every now and then he'd say to me that the elves had visited us and then we'd hunt around the garden looking under bushes and even in the trees until we'd find a tiny little book. Really tiny; the size of a matchbook. It was full of drawings and a story about a boy named Adam." He shook his head as if still in awe of their find. "The pictures were always so detailed and it took me ages to figure out Dad did them for me. I still have a couple of them."

John smiled, watching the joy in Adam's face, but he said nothing, not wanting to break into the precious memory. After a brief moment Adam shrugged and with a long sigh went back to looking at the sketchbook. Turning the page, he pointed at a picture of Jamie. "Who's this guy?"

Tilting his head for a better look John grinned at the almost childlike mischief that hid Jamie's gentle wisdom and explained. "That's Jamie. It was his mum who took David into the store. Jamie shares his sandwich with him every day and he's the one who convinced me to give your dad a chance."

"He looks like a good person," Adam mused, looking at the typically generous expression David had captured in Jamie's eyes.

"He is," John agreed. "He taught me a few things about human decency. I was all set to put profit before your dad's well-being. To be honest, I didn't even consider him as a person at the start." Actually stating that out loud to David's son shook John, but acceptance of his own flaws was something else he'd recently started to learn. He looked up at Adam and admitted, "Jamie made me think about how cold it got at night and how unsafe it was for people like your dad."

"People like my dad," Adam repeated quietly, trying to get it clear in his head that the father he'd known could be seen by society as a whole different category of human being.

John slowly reached over and ran his fingers along the twisted and broken spiral binding. "His sketchbooks were the only thing he had; his connection to you and us. He got beaten up pretty badly to stop them being taken from him. He lost everything else but saved this one. He asked me to bring it today to give it to you, Adam."

Adam sat and didn't lift his eyes from the book or make a move to answer, but John could see the tight clench of his jaw. It was something he'd seen in David far too many times. Resisting his long-held pattern of avoidance, John said softly, "It's okay, lad. He just wanted you to know that he loves you... always has."

Adam nodded and carefully slid the sketchbook into his school bag. John felt an unexpected twinge of anxiety when the book disappeared from his sight but assured himself that this was what David wanted and his son had a right to it.

SIDE by side at the kitchen sink, one washing and the other drying, John filled David in on the final details of his conversation with Adam.

"He said you were a dag, you know." John chuckled at the "Aussie-ism" and gave him a sideways glance, still trying to picture David in that role.

"He's right." David grinned but kept his eyes down on the tea towel moving rhythmically over the rim of the white dinner plate.

"Said you used to make up gross jokes."

"I did," David replied this time with a light giggle.

John shook his head, bumped him gently with his hip, and said softly, "Dag."

This time David actually laughed and bumped him back. It was a small gesture, but enough to make John's heart swell. He stood and grinned at David for a moment before dipping a couple of fingers into the dishwater and scooping a well-aimed soap bubble at David.

Looking down at the bubbles popping to spread a dark wet patch on his T-shirt, David raised his eyebrows, looked John straight in the eye, and flicked him with the towel.

"Oh, it's like that, is it?" John growled and rounded on David, who instantly took a step back, still chuckling. But rather than grabbing at the towel, John's hand cupped the back of David's head and he leaned in to snatch a kiss. Their teeth clashed a little as they smiled through the kiss, but neither minded.

David's hands moved forward to rest lightly on John's hips and this time *he* initiated the kiss. It was slow and tentative at first, but deepened when their tongues found each other. The damp towel dropped to the floor as David tightened his grip and pulled John closer, pressing hard against him. Their playful struggle changed into a sensual dance as their hips slowly slid together while they breathed each other's air.

John's hand slipped under the hem of David's T-shirt, brushing over ribs now barely evident beneath the smooth flesh. He nipped lightly at David's bottom lip while his fingers dropped lower to trace the outline of David's budding erection through the worn fabric of his jeans. John slowly eased the zipper down and slid his hand between denim and heated skin to press his palm against the hardening flesh. When David turned his hip into the touch John curled his fingers to feel the weight of the needy cock.

David's head tipped back; half-open eyes focused on John while he moaned and pushed his hips into each movement of John's hand. Although the obvious desire in David's eyes surprised John, he went with their need and slowly moved them the few steps back to the wall. Strong hands moved from the open jeans to grip slender hips. In a single near-urgent action John quickly turned David to the wall to lean hard against him while sliding lips and tongue over the light sweat on the back of David's neck.

The faded wallpaper against his cheek shifted. *Rough concrete scraped an already fist-bloodied cheek and David tensed, waiting for the pain.*

It was the sudden stillness that alerted John more than anything else. His breath was ragged when he whispered, "Dave?"

No response.

The realization of their position, of what it might mean to David, swept through John, leaving him filled with fear-driven nausea. His breathing hitched and faltered while he tried to calm himself against David's back. Although his instant reaction was to haul David away from the wall and splutter out heartfelt apologies, John hesitated and listened to something more instinctual. Easing off just enough to release some of the pressure, John leaned gently against David, his hands soft as they brushed lightly over the unresponsive body.

The first few words made no sounds and perhaps no sense while John tried to settle himself. Gradually he found his voice.

"I don't know where you are right now, David, but I'm here if you need me. Look for me, Davey. I'm here," he finally managed to whisper. He repeated these and other words over and over, trying to keep his tone calm and level.

Clutching, grasping hurting fingers slowed... changed... gentle and soft, not pushing, not tearing... words of threat and filth found disappeared into an accent... they whispered and caressed forcing the other words into silence....

John.

The tension under his hands slowly began to subside and John rested his forehead lightly on David's shoulder. "That's it, Dave," he murmured, giving in to his own relief. "You're here with me and I'll never hurt you."

John slowly slid his arms around David's waist and eased him away from the wall, keeping him close against his own body. David stood disoriented. Though his eyes were open he wasn't yet seeing the room. He closed them and listened, listened to the northern accent made soft by the gentle tone. David continued to lean against the warm body that issued that low rumbling voice and began to understand that he'd found his way back to John. Consciously slowing his breathing as he'd been taught, David let go of the last threads of the other reality and whispered, "I'm sorry, John."

"Oh, David, you have *nothing* to be sorry for," John reassured him, his voice cracking just a little. He took a deep breath and raised his head. "Absolutely nothing."

He carefully brushed David's hair behind his ear and placed a chaste kiss on his neck. "Would you like to lie down for a while? I can put the kettle on and make us a drink."

David listened, took a breath, and straightened. He glanced at John and nodded.

"Come on then…. You'll feel better in your own bed. I'll make us tea and be in in a minute," John babbled as he walked with David to the door of the bedroom, his hand resting lightly on the small of his back until David gave him a tired smile and wandered into the dark room. It was only when he made it into the kitchen that John felt the shaking seize his body. He slumped against the kitchen bench, shoulders bent, and seemed to crumple. The sounds he made were small as they bounced around the otherwise silent room.

Slowly, very slowly, John became quiet and the shudders eased. He was tired to the very marrow of his bones and at that moment knew he needed to be near David.

He straightened and looked toward the bedroom, but he hesitated; part of him needed to make their tea first. He roughly scrubbed at his eyes with the palm of his hand and set the cups on the counter, each with its own saucer and teaspoon. Even though he knew it would still be sitting un-drunk and stone cold in the morning, he went through the entire process of properly preparing the beverage.

When the tea was ready John stood and looked at it. He shook his head and walked out of the kitchen, leaving the full cups where they sat.

The only light in the bedroom came from the waning moon in the corner of the window. John could just make out David's body beneath the quilt. He slowly shed his clothes and snuggled in behind David, where he carefully put an arm around him. Many layers of anxiety dissolved when David leaned back against him with a quiet "Hey."

"Hey yourself," he murmured and kissed the bare skin of David's shoulder. "You okay?"

David turned his face enough to see John and gave him a small nod. "I'm okay."

John heaved a long sigh and held David closer. "While I made the tea, I was thinking about the first time we made love. I was so scared for you… and me."

David frowned, but John continued. "I was so scared I'd hurt you. We were like this, me behind you, and I wanted you so much." His hand moved down to gently caress David's hip bone, subconsciously mimicking his actions of that night.

David closed his eyes and let John's voice and touch bring it all back to him. "I knew you wouldn't hurt me, John," he mumbled, understanding that it was one of the few things he did know at the time.

John's fingers splayed out over the pale skin, reading the changes beneath them. The bones weren't quite so angular and they didn't need to hesitate over the purple and yellow blemishes of a recent beating. This time John's fingers didn't tremble and were sure of their touch; this was David, the man he loved and who loved him back.

CHAPTER 27

YOU learn fast on the street. David had wandered for days with no purpose or even an understanding of why he was there. He just knew he needed to walk.

But he learned quickly to keep his eyes down when around large groups of teenage boys partying their freedom on a Friday night. Communication with other humans was rare and generally to be avoided.

Give *nothing* away about yourself and you might remain safe.

David knew the times public toilets were locked after dark; then it was parks, alleys, and vacant lots. He watched old-timers stuff their clothes with discarded newspapers in bitter weather and followed suit. Anything to stay warm and survive another day where the sun may come out.

David knew he'd never lose what he'd learned. Even here with John snoring lightly against his back, it would stay with him despite their skin sharing warmth in the first gray of dawn.

"I LAY in bed and watched him sleep last night," John said softly with an embarrassed shrug, not even sure why it was relevant. But Barbara smiled, understanding that he'd get around to what he wanted to say when he was ready.

"Last night...." John stopped and gave a slightly frustrated glance at the ceiling. "Things have been going so well. Then last night I think I pushed him... David, too hard. We were um, *playing around* and we got carried away. I held him against the wall and he kind of disappeared. It was as if he went into himself. I *frightened* him, Barb, and it was only when I stopped and talked to him that he was able to come back."

Barbara shook her head and reached over to touch his hand. "No, John. That's not totally true. It wasn't you that frightened him. There are places in David's memories that I'm sure neither of us would want to be. They're going to surface from time to time and, as scary as it might seem, that needs to happen."

It was John's turn to shake his head. "I don't understand. How can what I saw him go through last night help?"

"Burying things doesn't help. You two are very similar in that way. Far too similar in fact," she said, as an almost cheeky smile crept into the corners of her mouth. "The main difference is that you were given some good advice and found your little store before it all became too much for you."

She sat back and sipped her coffee to let John mull over the concept. Finally he nodded his acceptance and she continued. "He's learning, John; learning how to cope with both his past and his present. I don't think he's ready to deal with thinking about his future yet. You know I can't tell you what we discuss in our sessions, but he's working so hard at it. And from what you just told me it's helping... *you* are helping. Don't look so surprised! What you did through instinct, talking to him, was what he needed to help him find a way home when he got lost."

When he got lost.... John knew that was true because that's exactly how it had felt. Looking down at his hands, John voiced the one fear that still ate at him. "What if I can't always do that?"

"Then you can't, John," Barbara answered with total and somewhat unnerving honesty. "But I believe he's not the same man who slept here clutching his sketchbooks. David won't always hide now. He'll look for *you*, John."

"Fuck," John cursed quietly and tightened his fingers around his mug.

But Barbara just gave him a small laugh and asked, "So how are *you* doing, John?"

"Me? I'm okay," John replied as if to deny his white knuckles.

"Of course you are," Barbara commented with a raised eyebrow, making John laugh.

JAMIE hunched over the counter flicking through a magazine, not really taking time over any of the articles, but doing that aimless browsing we adopt when avoiding onerous work tasks. A shadow passed over a picture of a celebrity who was trying to prove that they'd eaten at least once in their lifetime and Jamie looked up to give the elderly customer his best smile. "Adele, what can I do for you today?"

She gave him a slightly confused frown and placed a small parcel on the counter. Jamie looked at it and then back to the woman, wondering if he was supposed to know what this meant. "Is that for me?"

Adele shook her head and pointed to the front of the store. "A young man was sitting outside and gave it to me to bring in for his dad. *David,* I think he said. That's the quiet man who stays near the old books, isn't it? Didn't look big enough to be dangerous, the package I mean, so I brought it in."

Jamie immediately looked in the direction she'd indicated but saw no one through the window. "Um, can you do me a favor and look after the store for a minute?" Jamie asked, already heading toward the door.

"Look after the store," Adele muttered and moved behind the counter with an air of authority. "I worked in retail for over forty years; I could *run* this store."

Jamie rushed out onto the street, but could only see a group of mothers listening to schoolyard tales as they walked their children home. "Shit," he cursed quietly but still received an admonishing glare from one of the women. Jamie muttered a quick sorry and gave her an apologetic smile. It was then he saw past the group to spot the back of a teenage boy disappearing up the street.

It was only a glimpse, yet it was enough to send Jamie jogging up the street until he was able to stretch out his arm and touch the boy's shoulder. "Adam? It is Adam, isn't it?" Jamie asked hopefully when the young man stopped and turned toward him.

Adam gave Jamie a long look before finally nodding. "Yeah. I, ah, I don't want to cause any trouble. I know I'm not supposed to be here."

"It's okay," Jamie said quickly, seeing how flustered Adam was at being approached. He nodded toward a nearby bench and starting walking, watching to make sure the teenager followed him. "I'm just surprised you knew how to find us."

"It was pretty easy," Adam started quietly. "I mean, I knew John's name and that he had a bookstore so it didn't take me long to run a few searches on the Net." He glanced sideways at Jamie and shrugged.

"Fuck, I can barely do e-mail stuff." Jamie giggled, even though he was actually quite proficient on a computer. "So you found your dad?"

"Yeah, but I know I need to give him time; John and I have talked about that." Adam looked down at his hands and picked at a bit of dry skin next to his nail, threatening to make it bleed. Jamie nodded a little sadly. "Your dad is such a good person, Adam. He's worth waiting for, and he'll get there. So why the present?"

By this stage Adam had decided that he liked this Jamie guy and that his dad had got him just right in the sketch. He smiled and announced, "Today's his birthday."

Jamie stared for a second. "Yeah? Shit, he kept that pretty quiet. But knowing Dave I guess that shouldn't surprise me."

"I just wanted him to have something. To know I'm thinking about him," Adam suggested, not sure if he was expressing how he really felt. "That's okay, isn't it? He'll be okay with that?"

Jamie had no idea *how* David would react to the realization that his son knew where he was but chose to reassure the worried teenager. "I think it'll mean a lot to him, Adam."

Adam nodded and looked down the street to where he could just make out the front of the bookstore. "Is he in there now?"

Briefly following Adam's line of sight, Jamie quietly confirmed, "Yeah. Dave's in his favorite old leather chair with his nose buried in a book."

It took several rapid blinks to clear the moisture that welled in Adam's eyes at the scene he could so easily picture, and it hurt to know his dad was that close and he couldn't talk to him. "I miss him."

For an instant all Jamie wanted to do was to grab Adam's hand and walk him through the door of Margins and sit him in the battered chair next to his father, but he knew he couldn't do that to David. He'd come so far in the past year; each small step took courage and those steps had to be his own. "He misses you too, Adam," Jamie sighed. "He wants to be part of your life, but give him a bit longer, yeah?"

Adam nodded and stood up. "I know, more time. I better get going. My mum will be expecting me home. Tell my dad I said happy birthday, okay?"

"I will... *and* give him a hard time for not telling us." Jamie smiled and patted Adam on the back before turning toward Margins.

"The wanderer returns." John grinned at Adele but made it very obvious the comment was directed at Jamie. Without even acknowledging the dig, Jamie bent forward to give Adele a quick kiss and said, "Thank you. I managed to talk to him and everything's all right."

"That's good," she whispered as if they shared a secret, and then said a little louder, "Keep me in mind if you ever need advice on retail; did it for years, you know." She gave them a cheeky smile and walked very straight-backed out of the store.

"Now what was that all about?" John asked, standing with arms folded and a curious grin on his face.

"It was Adam," Jamie whispered and shoved John toward their little kitchen. "He was here."

The color visibly drained from John's face. "Fuck. What happened? Is Dave all right?" He instantly made to move out the door but Jamie quickly held up his hands. "Dave doesn't know. Adam didn't come in."

Dave doesn't know. "Okay... okay." John rubbed his fingers over his mouth, taking a moment to process the situation. "Why was he here? What did Adam want?"

Digging the little parcel out of his pocket, Jamie showed it to John and said, "It's David's birthday."

John looked from the parcel to Jamie and then out to the store. "He didn't say anything." John's voice was quiet and held a tinge of hurt.

"Maybe he doesn't know?" Jamie offered. "I mean, he doesn't seem to follow a regular calendar. He only found out it was nearly Adam's birthday by accident, remember, and he'd see that as more important than his own birthday."

John nodded sadly; he remembered that only too well… and what David had resorted to to see his son. Finally he turned back to Jamie with a very determined look and said, "Dave has a present to open from his son."

David was sitting buried in the second book of a trilogy, boots beside the chair and a leg curled beneath him. It was a familiar sight to John, but it still had the power to make his heart rise into his throat. "Do you know what day it is, Dave?" John said quietly and sat next to him. When David just nodded, John pushed the little package into his hand and admitted, "I didn't know, but Adam did."

The tension in David's body was instant; he stared at the package as if it contained all the ills of the world.

"He brought it for you," John explained carefully. "He didn't come in, Dave…. Adam's a good boy."

When David didn't move John began to gently rub his hand over the knotted muscles at the back of David's neck. "You want me to leave it with you?"

The question took a while to register and David's eyes drifted up to John's before returning to his hands. Slowly his fingers began to peel off the tape; three pieces in all. Next the blue foil wrapping was folded back and David held in his hand a tiny book.

John leaned forward to get a better look. "It's an elf book." The comment was whispered but held the awe David remembered in little Adam's voice. He looked up at John and smiled. "Yeah… it is."

Together they sat in the leather chairs and read through the story of a teenage boy called Adam who had searched for a misplaced treasure only to find he hadn't lost it at all.

THE insistent ring finally broke through the dreams of sleep. With a groan John threw back the covers and grumbled all the way to the living room, ready to give the caller a serve.

"Hello, may I speak to John McCann please?" The voice was that of an elderly woman trying hard to mask a prominent accent in a "proper telephone voice".

"Speaking." John frowned; the familiarity of the voice took away the last of his anger even though he couldn't quite put a face to it.

"Hello, pet. It's your Aunt Annie."

John was quiet when he slid back into bed. David lay on his side and watched John settle without a word of who was on the phone. "You okay?" he whispered, hating how his voice echoed in the silence of the dark room.

At first there was no answer and the question seemed to hang between them, but finally John said in an oddly matter-of-fact voice, "My dad died."

When nothing else was said, David shuffled the short distance between them and leaned into John's back. His fingers gently threaded through fine blond hair that took on a bluish-silver hue in the moonlight of the open curtains. With lips inches from the pale curve of John's ear, David murmured, "You need to go home, John."

There was the barest shake of his head then said a soft, "I don't know."

John felt sick to the pit of his stomach, but concentrated on the gentle caress and gradually began to hear the soft hum of an unfamiliar tune. When the words started he didn't recognize them but let them wash over him until the churning eased.

Softly he whispered, "I didn't know you spoke Spanish."

"I speak Spanish."

Maybe some lessons can be unlearned and survival is more than staying warm? Sometimes you need to let your guard down and give a little more of yourself.

CHAPTER 28

JOHN dropped the empty plastic cup into the garbage bag as the cabin crew moved along the aisle to prepare the plane for landing.

He glanced down at his watch, already edgy for that calming cigarette, and caught the empathetic smile of an equally edgy businessman nearby. Returning the smile, John closed his eyes and took a deep breath.

PACKING had been something of a blur.

David sat on the edge of the bed and watched quietly as John bustled around the room, retrieving, folding, looking more than a little lost.

"I don't have to go, you know, Dave," John muttered as he looked up from the printed e-ticket.

"Yes you do." David's voice was calm and steady.

"I don't like leaving you."

"I'll be okay, John. You need to do this."

John knew David was right but it didn't make leaving any easier. He glanced at the stuffed backpack leaning against the chest of drawers and felt a tinge of the old fear. Following his gaze, David said simply and quietly, "I'll be here when you get back, John."

John nodded and pinched the bridge of his nose, fighting the headache that had been threatening all morning. His eyes were still closed when he felt arms encircle him and David's warm breath on his cheek. Letting himself be held, John leaned heavily against David before easing away and clearing his throat. "Keep your cell phone on and I'll call when I get there," he said in a businesslike voice, only to sigh when he saw the rather sheepish shrug it garnered. "You've no idea where it is, do you?"

Not expecting an answer, John half-grinned and shook his head before pulling his own phone out of his pocket. "Don't lose it.... I'll pick up another one and call when I get to Heathrow."

THE "fasten seat belts" sign pinged on, pulling John back to the cramped cabin. He sighed with the knowledge that David was half a world away and he was instantly hit with a wave of helplessness. Even more than that, John felt alone.

DAVID remained on the sidewalk for a long while after watching John's cab pull away. He was reluctant to go inside. The apartment would be empty.

He slumped against the cold bricks, ignoring the strange looks of early morning passersby as they made their way to work. With eyes safely downcast, David rhythmically scuffed the heel of his boot against the wall while gathering the courage to go inside.

You told John you'd be all right... so be *all right.* David frowned, pushed away from the wall, and wandered up the stairs to their apartment.

With the rush of packing over, the apartment was quiet, empty. After standing a little lost in the doorway David found himself wandering around the living room like he had during his first days with John; looking at the other man's belongings. Missing him; needing him to say it was okay.

He huffed a frustrated breath. *I'm past this now.* He refocused and actually looked at the photos. Things *were* different. Next to the photo of John and his grandparents was a silver frame with a snapshot of John and David on the couch eating Chinese from takeout containers. David smiled, remembering how Jamie took the shot before they even realized what he was doing. His fingertip traced over the grainy image.

Maybe he *could* be part of all this now?

A sudden knock on the door startled him. David quickly moved away from the shelves to lean against the kitchen counter, not intending to answer.

Jamie stood and listened for a minute, then, rather than knocking again, said gently but loud enough to be heard, "Dave, it's me… Jamie."

David grinned and walked over to the door, opening it a crack. "John called you, huh?"

"Of course. The boss has to keep me in line if he's gonna be away," Jamie joked, waiting for David to allow him in. "And yes, before you ask, he did ask me to keep an eye on you. You know what he's like."

"I know." David smiled, the thought already making him feel a little safer.

Jamie cocked an eyebrow and held up a familiar brown bakery bag. "So here I am, breakfast bagel ready to share, and looking for a cup of hot tea."

THE sitting room had that old-fashioned smell; over-brewed tea and stale potpourri. Not a surface was left bare; shelves were cluttered with faded photographs and mismatched ornaments. John glanced around, remembering visiting his aunt as a small child and being told by his gran that he could look but not touch. It was a whole different world and one he thought he'd left behind long ago.

Aunt Annie sat beside him on the old but neat sofa and took his hand. "He never wanted to leave you, John," she said softly in a Geordie accent that sounded less exotic than it did when John was a child who'd never ventured further than his grandfather's Yorkshire allotment. "Things were different back then."

Looking down at the pale translucent skin of her wrinkled hand, John shook his head. "It doesn't matter now."

"Of course it matters, and don't think you can get away with that with me, John McCann." Aunt Annie looked at him over her glasses, a look John remembered all too well.

He laughed quietly. "I never could, could I?"

"No." She patted his hand and stood up to refill his cup from the cozy-covered teapot.

John grinned at the delicately painted china lady perched on the wide crocheted skirt. It always sat atop a "good" teapot; like the one he only got to drink from when he was home sick and his grandmother tucked him up on the sofa in front of the TV.

"The good teapot," John smiled.

Annie chuckled and set it back on the sideboard. "I think you deserve it today."

"Yeah," John murmured, picking up the cup.

"You were always his son, John," Annie said softly. "Even though he wasn't always able to be part of your life you were his little boy."

John simply looked away. "At least I'll get a chance to say goodbye this time."

FRUSTRATION and anger fought for supremacy over anxiety. David sat and stared at the plate of cookies in the middle of the table. His sessions with Barbara were never easy and he'd almost backed out today.

Too hard....

"What are you thinking, David?" Barbara asked after watching him for a while.

David shrugged and grumbled, "Nothing."

She sighed and waited. He could be obstinate in his denial but waiting frequently achieved more than pushing.

"I sometimes feel like I almost have a grasp on things," he muttered so quietly that Barbara had to strain to hear. "I can think clearly... then it's gone again."

"What gets in the way?"

Finally David looked up and gave her a slightly sad smile. "Me."

"Uh-huh." Barbara smiled back. "And we both know you're getting there... *if* you let yourself."

LOOKING around the room was disconcerting. John had met very few of his father's family and, now surrounded by cousins, he was a little overwhelmed by his resemblance to them. He smiled, shook hands, and made small talk. The older ones told him stories about his father while the younger were more interested in his life in Australia. Annie watched and waited until she could gently ease him away with the excuse of helping her in the kitchen.

"Thanks," he smiled and shook his head. "It's all a bit too much in one hit."

"They all want to know about the relation who made it big in Australia." Annie returned his smile and lifted down the tea caddy. "But tell me, did you ever think about coming back here, John?"

John shook his head. "It was easier to get away; people judged you here and I never wanted...." He stopped. Holding the kettle under the tap John watched the stream of water as he thought about how to continue. "I knew it could be difficult for Gran and Granddad."

Annie took the kettle from him and put it on the stove. She led John over to the table and indicated for him to sit with her. "John, love, your gran always knew."

"She never said anything," John whispered, frowning down at the starched table-cloth.

"You were always a private boy, John, and your gran understood that," Annie commented. "But it doesn't mean she wasn't watching out for you. When you were with that lass in Australia she worried that you weren't being true to yourself."

John gave a slightly nervous laugh. "Marian and I were... well, we were never really a couple."

Annie nodded. "Before she passed, your gran said to me that you hadn't found the right one yet... but you would if you let it happen." When the color rose in John's cheeks, Annie leaned forward in her seat and asked, "So are you going to tell your old Aunty his name?"

"David." John grinned as the blush spread further across his face. "His name's David."

"A good name." Annie winked.

THE day had felt long. A sketchbook lay on the other side of the bed, the worn pencil nub sitting on a half-drawn face. The light had faded and although David knew he just needed to lean over to turn on the bedside light, he lacked both the motivation and energy.

He closed his eyes and sighed. David had spent a long time alone but lately he'd grown accustomed to having a warm body next to him, being part of someone's life.

He missed John.

Slowly David's thoughts drifted until his breathing slowed and his eyes became heavy.

The buzz of the cell phone startled him. He sat up on the bed for several seconds until the blood pounding in his ears cleared enough to understand what the sound was.

John. He grabbed at the phone and flipped it open with an expectant "John? Hello?"

Adam did not expect to hear his father's voice. "Um… Dad?"

David was paralyzed; he could neither speak nor move.

"Dad? That's you, isn't it?" Adam whispered, listening to the breathing on the other end of the phone.

When there was no response other than panicked breaths, Adam pleaded quietly, "Please don't hang up."

The pain in David's chest was palpable as he listened to his son. He wanted to reply, tell Adam he was okay, but for that he'd have to speak, and speaking wasn't an option.

Squeezing his eyes tightly against the threatening tears, Adam clung onto the phone. But then he heard it. A soft tap in the earpiece, and he allowed himself a little bit of hope.

Adam remembered days when he was so angry with his parents over something that seemed all-important at the time that he would sit at his desk wound so tight he knew he would explode if he was made to talk. His mum raged and carried on, but his dad never tried to make him answer. Instead he simply gave Adam the option to tap on the desk; once for yes and twice for no. It usually resulted in him banging the desk so hard it vibrated against the wall, but it worked. As his dad talked the taps got lighter until Adam knew he could say what he felt without losing it completely.

"Thank you," Adam murmured into the mouthpiece. He flopped back onto his bed and asked, "Can I talk to you Dad? Maybe tell you about school or something? Would that be okay?"

David's finger touched the phone once. Not very loudly, but enough for Adam to smile and start retelling his day.

IN a single bed far away, John finally drifted off to sleep, his packed bag leaning against the wall in anticipation of an early long-haul flight.

CHAPTER 29

"WE did good," Jamie announced as he pushed the cash register closed and locked the drawer. "You know, I sometimes think that John doubts we can manage without him. And we just proved we can."

Just barely, David thought to himself, but was pleased that they'd made it through another working day on their own.

"So what do you have planned for tonight, Dave? Big party?" Jamie asked, knowing full well that David would simply closet himself in the apartment and wait it out until John came home. And that was still likely to be a day or two away.

David grinned and said, "*Huge* party with me and my closest friends."

"I'm invited then!" Jamie laughed as he started switching off the store lights. "Actually I'm at a loose end tonight and was wondering if you'd like some company?"

"I'm okay, Jamie…. Really," David confirmed with a warm smile.

"I know," Jamie said and pulled a face. "But… oh look, indulge me, yeah? Maybe just a walk or we could grab something to eat?"

David knew Jamie meant well and, though he would never admit it, got a little lonely at times. "I wouldn't mind a walk." He shrugged with a smile and stepped through the front door while Jamie set the alarm code.

The walk was more of a stroll but it gave David a chance to unwind and clear his head. He blew out a breath and watched the white puff of air as it slowly disappeared. "Winter's setting in," he commented and pulled his jacket a little tighter.

Jamie slipped his arm through David's as he said, "I'm glad you have somewhere warm now. I used to worry about you out here."

David just nodded and pulled Jamie a little closer.

"I asked my mum once if I could ask you to stay with us, but she told me you wouldn't and I might embarrass you by asking." Jamie came to a halt and looked at David. "Was she right?"

With a slight frown, David moved them to the ledge on the edge of a store window and sat down. "I think she might have been," he said still thinking it through. "It wasn't so much that I'd be embarrassed. Maybe more that I couldn't be around anyone back then." The frown deepened because he knew his explanation wasn't clear. David scuffed the toe of his boot over a blackened cigarette butt before looking back at his friend. "You and your mum were the first people who saw me as a person in a long while. I felt safe in Margins, and I didn't want to mess that up."

"Mess it up how?" Jamie asked.

"The mess is in here, I suppose," David muttered and tapped lightly on his head. "You're good people and I...." He shrugged; what else was there to say?

Jamie didn't look totally convinced but he leaned against David and said, "Well, I suppose John was just as messed up but in a different way, huh?"

The frown lifted from David's face and he laughed. "Don't let *him* hear you say that."

"Oh, I won't," Jamie giggled. "But it's kinda true. John had no clue how to actually live his life when he came to Margins. All accounts and business meetings; real relationships weren't part of the agenda. I think he was scared of you at the start because you made him feel something and there was no column for that in his accounts ledger."

"I was pretty scared too," David admitted. "I couldn't understand why he'd want to be with me. I mean...." He stopped and debated whether or not to say what was playing through his mind. Finally he admitted, "I knew you two had a night together and you said it was nothing, but it did make me wonder why he even looked at me after being with you."

Jamie was more than a little stunned. He shook his head and stared at David. "It wasn't even a night, Dave. John couldn't get out of my place fast enough; fuck, he didn't even kiss me. We had some fun, blew off some energy, and nothing more, whereas he *loves* you. You've been so good for him."

"It's mutual," David murmured, breaking into a broad and somewhat sheepish grin.

"Oh God." Jamie groaned happily and squeezed David's arm. "Let's get going."

David nodded but didn't make a move. His hand found Jamie's and he asked, "Did it bother you that John didn't stay?"

"Didn't bother me so much," Jamie mused. "Just made me wonder what was going on with him. I think I told him that he should spend his time with someone he loves... or was it not spend his time with someone he doesn't love?" He shrugged and laid his head on David's shoulder. "I think he listened to me."

"I think he did." David smiled, hoping that whoever found Jamie would deserve his love. "Hey, you wanna go somewhere with me?"

"Um... yeah?" Jamie said suspiciously.

"Come on then." David stood and led Jamie down the street.

AS Jamie handed a plate to the last person in the queue, he turned and grinned at David. Someone else also smiled and David felt a hand gently touch his arm. "I was surprised when I saw you two arrive," Barbara whispered. "But it really was a big help to have a couple of extra pairs of hands."

David smiled back. Although he was so weary all his joints literally ached, David felt good.

"Come and have a drink with me," Barbara suggested, easily seeing how tired he was. "I think Jamie's quite happy helping Brian clean up."

Glancing over his shoulder, David could see his friend involved in an animated conversation with the young social worker. He followed Barbara through to the staff kitchen.

Handing him a mug, Barbara said, "Thank you for tonight; there are never enough volunteers in these places. Most people drop by on Christmas Day and believe that gives them the right to forget about us for the rest of the year." David smiled in his usual self-deprecating way and sipped the hot coffee. Barbara just chuckled and reached for the cookie tin. Armed with a chocolate chip cookie, she commented, "You're doing better, aren't you?"

Looking down into his mug, David admitted quietly, "I think I am." He leaned over and took an offered cookie. "When John left I... I dunno."

"You lost your safety net?" Barbara suggested.

"Yeah."

"But you're doing okay, aren't you?" Although it was framed as a question both of them knew it was a statement of fact.

David grinned and nodded. "I think I am."

"Next question," she stated and smiled at David's near playful grimace. "And this is a tough one."

"Okay, let's hear it," he said with a smile, but mentally braced himself for what Barbara was likely to ask.

"How are you going to move on from this?"

A simple enough question, David thought. *So why is it so hard to answer?* "I'm not sure, Barb," he finally said, while rubbing his hand in slight agitation over the back of his neck.

"Come on, Dave; you know what you need to start thinking about." Her voice was calm, assured, and pushed David just enough that he had to focus.

"Adam." The name came easily; easier than David thought it could. He looked up at her and nodded. "I think I'm getting closer to... closer to being able to talk to him."

Barbara smiled and reached across to give his hand a gentle squeeze. She didn't touch David often, but he was moving through so many obstacles that she felt he wouldn't object. "You don't have to do it all at once, David; just a little at a time. Keep yourself in a safe place—in here." She patted him lightly on the head. "And open up only what you feel you can deal with. It *will* get easier."

"Promise?" David asked with a smile that could have been cheeky if there wasn't a tinge of sadness to his voice.

Barbara raised an eyebrow and grinned. "You definitely know me better than that."

CHAPTER 30

JOHN turned the engine off but didn't get out of the car. He sat in the dark of his parking space and pulled out a cigarette. The flame of the lighter flared, briefly illuminating the interior then snapping back into darkness. Exhaling a long stream of smoke John leaned against the headrest and closed his eyes. He'd taken an earlier flight to get back to David, but now he was here....

He said he'd be here when you got back, McCann.

John stabbed the cigarette into the ashtray. *He'll be here.*

The apartment was in darkness when John closed the door behind him. He left the lights off and made his way to the bedroom. The door was slightly ajar. John stood and listened as he peered into the gloom, but even before he saw the full backpack leaning against the chest of drawers he *knew* David was there.

Carefully, quietly, John undressed, all the while watching his sleeping lover until he realized David's eyes weren't closed at all and there was a gentle smile on his face. Laying his pants over the armchair, John grinned and whispered, "I didn't want to wake you."

David simply nodded and waited for John to climb into the bed beside him. As the mattress dipped, David relaxed for the first time in days.

"You okay?" John asked, feeling a little awkward.

"I'm okay," David whispered, still smiling.

John nodded and tentatively reached out to push a strand of hair from David's face. He wanted to touch him but something, perhaps the distance of the half-world he'd just traversed, made him hold back.

The two men lay in silence watching each other until David murmured, "I missed you, John."

"Oh fuck, Dave." John rapidly closed the distance between them and took David's face in his hand. "I missed you so fucking much." Their kiss was soft, but the gentle movement of their lips contained all the need and worry of the past few days.

Slowly, David's hands moved to John's body. His fingers reacquainted themselves with the smooth expanse of fair skin, touching then moving on to touch somewhere else. Although John's tongue met David's in the kiss he held back to let the other man lead.

Recognizing the almost tentative nature of the touches, John pulled away just enough to whisper, "It's *all* okay, Dave." David gave a tiny nod and reinitiated the kiss. This time it was stronger, more insistent. His leg slipped carefully between John's until they straddled each other's thighs.

"Feels good," John moaned when David started a slow rock against him. His hands cupped David's arse to hold him close, sliding his nose over the sensitive skin where stubbled jaw met the heat of a pulse point. John felt himself sink into David's smell.

They moved together, without the desperation of the reunited, but of a couple who knew each other and were comfortable in the knowledge that the other knew them.

When they came it was quiet, just puffs of breath into each other's mouth.

As the first signs of dawn filtered through the window they'd begun talking, that "real" kind of talking that only seems to occur in the early hours of the morning. "It was... I dunno, *strange*," John said as he stared into the growing light trying to grasp exactly what it *was* like. "It was where I'm from, but not where I am now. Does that make any sense?"

David nodded and moved closer to rest under John's arm. "It makes perfect sense," he reassured, flexing and stretching his fingers until they barely made contact with John's cheek, the pads lightly brushing over a faint laugh line.

John smiled his small half-smile that David had come to recognize as a sign of uncertainty. "I told my Aunt Annie about you... that I love you." John's voice held a quiet wonder that'd he'd done something either very brave, or very foolish. "I was scared to death, but she said she knew

I wasn't the 'type' to marry and have kids... even when *I* didn't really know." John chuckled at the euphemism she'd used and turned to catch David's palm with his lips.

"I think I always knew," David whispered, as if sharing a long-held secret.

John frowned at the admission and though he rarely pushed David on his past he had to ask. "Why'd you get married then?"

David didn't need to consider his answer because it was so obvious to him. "I loved her. Still did when I left, I think." He gave a small shrug at the look John gave him. "I was... *am* gay, John, but it didn't stop me loving her, and I liked being married, having a family." He paused and frowned, knowing what he was about to say had never actually been spoken out loud. "But I don't think she ever loved me."

It was a simple sentence but one that held so much hurt John couldn't answer. *How could she* not *love you?* The question seemed so glaringly obvious yet it was one John knew he couldn't ask.

After a few moments of silence John asked quietly, "Why did she marry you then, Dave? Was it Adam?"

David shook his head. "I've been thinking about that and I dunno. I guess I gave her what she needed at the time. A home, a family, and a husband with a good job. I was useful."

Useful? What the fuck does that mean? John ignored his past approach to his relationship with Marian and ached to verbalize his distaste, but the opportunity was gone when David asked, "Did you find out why your dad left?"

"I suppose I did," John mumbled then sighed.

David nodded and lay watching the steady rise and fall of John's chest.

"I missed my dad growing up. Not all the time, just sometimes," he said and curled his fingers through David's hair. "Sometimes I just wanted to tell him things or maybe wanted him to know how I was doing. It was rarely the important things because I had my grandparents for those, but more the everyday shit." He shifted on the bed and pulled David closer. "I used to lie awake and wonder where he was; if he had a new family, if he ever thought about me. I never told Gran that, of course. Maybe I should have. Maybe I could found out before now that his new kids are my family, too, and he didn't go to leave me behind."

Light caresses graced John's chest as he spoke. He glanced down, knowing where David's mind had wandered, and pressed his lips to the hair that had fallen back over David's forehead. "He's a good boy, Dave. He'll wait."

"He talked to me, John."

The statement was so quiet that John wasn't sure he'd heard it correctly. Hauling himself, and David, a little higher against the pillow, John asked, "What do you mean he talked to you?"

David shrugged as if it was nothing, but both knew that wasn't true. "On the phone. He called. I thought it was you."

Fuck! John took a moment to give David, and himself, a little breathing space before asking as casually as he knew how, "Was it okay? I mean, what did you talk about?"

The muscles in David's jaw worked silently for a moment before he mumbled, "I didn't really say anything, but I listened and he knew I was there." John lay very still; tense to the point of pain waiting to hear more, desperate to ask for more. But he knew to listen. David's eyes slid shut and he breathed against John's skin. Slowly the words began again, "He told me about school, about a girl he likes, and...." The room grew silent as David's face contorted with the threat of tears.

"Oh fuck. It's a good thing, Dave. It's a *very* good thing," John whispered with near urgency. "He loves you. Wants you in his life and this is a start." Taking a breath, John pressed his cheek against David's hair. "Fuck, Dave. That would have meant so much to him."

Focusing on the gentle rhythm of John's breath wisping through his hair, David slowing began to release the knots of tension constricting his throat. "Did you know your dad loved you, John?"

"There's a question," John said almost flippantly, but fought the urge to leave it at that; something he'd become very good at over the years. "To be honest, Dave, I don't really know." Shifting a little, John eased them down, pulling the quilt around their shoulders. "Sometimes I believed my gran when she said he did; other times...." He sighed,

fatigue finally catching up with him. "But maybe I can live with that now?"

ADAM'S grin said it all. John couldn't resist giving him a good-natured shake of the head as he ordered their drinks and sat down at what was now their regular table. "I heard you spoke to your dad." He chuckled, the smile still creasing the corners of his eyes.

"He told you? What did he say?" Adam sat forward, barely able to contain his joy.

John thought back to their quiet conversation in the early hours of that morning and said, "Just that you'd called. He thought it'd be me."

Adam nodded. "He said your name when he picked up.... I thought he'd hang up when he knew it was me. But he didn't." Smiling at the waitress, Adam took his drink and fiddled with the straw, watching the bubbles detach from the wall of the glass and float to the surface. "I was so scared he'd hang up on me. It was as if I couldn't breathe when I heard him and I didn't know what to do, John. We used to talk all the time when I was a little kid and now, it was my *dad,* but at the same time it wasn't."

"He's still your dad, Adam," John said, well and truly relating to what the teenager was trying to come to terms with. "No matter what he's been through he's still your dad. Even if he can't be there with you I know he liked hearing you, Adam, being part of your life."

Adam looked up and asked, "Did he say that?"

John gave a single sad chuckle. "You know David; he doesn't say much of *anything*. But it was pretty clear how he felt."

With an expression that was part smile and part grimace Adam mimicked David perfectly.

"Oh I know that look all too well." John laughed. "But believe me, Adam, it meant a lot to him and he misses you."

"Then why can't he fucking *talk* to me?" Adam blurted out, but quickly regretted giving voice to thoughts he'd tried so hard to repress. "I'm sorry, I'm sorry. I really do understand, but he's my dad, John.

Sometimes I need him to be my dad. I was just a kid when he left. I'm *still* a kid. He was meant to be the strong one...."

"I know," John whispered and leaned closer to briefly touch Adam's shoulder. "Sometimes life just doesn't work out that way."

JOHN thought about Adam a lot during his drive back to the bookstore. He'd been taking it all so well that John had almost forgotten that Adam was still just a boy, a boy who'd effectively lost his dad. It was just another reminder that life wasn't that neat little jigsaw puzzle with a picture-perfect goal at the end.

He pulled the car to the side of the road, his thoughts not yet quite clear enough to relate any of the conversion to David. John released a long sigh. *How did you think this was all going to pan out? Dave would keep improving, he'd meet up with Adam, and... and what?*

John didn't have an answer.

THE tinkle of the shop bell and instant dimming of street noise settled all but the smallest amount of the anxiety that had balled in John's chest. Margins was warm and he stood for a moment to let the smell of paper and brewed tea waft over him. John smiled and wandered into the kitchen to fill his mug from the teapot he knew would be at the right temperature for drinking.

David and Jamie were sitting in the old chairs when John rounded the bookshelf. He winked at David, who was listening to a wide-eyed Jamie exclaim, "And then he fuckin' bit me!"

With a roll of his eyes John threw a paper bag into the storyteller's lap. "Here, I brought back a couple of doughnuts. They might shut you up for a while; although somehow I doubt it."

Jamie simply grinned, pulled out one of the doughnuts, and placed it next to David's half of their sandwich.

CHAPTER 31

THE wind tugged bitterly at John as he sidled up to David and murmured, "So… will you let me buy you that jacket now?" David smiled but shook his head and continued walking down the aisle between the trestle tables of the market. When they reached the rack of winter jackets, John shot David a look and grumbled, "You're a stubborn bastard, aren't you?"

David grinned and pulled a face, unaware that the stallholder had moved up behind him. The hand on his shoulder was innocent enough, but David froze at the touch; his eyes locked on some empty space in front of him.

It took a moment for John to realize what just happened, but no time at all for him to divert the stallholder's attention to another customer and get him away from David. While the man rummaged through his stock for a requested size, John moved to David's side and said quietly, "He didn't mean anything, Dave."

David glanced down at his feet and nodded. "I know."

John watched David carefully, waiting for the focus to return to his eyes. Keeping his voice low and calm, he reassured him. "He's gone now."

Another small nod and he whispered, "I know." This time, however, David looked up and met John's eyes.

"You do need a new jacket though." John smiled, leaning in to give David a light bump, relieved when his smile was returned.

Letting out a long breath David shrugged and admitted, "I guess I do."

"So…." John started playfully, recognizing that David was back with him. "You gonna let me buy it?"

David just looked at John and with a cheeky tilt to his head he made a show of pulling out his own wallet.

With the new jacket safely folded in a generic white plastic bag, the pair headed for the warmth of the café. Before they reached the door David glanced at the nearby public toilet block and said, "Just gotta pee. I won't be long."

"Sure. You want a tea?" John asked as he felt the welcoming rush of warm air from the café's open door. With a raise of his hand in agreement, David wandered through the battered and graffiti-covered door of the male toilets.

David smiled at his slightly blurry face reflected between the scratches on the bathroom mirror, then set about washing his hands. He was nearly done when he became aware of movement in the room and glanced back at the mirror to see a figure standing very close behind him.

"New territory?" the man asked cryptically. There was familiarity to the voice, but definitely not that of a friend.

David instantly dropped his gaze to his hands. He focused on the last of the soap bubbles as they popped and dissolved under the stream of water. "I'm sorry. I don't know what you're talking about," he mumbled.

The laugh David heard was one of total derision and bile rose in his throat. "Sure you do," the man whispered, his breath hot over the back of David's ear. "So do you charge more for a blow now you're all shaved and pretty?"

"I don't know what you're talking...." David breathed through gritted teeth only to be cut off.

"Shut it," the man hissed. "I liked you better when you didn't talk; couldn't talk 'cause you were on your knees in the piss with your lips wrapped around my cock."

No! David straightened up and shook his head. "No... not me." He spun around and glared at the man, who saw only the anger and none of the fear. "That is *not* me now!"

Not understanding David's reaction, the man quickly stepped back. He wasn't used to this kind of response; sullen acceptance or a barrier of shame, but not what he perceived to be aggression. "Well, plenty more whores around." He sneered, spat at David's feet, and quickly exited the toilet block while trying to keep his façade of control intact.

Drops of water fell from trembling fingers as David stood and watched the now-empty doorway. A wave of nausea hit and David gulped in air until it passed enough for him to turn back to the sink.

He leaned heavily on the porcelain bowl; the tap was still running and David watched the water rush into the rust-stained drain. When the shaking of his knees finally subsided and regained the ability to support him, David reached out and filled both hands with water. He immersed his face until the water slowly trickled through his fingers, then stood breathing into his wet hands thinking the same thought over and over. *Not me now.*

Squeezing his eyes shut, David lowered his hands. It took him several moments to get the courage to open them and look at the mirror. Looking back wasn't the smiling man of only minutes before, but it also wasn't the disheveled homeless man who did tricks to survive. David tore off a section of paper towel and dried his face and hands with rough swipes, all the while staring at his reflection.

Not me now.

The pale eyes simply looked back at him as if in defiance of the claim. *You haven't changed. Yes, you're clean and lice free, but he recognized you for what you are.*

David shook his head. *No. Please.... That's not me now.*

As if to back his plea, David stripped himself of his old jacket and threw it in the trash. The thin plastic of the bag collapsed in around his damp hand as he reached for the jacket. It took several shakes but the garment finally emerged and the bag fluttered to the floor.

With his new jacket on and zipped, he stood his ground in front of the mirror. *I bought this. I earned it.* David's chest heaved while the thoughts were repeated.

Slowly his sight left the mirror and he stepped away from the sink.

JOHN was just carrying the tea to a table when David entered the café. *It's okay. Sit with John. It's okay now.* He sat in the old wooden chair desperately clinging to that thought.

"Jacket looks good." John grinned and pushed a cup across the table. He took a sip, grimaced, and reached for the sugar. Piling in a couple of spoonfuls, John looked over at David and said, "You know, Adam was pretty excited about being able to talk to you and I was thinking that maybe you could make it a regular thing?"

The rhythmic clink of the teaspoon as John stirred his tea all but drowned out John's suggestion. David knew something had been said about Adam, but what it was was lost to him as he watched the silver spoon swirl through the contents of the cup.

Not realizing David wasn't following what he'd said, John continued to talk about possible scenarios for the one-sided conversations with Adam, and maybe a hint that David could gradually join in. The spoon stilled and he laid it on the table to take an appreciative swallow. "They do good tea here." He smiled and gave David a quick wink. "You know, I'm sure it really helps him to know that you want to be part of his life again."

Part of his life again. The light in the café glared a sickly yellow; it irritated the periphery of David's vision. He tried to blink it away while he picked at a small fiber caught in a splinter on the edge of the table. As his cold fingers kept slipping off, his agitation grew.

The smiled slipped from John's lips and he carefully reached across the table and closed his fingers over David's to still his hand. "Drink your tea, Dave; it'll warm you up."

David slowly withdrew his hand from under John's and wrapped it around the hot cup.

He didn't look up.

What's going on, David? John sat quietly watching his lover, well aware that the mood had changed again and David was struggling. *This can't still be over what happened at the market....*

He was about to ask when a group of teenage girls entered the café laughing and chatting. Just the sound of happy teenagers, but it jarred

David's raw nerves. He stood up with an abruptness that spilled tea into the white saucer.

It was too loud, too... *too much,* and he had to get out.

The girls mouthed abuse as he pushed past them and out the door, but John sat staring, his fingers still clutching his tea. *What the fuck just happened?*

When the door swung shut John gave himself a mental shake, threw a few notes on the table, and quickly followed, half-expecting to find the sidewalk empty.

David paced a few steps, then turned and paced some more. He needed to move, but didn't want to leave. Confusion warred with reason.

John's relief at seeing David was quickly replaced with concern; he'd seen David agitated before, but not like this. "What's going on, David?" he asked, edging into David's line of sight. "Things are getting better. You have a home, you and Adam are communicating...."

David took in half-words, not able to make sense of what John was saying above the static of his jumbled thoughts. His arms hurt and he rubbed at them, turning away from John. He wanted John to stop... needed John to stop, to leave him alone....

Not knowing what else to do, John reached out and put his hand on David's back. Physical contact had worked before and brought David back to him, but rather than settling with the touch it had the opposite effect. David pulled away violently and held up a warning hand for John to back off. David's face held a mixture of fear and frustration, but also something John had not seen before: anger.

"David?" John said the name quietly but his own hurt and confusion were clear.

David turned and looked at John. He wanted it to be okay, to take that expression from John's face, but at that moment in time there seemed no way he could make that happen.

With a frustrated shake of his head, David lifted his hand to his face, where it rubbed anxiously at his cheek and lips until it finally settled to cover his mouth.

Fuck no. Don't let this happen. A chill started to settle in John's gut. He could see where this was heading and felt completely helpless to stop it. "Come home, David. Please," he pleaded quietly and half-held his hand out.

This time David nodded, but didn't move toward John. Slowly he turned and walked away.

John stood on the sidewalk and watched where the back of the man he loved disappeared from view.

CHAPTER 32

"AND he just fucking walked away."

Jamie sat and watched John as he spoke. His friend was slumped forward in the chair, hand cradling his temple and agitated fingertips pushing into his hair.

"But he nodded, right? When you asked him to come home?" Jamie asked, trying to either clarify the situation or at least John's perception of it.

John's hand slipped down his face and over his lips where they stayed for a moment while he thought that through. Finally he glanced up and said with little conviction, "Yeah, he nodded."

"So why are you here with me, John?"

The question was a difficult one to answer, but ultimately John knew why. "I can't be there alone. Not anymore."

Please don't give up now, John. Not when you're so close.

The pair sat in dejected silence until John reached for his cigarette packet and lit up. He took a long draw and let the smoke drift out between his lips as he spoke. "Is it always this hard, Jamie? Or am I just the *lucky* one?"

Jamie rolled his eyes at John's miserable sarcasm and replied, "How the fuck should I know? Serial one-night-stand guy, remember?"

"I'm starting to think you have the right idea," John muttered, but reached out to cup the back of Jamie's head and pull him forward to plant a kiss on his forehead.

"No chance," Jamie denied, shaking his head. He took John's cigarette and put it between his lips briefly before stubbing it out. "Sure, you have to fight for what you have with David; but I'd swap places with either one of you in a second. Not that I fancy you, boss, so don't get any ideas in *that* direction." Jamie grinned and gave John a wink.

John's lips curled but there was no smile in his eyes. "Are you telling me to go look for him again?"

Jamie's lips tightened in thought and he got up to empty the ashtray. With his back still turned, he let out a long sigh. "Maybe not, John."

The answer wasn't at all what John expected and his stomach lurched. "But you told me once to keep bringing him back. Bring him back until he stayed, you said."

"Maybe I was wrong?" Jamie reasoned and returned to his seat. "Maybe this time is different?"

Please don't say that, Jamie. Cold emptiness began to fill John as he murmured, "So I just let him go?"

"*Fuck* no, John," Jamie said and pulled him into an awkward hug. "You go home and wait for him to come home. He won't know where you are if you're hanging around my place."

"And if he doesn't come home?"

"He nodded, John. He'll come home."

THE streets passed unnoticed as David continued walking; he'd walked them so many times before that what was around him didn't seem to matter. The need to move was all he felt until a fellow pedestrian grabbed his sleeve to stop him from stepping onto the busy road. "Watch where you're going, man," he grumbled as the traffic hurtled by. David looked up at the man and blinked before stumbling a step back. He remained standing when the light changed to green and people jostled past onto the crosswalk.

By the time the light returned to red David had moved to a nearby bus shelter to lean heavily against the metal frame.

"Excuse me. Are you all right?" The face of a young woman swam into focus in front of David. He looked at her, not able to understand why she was there; why she was talking to him.

"Do you need me to call someone for you?" She persisted, seeing that things were definitely not all right with this man. David frowned. *People don't stop; they look away, pretend not to notice, don't let me invade their safe warm existence.*

When David didn't answer, she took a half-filled bottle of water from her shopping bag and pressed it into his hand. "Have a drink and sit down." She shuffled him into the bus stop and sat beside him on the bench. "Go on, take a drink," she encouraged and reached over to unscrew the cap when David just stared at the bottle in his hand. "It's okay; it's only water."

David slowly lifted the bottle of water to his lips and took a mouthful. The cool water slipped easily down his throat. He blinked and swallowed another mouthful, quenching a thirst he hadn't realized he had. "Thank you," he muttered, eyes still on the little plastic bottle.

"You're welcome." She smiled. "Now are you all right to get where you're going? Do you need me to call anyone?"

I don't know.... "I'm okay, thank you," David lied and made to give the bottle back, but she lifted her hand in protest. "You hold onto that and sit a minute," she said, glancing at the bus pulling into the bay. "My bus is here. You sit a while, get your bearings."

The shadow created by the bus moved away and David sat alone in the bus shelter.

JOHN was on his third glass of scotch by the time the sun set. The tiny apartment seemed cavernous as he sat alone on the couch. His car keys lay ready on the coffee table next to David's sketchbook.

In the early hours of the morning John finally drifted into a drunken sleep.

WINTER nights felt very different when you were on the wrong side of the window, but David quickly fell into old survival habits. He found the deep alcove of a doorway, glanced briefly at the other man already settled in one corner. A look of resignation and a little wariness passed between them as David hunkered down opposite him. The tiled floor was cold through his jeans without a crushed cardboard box to take off the edge.

He drew up his knees, making himself as small as possible in an attempt to conserve body heat, and settled into an uncomfortable doze.

JOHN woke to a gentle shove and a hand offering headache tablets. He squinted against the morning light, blinking until he could make out Jamie's silhouetted figure. He gratefully took the pills but when he reached for the dregs in the whisky glass he was stopped and Jamie said, "Not a good idea. Here, try this instead." A glass of water replaced the whisky.

The pills were downed with a grimace of disgust and as the cold water hit his stomach, John fought an instant wave of nausea. Jamie sat and patiently waited for John to speak. Through dry lips John finally muttered bitterly, "I didn't look for him and he didn't come home."

"I'm sorry, John," Jamie answered miserably, not sure if he'd suggested the wrong thing to his friend even though it still felt right. "But I think it has to be up to David now."

John shook his head and instantly regretted the action when the sick thump intensified. "That's the problem though, Jamie. Is David even *capable* of sorting himself out enough to come back? I mean, you didn't see him yesterday."

"No, I didn't," Jamie started quietly. "But don't underestimate him, John. David is not only smart, but he's strong." When John shot him a doubtful look Jamie stood his ground. "Think about it, John. Think about it without the hurt and without being pissed off at him—"

"I am not *pissed off* at him," John interjected angrily.

But Jamie continued. "Of course you are; after all you've been through with him you have a right to be pissed off. However, right now you need to let that go and think about all the shit David has dealt with, how far he's come. Think about the times he's opened up to you and let you in, then tell me he's not strong."

It was difficult to bypass the hurt and headache, but John knew Jamie was right. "I'm still worried." He sighed and downed the rest of the water.

"Me too," Jamie admitted.

JOHN? David stirred when someone walked past him, but as he tried to unwrap his limbs from his body the pain was instant. He groaned and moved a little slower, giving his body a chance to recover and his muscles time to warm up. When he made it to his feet the others in the alcove had already left and David looked out at the passersby, unsure what to do.

Through habit more than conscious thought, David found himself at the door of the shelter just as Barbara arrived. "Hello, David." She smiled and pushed the door open for him. "You here for a visit or to replenish our book stock?" She kept the well-practiced smile on her face even though she could see that David didn't quite seem to understand what she was asking. "You want to come in, luv? Maybe have a hot drink and something to eat?"

He glanced into the shelter and frowned. "I don't know."

"Come on then. Come in with me," Barbara said and with a light touch guided him through to the main dining area.

Barbara watched as both his tea and breakfast remained untouched. *What're you thinking, David?,* she pondered as he occasionally frowned in thought. *What are you working out?*

He sat like that for most of the breakfast session, but as the others drifted off she noticed a slight change in his awareness of his surroundings. David was looking at the books on the shelves against the far wall or, more particularly, the elderly man straightening them up.

Barbara moved to the table and sat beside him. "The books are a huge success, you know," she said, purposely leaving it open-ended so David could comment if he wanted to. Together they watched the man pull some tatty books from his bag and leave them propped on the section of shelf reserved for new titles. "You've really started something good here." Slowly David's eyes moved away from the shelf and settled on Barbara. "It's a start and others are building on it," she said and smiled at him.

"It's a start," he mumbled, "and that's okay."

"It's okay," Barbara confirmed and looked back at the books even though she knew that was not what they were actually talking about anymore.

They sat together like that for quite some time until David asked, "Will I ever be like I was?"

"Nobody is ever like they were, David," Barbara said with complete honesty. David nodded, getting the answer he expected. "But if you're asking for specifics," Barbara continued, "things could get easier over time, although there generally isn't some huge epiphany and everything suddenly clicks into place. Makes a great ending for a movie, but unfortunately life usually isn't like that. Can you tell me what brought this on?"

"I thought I was doing better," David said with a still-confused frown. "But... I dunno. It was too much and I couldn't think. I had to be on my own to think." He sat quietly, not yet ready to go into all the details.

"So what now, David? Right now at this point in time, what do you want to do?" Barbara understood she was pushing him to make a choice and sat ready for the fallout if he couldn't.

"I want to go home." The answer was spoken clearly because it was the one thing of which David was certain.

JOHN made it to the phone before the end of the second ring and Jamie watched anxiously as he listened to the caller, nodding occasionally. When the call ended John stood with his head bowed for a moment or two before saying, "That was Barbara; he's at the shelter."

"Is he okay?" Jamie asked, attempting to mask his apprehension.

John sniffed and turned around. He straightened his shoulders and said, "He wants to come home."

"*Here* home?"

"Here home," John confirmed with a smile that almost wasn't a smile at all.

Jamie nodded. "Home to you," he said, smiling, and pulled John into a hug. "But you're still drunk and I'm driving, yeah?"

John chuckled into Jamie's shoulder and mumbled, "Anything you say."

CHAPTER 33

THE scratchy music of the radio that had drifted slightly off its station and external traffic were the only sounds in the car. Even Jamie was quiet. John sat in the passenger seat just able to glimpse David in his peripheral vision. He could see David staring at the passing streetscape and regretted his decision not to join him in the backseat. With a tired sigh, John thought back to his quiet conversation with Barbara at the shelter.

As soon as they'd walked in, she had signaled John over, letting Jamie make his way to David.

"He wanted me to call you, John," she said cautiously, immediately noting John's rough state. John simply nodded and rubbed a weary hand over cheek and chin. His stubble scraped his fingers.

"Do you want to go to him or can we have a little chat first?"

"We can talk."

Tread carefully, Barbara warned herself, and motioned to the doorway of her office. "David had a setback," she started and held her hand up to John when he shot her a frustrated look. "Bear with me here, John. David had a setback but—and here's the important part—he worked his way through it."

John gave her a curious if somewhat disbelieving look so she continued. "Something set him off and he had to walk away for a while but he *needed* to do that. I understand how hard that was on you...."

"Do you, Barbara?" John interrupted bitterly. "Do you really understand what it's like to love someone so much and watch them run away again and again?" He knew it wasn't Barbara's fault. None of this was her fault, but he couldn't seem to stop himself.

They sat in silence for a moment before Barbara sighed and said, "I *do*, John. I came into this job for a reason and perhaps that's to try and help where I couldn't before."

John's head fell back and he stared at the cracked cornice of the ceiling. "I'm sorry, Barb; it's just… well, I'm not very good at this."

Barbara smiled and reached out to rub John's arm. "You are, John. A lot more than you give yourself credit for. And you're allowed to be hurt and angry."

He tilted his face toward her and smiled. Not much of a smile, but a smile nonetheless. "Thank you," he said softly, surprised that the acknowledgment of how he felt, and perhaps permission to feel it, actually broke down a little of the pain. "Okay. So where to now?"

"Now you need to see that David was *not* running away from you. Something, and I don't know what, triggered a flight response, but I watched him think it through and bring himself back." Barbara's smile broadened. "That's a pretty big leap forward, John."

"Then he wanted to come home," John said thoughtfully.

"It was the one thing he asked for."

"Good," John said and stood up. He pulled Barbara into a hug that lingered a little longer than that of a man confident with what was happening. "We better head home then."

ALONE in the apartment, John wanted to talk, wanted to break the silence that was shrouding them. But he simply didn't know what to say. He moved to the window and stared out. Jamie had parked his car and was heading down the lane to open Margins. John saw him glance up, grin, and give a small wave. A hopeful wave?

But John closed his eyes and when he opened them again his focus had shifted onto the window's reflection of the quiet man standing watching his back.

"You keep leaving me, David," John said, meeting those pale eyes in the glass. There was no reply. "But I didn't go looking for you this time."

The words were factual and spoken without bitterness. David felt a twinge of fear, but only a small one when he answered, "You didn't need to, John."

John nodded and turned to look directly at David. He took a deep breath, held it, and then nodded again. A wave of vertigo and nausea washed over him. John slumped none too carefully into his armchair and closed his eyes to wait for it to pass. He sat and concentrated on his breathing, barely hearing David move through the room. Nothing was said but a cool, damp cloth was placed across his forehead and his closed eyelids. Gentle fingers smoothed it; over his right temple first and then the left. John sighed and relaxed into the touch.

"Barbara explained that you weren't running away from me," John stated and felt the fingers falter slightly before regaining their calming rhythm.

"*Never* away from you." The muttered reply was so quiet but contained such an intensity of purpose that John's eyes stung with tears behind the cloth. He reached up and took David's hand while sliding the cloth away from his eyes. "I think I want to lie down. Join me?"

With shoes kicked carelessly on the floor at the base of the bed, they lay together, close but allowing some space to breathe and talk.

"Back at the market," David started, talking almost as if telling John a bedtime story. His voice was hushed and his eyes stared at a distant point in the ceiling. "A man approached me. A man who knew me before I met you. Except I understand now that he didn't *really* know me at all. What he asked for I couldn't—no, wouldn't—do." John lay still and listened. His usual fear of David's past wasn't there. John listened and let himself hear it without his constant need to make things right.

"I made him leave and went to you. For the first time I started to believe there really might be a way forward, John. I think maybe that's what scared me."

David turned and looked at John before continuing. "Survival became a habit and all of a sudden there was so much more.... I couldn't think."

"I kept talking, didn't I?" John whispered. "Going on about how good it could be? About getting you and Adam back together again?"

"Yeah," David confirmed, but with a small smile. "I'm not who I used to be, John, and I now know I can't be that person again."

John turned and looked at him. "I didn't know that person, David. But I'm slowly getting to know you."

David nodded and smiled when John's fingers found his. "I don't think you're the same person either, John."

"That I'm not, Dave," John said with a small grunt and wry grin. *That I'm not.*

For a brief moment David's eyes flicked away and his lips slightly tightened in thought. When he looked back, John saw something new in his demeanor. *Determination perhaps?* "There's something else I think I've figured out. I think that maybe I can be Adam's dad again."

Oh, fuck yes. John beamed and cupped David's face in his hands. "Do you have any idea how much I love you?"

"Must be a hell of a lot if you're willing to put up with all my shit," David muttered happily.

With a somewhat weepy laugh, John pulled him closer, only to have their embrace interrupted by the insistent chime of John's phone. "Argghh. Perfect timing." John groaned and rolled over to pick it up.

"Hey, John; I just called to see if you could tell Dad about my exam results." The teenage voice was quiet but sounded pretty pleased with himself.

"Hey, Adam." John smiled at David and raised his eyebrows in a silent question. When David held out his hand, John said happily, "How about you tell your dad instead of me?"

He handed over the phone and edged off the bed to give them some privacy.

John slumped back against the wall just outside the bedroom door and listened to the occasional taps onto the phone. He smiled and shook his head. The dull ache of his hangover still lingered but he barely noticed as he listened. Tap, tap, tap.

There was a long pause and John wondered if the call had ended. Then he heard it. Said very softly, but he could clearly make out the words: "Night, Adam."

All the hurt suddenly welled in John's chest and dissolved.

He looked across the room at the photo of the young John with his grandparents. He could just make out his protective stance and for the first time he questioned, *Was I protective of my gran or was I the one being protected?*

John smiled and whispered. "I found him, Gran. I found the right one."

CHAPTER 34

FROM the same table, in the same café John stared out through the fogged-up window at the little store where he'd spent the past year of his life. His gaze was just as unfocused as it had been then but this time, rather than resentment at being there, his mind was filled with all that had happened to him during the past twelve months. The shop still looked roughly the same, but *he* was nothing like the person that signed that short-term lease.

His sight was suddenly drawn to the men loading cardboard boxes tightly sealed with wide strips of masking tape into the white removals van. Jamie walked into view, checking the neatly written notes on each box and pointing into the truck to give the moving men unnecessary instructions. A smile played briefly over John's lips with the thought *Every job needs a gaffer and Jamie makes a great supervisor; that way he can be nosy without actually doing much.* He sighed and watched the young man smile, obviously flirting with the well-built removalist carrying one of the larger containers. *Why didn't I fall for Jamie?*, John wondered looking at the cheeky grin. *Life could have been a hell of a lot easier, a lot less complicated.* His fingers fiddled absently with the near-empty teacup on the table, turning it in slow circles on the matching saucer.

A new financial year and his temporary "sea change" was over.

A delicately feminine hand covered his and asked, "Penny for your thoughts, John?"

John's hand stilled and he looked at the woman sitting across the table. He smiled and shook his head. "Just considering the fact that the year is over and my decision is made." John then added with a sheepish smile, "I was also watching Jamie and thinking that the last twelve months may have been easier if I'd fallen for him instead of David."

He blushed at his observation but Maggie laughed and said, "Ah, John, I love my son to death, but I know he would have driven you round the bend in no time."

John's grin widened. "Yeah, I think you're right. There have been a few occasions where I could have happily throttled him." He looked out the window again to witness Jamie scribbling notes on one of the boxes, his expression turned more serious. "Mind you, I'm not sure what I would have done without him."

"He's a good boy." Maggie smiled, looking across the road at her son, and then squeezed John's hand. "So how are you now, John?"

John continued to stare out the window. *How am I now? Interesting question.* He finally came to a conclusion and turned to look at her. "You know, Maggie... I would have to say I'm good." A grin spread across his face at the admission. "Yeah, I *am* good. *This* is my life now and I'm happy with it."

Maggie patted his hand and released it to take a sip of her tea. She let out a contented sigh and said with an air of understanding, "I knew my little shop would win you over. I could tell you needed it."

John laughed but couldn't deny it. "It did at that! I honestly don't know how you could give it up."

Maggie looked over at Margins, her voice taking on a wistful quality as she said, "I've had my time there, John. I had a wonderful marriage and raised my son to be a beautiful person. What more could I ask for? Besides, it's your turn now."

"My turn," John murmured, testing the feel of the words. He looked across the road again to catch Jamie writing something with a thick marker on the forearm of the removalist. John squinted until he could make out what looked like a series of numbers. "Looks like Jamie has a new friend." John chuckled, tilting his head toward the scene outside. Maggie shook her head and said with obvious love, "That boy is incorrigible! Although from what he told me, he seems to have become firm friends with one of the social workers at the shelter. Brian, I think he said."

John's eyebrows rose. "Well, he kept that very quiet."

"That means it's important to him." She glanced at Jamie with an understanding that only mothers have of their sons.

Another man walked out of the store, carrying what looked to be a small but heavy cardboard box. He stopped and said something to Jamie then broke into easy laughter; John couldn't help smiling.

"I can't get over the change in him," Maggie remarked, also watching the relaxed banter between David and her son.

John couldn't take his eyes off David as he replied, "Yeah, in some ways he has really moved forward since you last saw him."

Maggie studied John's face and asked quietly, "In *some* ways, John?"

John watched David climb into the van to load the box, the smile still on his lips, but only barely as he answered, "He has his good days and his bad days. Today is a good one." John sighed and added, "He's a lot stronger than he was. More confident, but you know, sometimes I'm sure there are moments when he still thinks of himself as homeless."

"How do you mean?" Maggie inquired gently.

John glanced down at his hands, trying to formulate words that could explain a feeling rather than an event. Finally he shook his head and said, "I don't know, Maggie. Sometimes, not often now, but sometimes he just... pulls back, withdraws into himself as if he's not able to be part of my life." John stopped, took a breath, and continued in a quieter voice. "He's trying so hard and maybe I'm overreacting. He has this bloody backpack in our bedroom. It doesn't scare me as much as it used to, but every day I see it and every day it reminds me that there are times when he needs to know he can just walk out the front door." John drained the last of his tea and ran his tongue briefly over his bottom lip. "Even now he keeps his things in his pack... and sometimes I find half-eaten food stashed in there."

"I would imagine that's only to be expected, sweetheart. He *must* have a lot to be worked through and that's going to take time. To me, he's achieved so much in getting his life to this point. I still remember the terrified, shabby man I lured into the shop not so long ago. But he has *you* now, John."

John looked down at the few stray tea leaves stuck to the inside of his otherwise empty cup. A flush rose up his collar as heat suddenly welled in his chest at Maggie's words. "We have each other. He's done just as much for me."

Maggie touched John's arm and whispered conspiratorially, "I always knew he was a special one."

A special one, John thought. *Very special.* He whispered back, "I know."

Suddenly aware of someone standing next to him, John turned to see the waitress hovering with a fresh pot of tea. She smiled, lifted the pot, and asked, "Refill?" Both Maggie and John moved their hands to allow her access to their empty cups.

Maggie watched John thoughtfully as he stirred a spoonful of sugar into his tea and said, "Jamie told me about David's son."

John sighed and rested his teaspoon on the side of the saucer. "Adam. I meet with him regularly and I think it helps. Helps both of us actually."

Maggie nodded, encouraging John to continue. He leaned forward in his chair and rubbed his fingers briefly across his mouth. "Adam needs his dad, but I guess I do for the time being. At least until David is up to building that relationship again."

"Has he spoken to Adam at all?"

"In a fashion, but I think we're getting closer to it really happening."

"You're a good man doing this for them, John," Maggie said, giving his hand another pat. "How is David coping with all of this?"

John grimaced slightly at the question but appreciated the comforting touch of her hand. "That varies. It isn't that he thinks Adam will reject him anymore; it's more that he's only just starting to believe that he *deserves* to be part of Adam's life. The other night he told me that he thinks he can start being Adam's dad again. The reality of that is going to be difficult for him, but if we take it slowly I think we'll get there."

Maggie knew all too well the bumpy road ahead for them. "Stick with him, John; I know it can't be easy."

John nodded quietly. *It hasn't been easy.*

She took a bite of her gingersnap cookie and chewed thoughtfully for a moment. "Whatever you're all doing seems to be working though, and what is it they say? Two steps forward...."

"One step back." John finished the well-worn phrase with a good-natured roll of his eyes.

"Yes, I know. I've always hated that old cliché too," Maggie said with a wink. "I believe that we should all be able to dance through life and only change the tempo now and then."

John looked at her and grinned broadly. "I think I can see where Jamie gets his outlook on life."

"I taught him well." Maggie laughed, wagging her cookie at him. "Actually, John, I'm surprised you're staying in the apartment when you have such a nice one uptown."

"I gave up the lease on that. This is where I want to be; this is home for me now," John replied. Then he added in a mischievous tone, "Besides, there aren't many places these days that have an old-fashioned tub big enough for two."

Maggie wiggled her eyebrows in a fashion John had seen Jamie do on many occasions and giggled. "Oh, believe me, John, I know.... *I know!*"

John shot her an incredulous look and burst into an enthusiastic round of laughter. "Maggie! You are a wicked woman!"

Mid-laugh, John returned his attention to the moving van and saw David standing across the street looking at him through the misted glass. David's smile was wide and open; it filled John with such an overwhelming joy that it momentarily took his breath away. *Yeah, today is a good day.*

Maggie sat in quiet recognition of John's expression, understanding enough not to comment.

Realizing he was being watched, John cleared his throat and his blush deepened to the point where Maggie couldn't resist a gentle laugh. "It looks like they've loaded the last of my things into the van. A quick trip to get the rest out of storage and we're done." Her expression saddened slightly at the thought of this chapter in her life closing.

John nodded. "Take a few minutes, Maggie. I'll settle the bill and gather the troops."

"Thank you, John." Maggie smiled as he got up and walked over to the cash register. She would miss her life here but knew what she'd said to John was true; her time here *was* over and it was their time now. Maggie took another nibble at her cookie and watched John walk across the street to slip his arm around David's waist. The smile didn't leave her lips as she thoughtfully chewed on both the cookie and the notion: *Their time now....*

MAGGIE shared one more cup of tea with John; one that was to be her last in the little kitchen of the bookstore before following her son to her car. John watched her go and took a minute or two to gather his thoughts. He leaned quietly against the doorframe and looked out at the street of small stores and cafés.

"Get inside, John; it's going to be a cold one tonight," Adele scolded as she walked past on the way to her bus stop. John chuckled and waved. "It's pension day tomorrow; I'll have the kettle on ready."

Before locking up, John glanced back into the cluttered store, at its heavy wooden shelves laden with books new and old. He chuckled. "A fucking shoplifter's paradise."

THE apartment was quiet. John threw his keys on the coffee table and walked through to the bedroom. Coming to an abrupt halt, he stared at the empty space against the chest of drawers. David's pack was gone. He took a step closer as if it would somehow magically appear.

Panic threatened for only the briefest second before John looked around the room. David's phone was on the nightstand as was his sketchbook.

Glancing back at the vacant space, John bent down to slowly slide open the bottom drawer.

They took up not quite half the drawer, but John smiled at David's clothes all neatly stacked and folded.

He strolled back through their apartment and heard the faint splash of water. His smile broadened as he tapped on the bathroom door.

"Room in there for two?"

EPILOGUE

ADAM sat and waited. *John said they'd be here at five and it won't be that for another ten minutes.*

He fidgeted in his seat, sitting up then slouching back down only to sit up again. First one napkin was torn into a neat spiral then another simply frayed around the edges. Adam was about to start on the bundle of sugar packets when the waitress appeared with his orange juice. With an apologetic smile he scooped all the paper fragments into his hand and placed them in hers.

"He shouldn't be long. He's never been late yet." She chuckled, having seen John and Adam meeting for quite a few months now.

"Yeah." Adam smiled back. "John's always on time." *But my dad was always late for everything.* Adam's stomach did a flip at the thought and he instantly pulled out his cell phone to check the time again. *Five past; maybe they're not coming.* Adam closed his eyes and took a long breath. *They're coming. John would call if they weren't.*

The thought had barely passed when the door opened and John appeared. Adam smiled but looked straight past him. He frowned at the empty doorway and looked back at John.

"It's all right, Adam. He's here," John reassured him and took a seat. "He needs a minute and I thought it would be a good idea if I came in and spoke to you first."

Adam nodded and glanced again at the doorway. "He's okay though, John? I mean, he still wants to do this?"

"Oh, he wants to do this. He's just… he's just a bit nervous, is all." *Scared to death is more like it.*

Adam didn't look convinced but decided he'd trusted John this far so he could wait a few more minutes.

John knew the meeting was going to be hard, and playing go-between had his nerves twitching. "I'll go and get him in a bit but before I do I want to make sure you understand that if he doesn't say much it's not because you've done anything wrong. He finds it difficult to talk sometimes and…."

The hint of a smile formed on Adam's lips and he said, "I understand, John. I really do." He shrugged, went to take a drink, then changed his mind and put the glass back on the table. "Do you think you should go and check with him? See if he wants to come in yet?"

"I'll see if he's ready," John said, hoping like hell David would be able to do this at all. With a brief nod, John stood and walked to the door. The short walk frightened him more than any he'd taken into hostile boardrooms or shareholders meetings.

David slouched against the wall. From his position he could lean over and peer into the café or watch the passing shoppers compare bargains. He chose the latter. But although his eyes were on the opposite side of the street all his thoughts were centered inside that café, on what he could possibly say to his son. When the door opened David could see John emerge in his peripheral vision. His stomach lurched.

"Hey, Dave," John said quietly. "You want to come in?"

John watched as David straightened, filled his lungs with air, and slowly exhaled. He turned and said, "I think I need to do this on my own, John. Is that okay?"

"Of course it is," John answered, not sure if he was pleased or disappointed, and stepped away from the door. He gave him what he hoped was an encouraging smile and said, "No matter what, Dave, just remember it's Adam and he loves you."

Pins and needles pinged through David's arms down to his fingers as he stepped into the café. Within an instant he saw the expectant face of Adam watching him. *He looks as scared as I feel.* The first few steps to the table were shaky but David made it to the seat opposite Adam.

From his vantage point just outside the front window John took a peak at David's progress across the room. "That's it, Dave," he muttered, feeling each and every step with him. When David finally sat, John let out his breath and his attention turned to Adam. "Talk to him, lad. You'll have to start this for him."

But Adam didn't speak. As hard as he tried, now that his father was there in front of him he just didn't know what to say.

The pair sat in silence for long enough for John to make a move toward the door, but as his hand reached out he saw another hand reach for Adam's.

Although his eyes were still downcast, David's fingers weren't hesitant when they closed around his son's. The grasp was warm and solid. It reminded Adam of when he was little and his dad used to take his hand to cross the road. It felt good.

"Your hands are nearly as big as mine now," David said quietly, sharing a similar memory. *Almost a man who might not need his dad anymore.*

"Yeah," Adam replied, his eyes flicking from their hands to David's face. "But I still bite my nails."

"Only when you've got something on your mind." David smiled and finally looked up to see the same smile on the face of his son.

John stood at the window, not caring that he was in full view of the café's customers. He'd watched with surprise when David made the first real contact and then spoke to the overwhelmed teenager and, as nervous as he looked, John could see that David was becoming "Dad" again.

He turned away from the window and couldn't resist a laugh of sheer joy, only to receive a scowl from a passerby. John just grinned back. When he returned to the window, both Adam and David were looking at David's wrist. He saw Adam laugh at something David said. John strained to see what they were looking at until it dawned on him. The little heart tattoo. He'd seen it so many times but never felt he could ask its meaning. There were so many things John hadn't asked.

When we get home, I'll ask.

A black cat for a witch may be a cliché, but add a whole bunch of tribal tattoos and an intolerance to garlic (seriously) and you have ISABELLE ROWAN.

Having moved to Australia from England as a small child Isabelle now lives in a seaside suburb of Melbourne where she teaches film making and English. She is a movie addict who spends far too much money on traveling… but then again, life is to be lived.

Visit Isabelle's blog at http://isabelle-rowan.livejournal.com/.

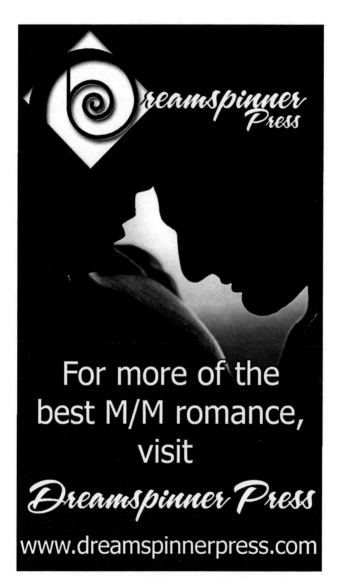